GRACE
ABOUNDING

GRACE
ABOUNDING

DONNA M. YOUNG

Grace Abounding
Copyright © 2019 by Donna M. Young. All rights reserved.

Unless otherwise indicated, all Scripture quotations are from *The Holy Bible, English Standard Version*®, copyright © 2001 by Crossway Bibles, a publishing ministry of Good News Publishers. Used by permission. All rights reserved.

Published by Donna M. Young
P O Box 76, Lawton, IA 51030
dmywriting@wiatel.net

Author photo by Elizabeth Rose Kahl

Book Cover and Layout by Christina Hicks
christinahickscreative@gmail.com

Published in the United States of America
soft cover: 978-1-947143-12-8
E-book: 978-1-947143-13-5
Fiction / General
Fiction / Christian General

http://www.donnamyoungwriting.com

PART 1

Likewise the Spirit helps us in our weakness. For we do not know what to pray for as we ought, but the Spirit Himself intercedes for us with groanings too deep for words.

Romans 8:26

You are the light of the world. A city set on a hill cannot be hidden. Nor do people light a lamp and put it under a basket, but on a stand, and it gives light to all in the house. In the same way, let your light shine before others, so that they may see your good works and give glory to your Father who is in heaven.

Matthew 5:14-16

CHAPTER 1

Drip, drip, drip. The sound, persistent and annoying, emanated from somewhere in the murky shadows and scratched at her subconscious. Drip, drip, drip. Her labored breathing became suddenly desperate and she gasped, frantically sucking in as much of the muggy air as her lungs would hold, while an urgency in her heart caused her to claw her way back to awareness. The sound of moaning soon followed and then shocked her as she realized it was coming from deep within her own throat. Feeling very much as though she'd been fed through a wood chipper and shot out the other end, Gracie's eyes opened to mere slits. Just enough to assure her she was still present in this earthly realm. Which, considering her current pain, wasn't necessarily a good thing. Her brain was having a difficult time comprehending what she was seeing in the semi dark. It looked as if the whole world might literally be turned upside down. She squeezed her eyes shut and opened them again. Nope, still upside down. Everything within her immediate line of vision, besides being topsy-turvy, was colored various shades of green and seemed to be dripping, soaking, sopping wet. She shook her head gently, to clear the cobwebs, and tried to remember.

Barely able to take another breath, due to an enormous pressure on her chest, she determined in her still dazed and semi conscious state that it was far too difficult to think while being simultaneously strangled and deprived of oxygen. So, reaching for the buckle on her combined shoulder/lap harness, which seemed to be the main source of her current strangulation, she released it. And fell like an over ripe piece of fruit, thudding, to the ceiling of the helicopter's cockpit.

Holding her ribs and rocking back and forth on the surface where she lay she took a deep shuddering breath. Then, shaking her head, and touching her scalp to find a large gash, and a fair sized goose egg there, along with a generous amount of a wet, sticky substance in her hair, she again tried to gain some sense of perspective... At this point, all she knew was that she was very thirsty, and the coppery taste of blood was so strong in her mouth, she had an urge to vomit.

With a start, she remembered. She was with her husband, Jason, and they were on a mission trip through the mountains and rain forests of Haiti for their honeymoon. There had been a storm and then a crash. Looking in vain for her beloved, she shouted, "Jason, honey, are you okay?" No answer. Had he been thrown clear of the craft? "Jason. Answer me." Again, no response. Not detecting any movement in the small, darkened space; Gracie's fear was so great, that her heart, pounding hard in her chest, felt as if it might escape its small, boney cage and take flight.

Feeling around frantically in the topsy-turvy space, it suddenly occurred to her that upon undoing her own belt, she'd fallen from above, so she reached upward. And, waving her arms around over her head, finally connected with Jason's limp body.

Hanging, bound within his harness, he was cold and wet to the touch. A strong smell of blood and urine filled her nose as her face drew closer to his body, and though she knew she was bleeding from at least one gash on her head, she was sure most of the cloying, coppery odor was coming from Jason's currently undetermined wounds. At this point, she couldn't tell how much of the damp stickiness was blood, and how much was perspiration caused by the extreme heat and humidity trapped with them in the soggy confines of their polycarbonate prison. Not without first adding some much needed light to the situation.

Fear gripped her again as she desperately searched for a pulse, a heartbeat, breathing, anything, and was unable to find any. Just when her mind was about to go on stress overload, Jason coughed, sucked in a beleaguered, and strangled sounding breath, and let out a soft groan. Realizing she'd been holding her own breath until she could assess his well being, she gasped again, and gulped in several more mouthfuls of hot muggy air.

Tears of relief tracked down her blood caked, sweaty cheeks, as she propped up her husband's flaccid body with her own, and released the latch on his harness. His limp weight dropped on her rigid form, and with controlled difficulty she guided him carefully to the ceiling's surface where she stood shaky and unsure of what to do next.

In the dim light she could see Jason's side of the cabin had taken the brunt of the damage from the recent crash, almost as if he'd planned it that way in order to protect her. That would be so like him, her sweet, unassuming hero. And from what she could detect, so far, he appeared to be pretty badly hurt. Though, again, without proper light it would be hard to diagnose the situation appropriately.

Grace had no idea how long their aircraft had been

down. Rain, clouds and towering trees were surely adding to the degree of darkness growing to surround her. But, since they'd left Port-au-Prince early in the morning, and from all evidence available it seemed to be closer to end of day, it might be safe to assume they'd been out of it for quite some time. Could they really have been unconscious that long? Well, coming from her own painful and traumatic past of comas and bouts of unconsciousness, she guessed the answer to that question would have to be a resounding "Yes".

It had all happened so suddenly. The storm literally came out of nowhere. Though admittedly this was Haiti's rainy season, and perhaps they hadn't been as aware of the unpredictable weather trends as they should have been, or as prepared as was necessary in this hostile environment.

One minute the skies were clear, and the next they were smack dab in the middle of a tempest so strong it took her breath away. Angels were near as always, but they didn't intervene, not yet, and that gave her some degree of comfort, causing her to believe they would survive whatever might happen next. After all, if she'd been in danger of death, her heavenly warriors would certainly have interceded, wouldn't they?

Jason had done his level best to both, ride out the storm, and maintain control of the aircraft. But, after lightening hit, and the chopper was swept into a sudden downdraft, windblown tree branches rushed to meet them. The jumble of blades hitting wood and foliage, and the mountains of chopped up leaves left plastered on the windshield, was the last thing she remembered.

In actuality, that lightning bolt was sent straight from the enemy, and had struck them directly in the control panel; rendering the chopper's engine as dead as a doornail. For Satan and all the demons of hell who were determined to do away with the young couple in any way possible, it was a long awaited win, and the hallways of hell were filled with resounding shouts of glee.

As the small craft flipped, end over end, through the island's rain forest; Jason and Gracie's heavenly guard did what they could to cushion the fall. At some point in the ensuing turmoil Grace had hit her head. And, from the size of the bump there, the amount of blood present and the throbbing pain that was still present, it had been a pretty nasty blow. Only God knew what would have happened, were it not for those duly assigned winged warriors. Neither Jason nor Grace would ever know how close they'd come to permanent eradication that day.

One thing she did know for sure, was that no one anywhere knew their coordinates. There'd been no opportunity to send an S.O.S. in the midst of the crisis. However, now was not the time to panic about that or anything else. Now was the time for action, so she took a couple of deep breaths and attempted to calm her racing mind and heart. There was suddenly much to do.

Dizzy, and nauseated, from the blood she'd swallowed, she dug around through piles of tossed and displaced personal belongings and supplies in the crowded, upside down space, searching for their bags; where she knew she would find a medical kit, flashlight, and other necessities. Darkness continued to descend, adding to the shadows, which made her already tricky search all the more difficult. After several failed tries, she finally lit upon the smooth nylon bag that held some of their smaller emergency medical supplies and realized she'd been holding her breath again, as she let out a relieved sigh.

Once turned on, the flashlight's brilliance danced and twirled throughout the cockpit, filling her small space with illumination, and expelling some of the grey semi darkness. Though momentarily blinded by the brightness, Grace felt a surge of hope at its presence. Gently placing Jason's head on a rolled blanket, she began to check him from head to toe. He was groaning loudly now, and she looked in the medical kit for some pain relief. Morphine calmed him and sent him sliding in and out of a confused consciousness. Sitting back on her haunches, tears filling her eyes as she examined her husband, she shook her head in dismay.

At least two broken ribs, and perhaps three. With the amount of difficulty he was having breathing, she wondered if he'd punctured a lung as well. She wasn't absolutely sure what she would do if that was the case, considering her limited medical training. Both bones, the tibia and the fibula, in his lower right leg were broken; with a portion of the jagged tibia exposed. She knew it would be imperative to set the leg, and cover the exposed wound. Disease could take over quickly in these warm and humid conditions. The emergency training they'd received in Port-au-Prince, before they were allowed to take off on this missions trip to the inner continent, would surely now be invaluable.

Closing her tired eyes as she remembered the way she'd balked and whined at the extra time expected by local missions authorities; to prepare them for any possible contingency; she had to admit she was often not nearly careful enough.

Anxious to be out in the wild, 'doing good' for the people of Haiti, she'd considered the emergency medical training they were expected to attend an utter waste of time. After all, when would she ever use that much extensive first aid? They were here to share the Word of the Gospel, not run a clinic. But, the authorities insisted they both attend the two week long training and certification classes. Now she could just about kick herself for her selfish foolishness. At the same time, she praised God for His wisdom in seeing that she had what she needed in spite of herself and her own 'good intentions'.

How many times in her life had she worked at cross purposes of the direction God was trying to send her, because of her blasted stubbornness. She knew it was more times than she could count. So anxious to be off doing His important work that she often didn't involve Him and His direction in her final decisions. Yes, even though she was an emissary of the Lord, she still found herself deciding what He would have her do, without checking in with Him first. She wondered in that moment why He even continued to put up with her.

She supposed her 'do it all' nature stemmed, in part, from growing up in charge. She'd spent so many years forced to be the care taker of her siblings, and anyone else who happened across her path, that she rose up too think she didn't need anyone. That she could do it all herself! After all, she'd proven herself to be very capable in the past. And in so thinking, she'd fallen into that nasty and confusing pit of 'self-sufficiency', when her sufficiency should always and only be in the Lord.

Their mission sponsors knew the conditions they would encounter in the mountain villages much better than she did. And, aside from being able to take care of their own health issues on the arduous trip, they would have a chance to bring medical supplies and the appropriate accompanying, if mostly basic, knowledge with them to the people of the mountain terrains. These were life saving pieces of a whole person approach to missionary work that were not normally available in that rough environment. So, obviously, much to Gracie's torment and rampant impatience, there was indeed a need to know the practical applications of those supplies.

She decided that once she could eventually manage a return to relative civilization, that is if they made it out of this situation alive, she'd have to take the time to thank those authorities for their insistence that she undertake the required preparedness classes. Their continued persistence then, might very well be the thing to save her husband's life now.

Haiti was currently experiencing very troubled times. Even before recent storms and disasters, villagers from the mountainous locations where they were headed had been forced to hike for days just to receive minimal health care, which was one of the reasons the people in the region depended so heavily on their village's local witch doctors. But, since the horrific earthquake of 2010, even more roadblocks stood in their way. Gravel roads, ancient paths and bridges all over the island, were blocked by downed trees and mountains of debris. And, even after years of empty promises by so many, were still not cleared of rubble by the government, or any of the international aid organizations who'd collected billions of dollars in contributions supposedly with the intent of helping the people of the island.

Travel was more difficult than ever and few islanders chose to undertake the dangerous trek to the city, choosing instead to nurse their wounds and illnesses in the relative comfort of their own homes, even when the results were most often death or permanent injury.

Now, eight years after the massive 2010 quake, which left over three hundred and sixteen thousand dead and in excess of three hundred thousand additional souls injured, the island was still struggling to get back on its own shaky feet. With recent storms adding to their difficulties, more than three million were still experiencing food shortages, and close to another three million had need of additional types of aid. Upwards of fifty five thousand continued to live in makeshift camps in the lowlands, with eighty percent of all available housing on the island destroyed. Schools, medical facilities and government buildings had been reduced to nothing but rubble, and sadly, remained that way.

Hurricane Sandy in 2012, three years of drought, and 2016's hurricane Matthew, which killed over an additional thousand Haitians, added to the almost total destruction of the island's already fractured infrastructure.

Haiti, an island which had always depended a great deal on agriculture for the livelihood and wellbeing of its inhabitants, could no longer function in that capacity. With irrigation systems destroyed, along with the bulk of crops from 2010, to 2016, that facet of the nation's identity might sadly never be reclaimed.

Meanwhile, rampant civil unrest, accompanied by a boiling over of anger in the populace, was the new mood in Haiti. Its people no longer trusted the 'so-called' humanitarian organizations, who had collectively raised those billions of dollars in aid, and which was never distributed to the citizens. Who could blame them for their lack of trust? Most of the island's wealth rested in the hands of a few select families, as the majority of its citizenry languished and starved. To top it off fuel prices soared and the high prices were creating an unsustainable cost of living for most.

Eventually, violent rioting broke out in the streets; and citizens, targeting businesses owned by those few wealthy families, were setting fires and looting stores. Recently one of the wealthy land owners had been caught and dragged through the streets, until his lifeless body was unrecognizable. These were the unpredictable conditions in which Jason and Gracie found themselves when they first arrived in Port-au-Prince several weeks ago. Conditions they were admittedly not even remotely adequately prepared for.

Their earnest desire to bring the Word of God to a confused and angry nation was sincere. For though a majority of Haiti's citizens claimed Christianity as their religion du jour, the local interpretation of Christianity consisted of Catholicism, with a whopping side kicker of Voodoo for good measure. And, since the couple knew the only true way to the Father was through faith in Jesus; they simply had to share the truth with those who were still confused. How could they not share their beautiful Savior? How could they possibly keep such a miracle of salvation to themselves?

Grace knew the added trappings of voodoo, or any other false religion, were always the work of Satan. His way of keeping minds turned from Jesus. And, she'd certainly experienced her fair share of run ins with him and his demon hordes in her life. But, she'd found that these ungodly measures were also sometimes used by those faithless individuals who thought they needed a backup, you know, in case the whole 'believing in Jesus' thing didn't work out. The only way to change that way of thinking, would be to help these people see the One True Christ. A Messiah they could believe in, not just the bits and pieces of 'religion' that had made up their belief system in the past.

The couple knew the road ahead would be rough, but they were willing to tough it out, as long as they were together. They'd noted, flying into Port-au-Prince on the day of their arrival weeks ago, one of the largest clouds of demons they'd ever witnessed in their ministry so far. A cloud so large they sat wide eyed, staring out the plane's windows, clear up until the moment they landed.

From a fair distance it appeared the entire island might be swallowed at any moment, in what appeared to be a black cyclone of epic proportions. That is, until they'd drawn close enough to see that the cyclone was actually thousands upon thousands of the enemy's hordes circling the land mass below.

Abundantly aware that Satan and his captains would go to any lengths to keep the two of them from sharing the Gospel with these desperate, hurting, and broken people, it was no surprise then that they found themselves in their current undesirable predicament. It was also clear that

Kakos, at Satan's command, was once again up to his evil plans, and had plenty of demons at his beck and call to help him complete his despicable mission.

For generations most Haitians suffered under varying religious misconceptions, and yes, they absolutely needed new revelation in that regard. But these days, one of the area's most common concerns was simply the ever present and ongoing struggle to survive.

Gracie knew their mission was ultimately to bring a God of love to a people who didn't have much to be joyful about these days. And the only way that was going to happen, would be to first show them He loved them enough to see their needs met. So, with a chopper full of supplies, and new knowledge to share, here they were. Or, well, there they were anyway, until this.

Holding the flashlight between her teeth she continued rummaging and scrounging through boxes and bags in the jumble of things strewn around her feet. Three twenty-four packs of bottled water, and she was pretty sure there was one more of those somewhere in the mess. Various bags of clothing, and some protein bars, plus jerky and trail mix made it out of the piles of rubble as she sorted. Amply aware she'd be thankful for all those items as time went on, she slid them aside into a comparative place of order. She also managed to rustle up the remainder of the medical supplies they'd packed for their trip. Trying to make Jason as comfortable as possible, she knew her next moves would be impossible without more morphine, so she readied another dose.

Not able to work efficiently with a flashlight hanging from her mouth, she rigged a holder for the lantern, and focused the light's beam on Jason's injured right leg. With quivering hands she sprinkled alcohol over the area, and proceeded to straighten his leg and line up the jagged bones. Finally satisfied with the appearance of her work, then dousing the area with another good amount of alcohol, she wrapped the injured leg in gauze, splinted and wrapped it again. Throughout the ordeal her face dripped with sweat and tears as Jason moaned, even crying out twice, right through the effects of the strong pain killers. When the procedure was complete she sat near her husband, shaking so badly she thought she might pass out, and stroked his fevered brow with a cloth soaked in a bit of water and alcohol from the partially empty bottle.

After a few moments of rest, and when some of the shaking subsided, she went back to work. Throughout her ministrations she'd found a number of cuts and bruises on Jason that needed tending to before she would consider taking care of her own. Once they were both cleaned up as well as she could manage under the circumstances, she sat back again, this time against a partially empty box of supplies. Now that Jason seemed to be a bit more comfortable, she allowed the tears to flow in earnest.

Oh, she wasn't crying for herself. She'd been in far worse situations than this, in her own life, and survived. She was crying for her husband. His breathing was tortured and she knew she'd have to do something about that very soon. But how to fix what was clearly a punctured lung, especially in these circumstances, without killing the man she loved? That was her present dilemma. As she sat, she leafed shakily through the first aid book she'd found in the medical supply chest.

The chopper had made its crash landing upside down and leaning nose first into an embankment. Grace knew their circumstances would have been made much worse if fuel tanks had ruptured, but was pretty sure their guardian angels had something to do with that positive outcome. Currently, she was searching for the radio. The flashlight's glow landed upon the control panel of the craft, and what remained of her fractured heart felt as though it dropped from her chest to her feet. Items flying through the cabin had crashed into the panel and dials there, crushing every helpful instrument in sight.

Then she remembered the satellite phone her dad purchased to stay in touch with them on their trip. But not locating the dark carry bag right away, she spiraled again into a panicky search for that elusive item. They'd talked on the phone; her parents, Jason and her; and took care of their "I love you" moments, just prior to leaving the coast and heading to the interior, so she knew it was here somewhere.

When her search finally revealed the black leather phone bag and its cover was quickly removed, she was devastated to see her last hope of communication smashed to bits just like the on board device. Told by the warranty manual that the phone was practically indestructible, she supposed that characterization probably didn't include damage from chopper crashes. It seemed the very thing that most likely saved their lives, their crash position, probably also destroyed their ability to communicate with the outside world. She would see what might be done with the cockpit's radio when the day offered a bit more light with which to work, but for now, she just didn't think her sanity could handle any more bad news.

In her heart of hearts she hoped a surgery for Jason could wait a bit longer. She'd found some help in the first aid book, located in their medical pack. And, the pictures displayed were very detailed. But, she was frightened to try a procedure of that magnitude in relative darkness, and in her present shaky condition. So, for now she would pray and try to get a little more rest.

Rain and storms prevailed throughout the night and with them came horrifying noises and bumps that shook and jarred the entire craft. Grace still didn't have any idea where their craft had come to rest for certain. For all she knew they might be on the edge of a precipice, or dangling from a tree. The only information she was sure of is that they were surrounded by branches and leaves that scraped and scratched at their metal cage, and that everything was very, very wet.

No matter how desperately she tried, sleep was elusive, so the night ticked away with no significant rest under her belt. Pretty soon a faint light, starting in the East, began to grow brighter. Hoping it might help her to see a bit better, even with downed trees and leaves plastered on the wind screen, she started to retrieve items she would need for the life saving surgery. Her window of time would be short, so this was the moment to take action, as it might be her only real chance.

Jason was still unconscious and his struggles to breathe were growing more noticeable by the minute. Grace decided she had to figure out a plan and get this done. In the dark her options had been limited, but now that there was a hint of daylight, she might be able to accomplish what looked completely impossible in the night. Traumatic pneumothorax was a more dangerous condition than Gracie imagined she had the skills to overcome, but with her husband's breathing deteriorating as he fought for air in the crowded space, she didn't believe she'd have a choice. So, as more morning light began to filter into the aircraft's cabin, she readied her supplies and steadied her mind, for the upcoming challenge. "Lord, you know I have no idea what I'm about to undertake. But, I think I can do it. I've always been strong and capable, so I believe I can pull this off."

Gracie hoped she'd retained enough information, from

the mandatory emergency medical classes she'd been forced to take by the missionary board, and the details from the first aid book, to pull this off without hurting Jason any worse than he already was. She was absolutely sure now, as Jason's breathing became more labored throughout the night, that he was suffering from what amounted to a deflated lung from too much air in his chest wall collapsing that vital organ.

True, a traumatic pneumothorax was very dangerous, but it was treatable, if she could only get her part of this right. She would have to relieve the pressure, by releasing the air in his chest wall that was compressing the lung. Dousing his bare chest with plenty of alcohol she felt carefully for the second and third ribs on the left side of his ribcage. From her reading she knew the space in between those ribs and near the sternum was called the second intercostals space. She placed her hands in what she hoped was the proper position to proceed.

Just as she was about to begin Jason opened his eyes and looked at her with an expression of total panic on his ghost white face. His mouth began to move with silent words. Words she couldn't quite make out. Every hair on her body stood on end and she was covered with goose flesh from head to toe. Gasping for breath Jason began to flail about. She reached for another dose of morphine, and injected the pain relief into his thigh, watching him slowly settle back down. "I love you Jason. You're going to be alright. I have got this, so just relax." Now, if she could only convince herself of the same assurance she'd just shared with the man she loved.

Hands shaking violently, and sweat dripping from her face, she paused and reminded herself to breathe. Her next steps would necessarily have to be done with calm and precision, as she couldn't risk nicking the lining of the lung. Using the utility knife, soaked in copious amounts of rubbing alcohol, that she'd salvaged from piles of stuff on the ceiling of the chopper's cabin, she carefully made an incision. Next, she inserted a plastic iv cannula into the recently made opening. The moment the small plastic tube met extraneous air, she heard the sound of whistling begin as the trapped air was released into the cabin.

And, the very instant the ensnared air left Jason's chest his breathing began to improve and his blood pressure, which had been dangerously low while in distress, slowly began to rise into normal range. Grace didn't want the air to escape too rapidly, which could cause further complications, but all seemed to be going well for now, at least as far as she could tell.

Trembling from head to foot, she picked up a bottle of water from the semi organized top of the wreckage to her right. Twisting off the lid she slid slowly down the inverted cabin wall and collapsed on a pile of clothing and supplies. Small sips to start. She didn't want to vomit, and still felt very much as though she might. But she also knew she needed to hydrate. She would rest a little now. Now that Jason's breathing was more normal. Plans for what came next could wait until she was feeling a little less overwhelmed and emotional.

Wings furled, their heavenly guard surrounded them. And now that the rain had stopped and it was bright enough to see more clearly outside the Plexiglas windshield, it was clear the area was, and had been, filled with masses of dreadful demons waiting to see if their evil plans had achieved the desired effect. Kakos was anxiously awaiting a report from his ground troops.

Fired from his 'Head Western Regional Demon' position after the previous rather pathetic and ineffectual efforts to bring Gracie and Jason down. Kakos was now assigned; along with Keres and any other underlings formerly allocated to the Western United States with him during that rather embarrassing time; to a career of tracking and bringing down the young couple who'd escaped his previous foul imaginings. His unit's sole purpose for existing now was to destroy Gracie, Jason, and anyone who was near and dear to them. So, here he was leading the hordes in Haiti. But he would also make frequent trips, accompanied by his underlings, back to Gracie's dear ones in the good ol' US of A, when conditions merited.

Things actually could have gone much worse for Kakos than this. He'd feared being sent somewhere much further south, if you get my meaning. However, the resulting demotion was devastating for Keres. Here she was, still answering to Kakos, the worst thug she'd ever had the misfortune of knowing, and him in a fouler mood than ever. She couldn't think of a worse hell than that. And, since she was already assigned to hell to begin with, she was fully aware of all its many levels. She knelt before her superior. "Speak Keres! What report have you?"

"I'm afraid, Sir, that it isn't news you will want to hear."

"Speak wench! Were they able to take down the aircraft?"

"Yes Sir. The aircraft is down. And there are even some injuries, but....."

"But what? Don't you dare tell me that they are still alive!"

"I'm sorry, Kakos. But yes. They are still alive. I don't know how, especially after all we threw at them, but that is the official word from the front." The scream, deep, penetrating and reverberating, was heard to the very depths of hell and beyond. "How can this be? Will I be defined by these two for the rest of eternity? What do I have to do to rid myself of this plague that is Grace and Jason, in order to redeem myself to Satan?"

"Sir, please, I know you're disappointed, but remember, Kakos, Grace and Jason are surrounded by their winged warriors. It's really hard for us to be effective against all that."

"I'm sick and tired of your excuses, and I will think of a worthy punishment for your failure later. Now that those two are down in the forest, hurt and vulnerable, there will be ways we can attack that even their heavenly guard can't predict. Now get out of my sight! I have to think." Kakos grabbed the younger demon by one arm and threw her with all his strength toward the chamber's entrance. She hit the exit with a loud thud, slid down the dark walnut door to the polished black marble floor and then slowly stood to her feet. She didn't dare look up, for fear that her boss would see the defiant, hateful look in her eyes. If there was a way to eliminate this demon from the underworld, and extinguish him forever from her reality, she would do it; but they were already in the last state of existence they would inhabit before the end of all things. So, she was stuck here. Stuck with him. And, stuck with the unfortunate, unending consequences of misguided, eternal decisions made long ago.

"Keres, one more thing."

"Yes Kakos."

"Does she know yet?"

"Not that we have been able to ascertain, Sir."

"Good. Do whatever you have to, to keep it that way. She mustn't find out, or our job will become much more difficult."

"I will do my best, Sir."

"And Keres."

"Yes Sir."

"I am sick of hearing their names. From now on, when you come to me with news of them, I don't want to hear their names."

"Very well, Kakos."

As Jason slowly regained consciousness on the day after his surgery he looked about the chopper's cabin bleary eyed and confused. It was obvious he'd retained little knowledge of the previous day and all that it encompassed. But, he was eager now, though admittedly very weak and tired, to hear about events of the past twenty four hours. Grace had used clothing and blankets from their supplies to make him a rudimentary, and admittedly very underwhelming, hospital bed. And, she hoped he'd slept more comfortably than she had in the few hours she'd attempted to get a little shut eye.

It had turned very quickly nighttime again, the previous day, after Grace had spent most of it performing lifesaving surgery, and then trying to get their shattered radio to work. It was all useless now, as the components were beyond repair, and she finally gave up, resigning herself to resting and watching over her husband. Throughout the day she'd viewed, through the cockpit's cracked polycarbonate windshield, demon hordes milling about outside their craft, held at bay only by the presence of golden warriors.

She'd watched with some relief as the shadows grew

and another day came to conclusion. If for no other reason than the inability to see those whose job it was to do them harm. Oh, she always knew they were there, lurking in the shadows, ready to leap into action at every evil opportunity. But, even though she knew they were defeated by the Name of the Lord, it didn't mean she couldn't get tired of seeing their horrid faces. Sometimes the stress of the burden she and Jason carried; that of the special gift of sight; was simply overwhelming. So, moments of quiet, where she could just focus on the blessings, were very important.

Grace had already determined that when she left the broken craft, to seek help for Jason, she would leave all the bottled water and prepared foodstuffs for her husband. He would have no way to find sustenance, so she wanted to be sure he had all the supplies that were available to them. He would be forced to ration, since she couldn't be sure how long the trip would take, but if he was frugal she hoped he could make it adequately until she returned. She'd located the water purification tablets amongst their survival supplies, so she would take an empty bottle and secure her water along the way. Those tablets would be essential for keeping her water free of water borne pathogens, which could cause severe intestinal problems and even death.

Being pretty resourceful she'd figure out the food as she traveled. They were currently using a plastic bucket in the chopper as a chamber pot, and Grace emptied the contents out the door each morning, but the smell was getting to be a very real issue. Jason would have no way to empty the contents after she left, and she worried about how overwhelming that particular issue might become.

It would be up to Grace to make a way out of their small sanctuary and into the hostile environment beyond the cracked wind screen, but she knew she'd be leaving Jason behind to fend for himself in his presently broken state, and wanted assurance he'd be able to tend to his own needs in her absence. Currently he couldn't move more than a few inches before being brought to a sudden halt by severe pain in his leg and chest. But, it was also apparent she couldn't stay here forever, as their food and water wouldn't last much longer.

Acutely aware that the same distance they'd covered in a mere four hours; using chopper power, on the day of their departure from Port au Prince; would likely take many days to traverse on foot through rain forests and over mountainous terrain. Gracie had no choice but to brave the forest.

By morning Jason's condition had improved a little more

and he was urging her to go. He wasn't terribly concerned for her safety, or his, as he was also aware of the gilded guardians still surrounding them. But he knew conditions could change at any moment. And, he was painfully aware his leg could soon turn gangrenous in the damp heat. The only likely way help might be secured would be to trust his wife to take care of things, and he knew she'd survived much worse in her life than a walk through the rain forest. He would just have to figure things out in the downed chopper in her absence.

He watched as Grace packed a few items in a nylon shoulder bag: a water bottle; purification tablets; two boxes of matches; a blanket and plastic sheeting; along with a string hammock, so she wouldn't have to sleep on the wet ground, and a sheet of mosquito netting; assorted cookware; the smaller of the two first aid kits; one of the flashlights and their only compass. She also strapped a small leather holster to her hip and thigh, and slid a hunting knife into the receptacle. The tool looked much larger, than its hilt to point length of eight inches, against the backdrop of Gracie's slight frame, but it made her feel a little more safe and comfortable. Better able to defend herself from possible threats as well as hunt for provisions. Grace had never taken any serious survival classes in her lifetime, only the mandatory medical knowledge courses required before embarking on this mission trip, but she'd been taking care of herself for years. And she knew God was watching over her as He provided her usual angelic protection.

At first light, she kissed her wounded husband, and headed out the choppers battered door; her winged warriors in tow and demons hissing and spitting as she passed.

The spirit of the Lord is upon me, because He has anointed me to proclaim good news to the poor. He has sent me to proclaim liberty to the captives and recovering of sight to the blind, to set at liberty those who are oppressed, to proclaim the year of the Lord's favor.

Luke 4:18-19

CHAPTER 2

S he hadn't completely lost who she was, at least not yet, but it was getting harder and harder to remember anything through the dark and blurry haze in her mind. Mike and Nancy had been worried about her since the night Jason and Gracie left on their honeymoon missionary trip. They'd gone as far as to take her to a family counselor, who claimed she was fine and probably just going through an adjustment period, so they were trying to be patient as she wandered the house in the middle of the night knocking things over and staring blankly at, well, nothing. Nancy felt a bit guilty about it, but they'd even taken to locking their bedroom door at night, just in case. The night she'd awakened to Anna standing next to her bed watching her had been completely unnerving.

Anna knew something was different with her, but couldn't put her finger on it. Evil thoughts, so evil, in fact, that she couldn't imagine they were emanating from her own personal brain matter, circled her mind at all hours of the day and night. She'd even gone so far as to sit in the upstairs window seat, as the sun slowly set in a pinkish, orange sky so beautiful it took her breath away, thinking of creative ways to torture and kill the two lovely people downstairs who'd taken her into their own home and loved her like one of their own. What was wrong with her?

It was simple actually. Anna was Kakos' contingency plan. If, for some reason he couldn't fulfill his duty to rid the world of Grace and Jason while they occupied a space in the rain forests of Haiti, he would mobilize her to take them out when they returned home. It was easy enough. He simply had to prompt her to set the house afire while everyone slept, and he could rid himself of the whole annoying, predictable clan in one fell swoop.

He knew it was risky. Keeping her hyped up with evil thoughts, and ready to do his bidding, while the young couple was not yet even at home. After all, that much malevolence crammed into such a small body, could cause problems he wasn't ready to deal with. For instance, she might go off the rails and do something crazy at school, as many of his former human tools had done. Those with the infilling had often become visible through school shootings and such, which made his further use of them impossible. Or she might even attempt some horrific plot against her new parents. And, if that happened, the authorities would become involved and take her out of the mix.

He knew from experience he couldn't capture the minds of either Mike, or Nancy, as their bond with the Son of God was far too strong. And Grace's sister, Lilly, well, he'd already tried to control her, to no avail, during the same period of time that he was tampering with the lives of her foster siblings, Bella and David. She'd proved to be a little stronger in faith than either her brother or sister and he simply couldn't break through that connection.

Tom, on the other hand, just kept the young girl at a distance. Prison had given him a keen sense of pervading evil. There was something about her that just plain gave him the creeps. Something different that wasn't there when they'd first met her at the soup kitchen, and wasn't there when Mike first brought her home for good. And, these days, whether they were working at the soup kitchen or doing chores at home, she didn't seem to be the same kid they'd all fallen in love with. He wanted to talk to Mike and Nancy about her, but what do you say when someone's kid gives you chills every time they walk into a room? He just didn't know.

Nana had been her constant companion and a valuable ally. And aside from her mom, probably her only real friend. They'd moved around a lot after she was born, and Nana always came with them. She was Anna's safe place, the rock on which her security rested, her soft place to fall. Nana was the one who told her she was smart; that she was pretty; that she was strong; and most of all that she was very much loved.

Anna was only six years old when Nana died. It was one of the worst days of her life. She heard all kinds of people tell her mom, at the funeral, that at six years old she probably didn't have a true concept of death. But she would beg to differ with them. When she saw her grandmother laying so still in the rosewood coffin at the funeral home; wearing her favorite pink dress, the one with the tiny daisies all over the bodice, and tucked about with cream colored satin; she reached out to touch her face. Shocked at the cold waxen feel of Nana's cheeks, she knew right away that the loving, kind, warm woman she'd known her whole life wasn't in there anymore. There was no way her body could have been cold like that if Nana was still there. She'd always managed to warm up every room she walked in to with her beautiful smile and nurturing ways. No, Nana was definitely not in there.

And, yes, she most certainly understood, six years old or not. It was exactly like the little frog she'd accidently squeezed too tight when she was only four. The one grandma made a small coffin for, out of an empty box of kitchen matches, lined with green felt left over from their home-made Christmas decorations. They'd dug a hole in the backyard of the house on Sycamore Street, and buried her small victim while she stood in the rain and cried. She'd wanted to dig him up and take him with them when they moved, but Nana explained that the little guy was probably nothing but dust by now.

Yes, she understood. Dead meant that her Nana couldn't hug her anymore, and couldn't regale her with more of her famous family tales. They couldn't laugh together anymore, or bake sugar cookies, or paint their fingernails. There wouldn't be anyone to braid her hair before school in the mornings with her Nana gone. It wasn't that Mom didn't want to do all those things. And, it wasn't that her mom didn't love her. But, her Mom worked three jobs and just wasn't around much.

Most of the really important pieces of her life, the ones that she knew so far, were from Nana's stories; and they gave her a sense of the intricacy of the world that she wouldn't have been aware of, if not for their very special relationship.

✝

Her mom never talked about Anna's father. But, Nana had told her plenty about him in her six short years. And even though she had to keep quiet about some of the (probably age inappropriate) stories Nana put out there, she was glad to know them. The colorful accounts that her grandmother shared helped her to decide what she would believe about herself, and what she wouldn't. She had to be careful not to let it slip that she knew things about Al; that was her father's name; because her mother had told Nana she didn't want her to tell what she knew, and Anna wouldn't have made trouble for her grandmother for anything in the world.

Nana explained to her, in intricate detail, how the Shasta mountains were ablaze the day she was born. And, in fact, that if you listened closely enough you could hear the pine trees popping and exploding, even clear down in the valley, as their sap overheated from the rampant wild fires.

The whole community was warned to evacuate, but not surprisingly, amidst all the stress, her mother went into labor early that same hot, dry, July day. Al drove them all to the hospital and after her mom was loaded onto a waiting wheelchair, they were ushered quickly into an elevator for a trip up to the waiting doctors in the obstetrics ward. Anna almost made her appearance during that elevator ride, but somehow they made it safely to a delivery room. Al stayed right in the room with her mom, but Nana was asked to wait in the hall outside, and spent the whole of Mom's labor pacing and fidgeting awaiting her precious new grandbaby.

Nana was always a little sad when she told this part of the story, but she felt it had to be shared for complete clarity of their ongoing situation. It seemed Al was disappointed that his little girl wasn't a little boy. And after he said some mean things to her mom, she cried and held her baby all the tighter. He left them at the hospital; Anna, her mom and her grandmother; to take care of some pressing business, and just never came back. They stayed in their room until it was safe to head home, and then called a cab, since Al had left them with no transportation.

Anna used to pretend to herself that perhaps her father had gone out to buy her a present and was swept up in the looming wild fires, never to be seen again. She wondered what he was like; since there were no pictures. Which of her quirky traits might be attributed to him, and if he ever thought of her. That is, if he wasn't actually swept up in the looming wildfires, never to be seen again.

Most of the time she chose to pretend he'd never existed. That maybe she'd even been created by magical fairy dust, or hatched from some ancient, mysterious egg. It was easier than being reminded every day that she just wasn't enough to cause him to want to stay. Who needed a father anyway? She didn't wish him harm, but the thought of him made her cry, so she just didn't spend much time thinking of him at all.

For her whole life it had always been mom working several jobs to care for their little family, and Grandmother at home tending to her. Because of the circumstances she didn't get to spend as much time with her mother as she would have liked, but when they did have an occasion it was always very special. A trip to the beach, a walk in the cool of the forest among the tall trees, or a visit to the local museum. And, always lunch afterward, just the two of them. With a great big banana split, and two spoons, for dessert.

She thought her mom was the most beautiful, the smartest, the hardest working, kindest woman in the world. And by the age of four she'd decided she would become very rich, so that her mom could quit working all those crazy jobs and stay at home with Nana and her. Then they would be able to spend as many days as they wanted making footprints in the warm sand, collecting leaves, and wandering together among the beautiful paintings and statues of the city.

There was no question in her mind that her mom loved her. She'd proved it over and over. Like when Anna was only five years old and she spent two weeks in the hospital. A nature buff, she'd always been a lover of animals, much to the dismay of the creatures she mauled in her desire to hug and pet them. Being an only child, with no other real playmates, can be a particularly lonely existence. So, she tended to pick up anything that crept or crawled, to keep as a pet.

She'd come across an old glass, gallon jar that already had holes punched in the rusted metal lid, probably left behind by some other small nature lover. And in an excited examination of the ivy growing on the side of the house where they lived, she discovered lots of potential friends.

She spent several days plucking spiders off the foliage and plopping them in the jar until there were so many critters inside she had to thump the jar on the grass before she could open the lid, or risk many of her new friends escaping. Being only five years old at the time, she wasn't entirely attuned to the needs of her new friends, or their carnivorous natures, and instead provided snacks of sticks and grass for them; leaving many very hungry spiders inhabiting the jar's space.

For some reason her mom wouldn't let her keep her jar in the house, so she stored it on a shelf above the washer in the garage. On a perfectly, beautiful summer day, after adding another dozen or so friends to her collection, she was walking from the climbing ivy to the garage, over the cement patio in the back of the house, talking to her little buddies through the clouded glass, when her hands slipped and she dropped her gallon jar. The quiet afternoon was pierced by the sounds of a loud crash, and a scream, as shards of glass sprayed the pavement. Now, one would think that upon release those little critters would have run for the hills. But, it was as if they had been watching the little girl, all this time, through the window of their glass prison, and were now looking for revenge for their mistreatment.

Instead, when given the opportunity, they ran right up Anna's legs. Thousands of spiders covering her, under her clothing, biting her, in her ears and her nose, and invading her hair. She screamed again, and when she awoke her mother was sitting beside her in a room with blue-green paint and faded murals of cartoonish looking, jungle animals on the walls. Hooked up to machinery that beep, beep, beeped to the steady rhythm of her heart, she looked over at her mother, confused.

Her mom, tears erupting from her red, tired eyes, relieved that she'd finally awakened, told her she'd been by her bedside for two whole weeks, waiting for her to regain consciousness. It was discovered, upon further investigation, that dozens of the eight legged friends in her jar were Black Widow spiders. The doctors told her mom that one bite rarely proved fatal, especial to a healthy person. But with so many bites the venom had a catastrophic effect on her muscles and nervous system. When the ambulance brought her in to the hospital she had been in such excruciating pain they'd started her on antivenin immediately, and rendered her unconscious with drugs that would keep her in a coma awaiting the results of the, hopefully, life saving infusions.

After that frightening two weeks, when she awoke, her Nana brought her a small stuffed monkey, with brownish red fur, a plastic face and soft felt hands and feet, that would be her constant companion for the next few years. And, when Nana came to visit in her hospital room, she told Anna of the day she'd been bitten. It seemed her grandmother was in the kitchen preparing lunch when she'd heard the screams. When she peered out the sliding glass doors to see what the problem might be, her mind couldn't quite comprehend, at first, what she was witnessing. She saw Anna laying on the concrete. She seemed to be covered with a fine layer of undulating fur, but that couldn't be. Then she noticed the broken glass surrounding her granddaughter.

Realization struck and she flew through the doors to grab the hose, turn it on, and spray Anna until she was pretty sure she'd washed away all the spiders. She checked for breath signs, picked up her small, soaking wet body, and ran inside to call for help. When Anna's mom got the call she ran from her workplace, flagged a cab, and rushed to the emergency room. By that time the bites had become red and inflamed and Anna's whole body was swelling into a hideous semi-replica of its former self. Her mother cried, and held her hand, horrified by the fact that she hadn't been there when her daughter needed her most.

After, what would later be dubbed, 'The Spider Incident', her mother worked a little less, and they spent a bit more time together. And though they were forced to make do with less, Anna didn't care. Now there were more walks in the warm sand, and more time spent in the cool of the forest. Trips to the museum and wonderful lunches at the little cafe downtown were a bit more common, and they all seemed a little less stressed. There is nothing like a near death experience to show us what's most important in life.

The following year, after Nana died, her mother met a man. His job allowed her to quit her three jobs and stay at home with her daughter, which at first seemed like a wonderful thing. But Anna couldn't help noticing the growing sadness she saw in her mom's eyes, and she knew that sadness was caused by him. She heard his shouting at night, and her mother's crying. She saw the marks on her mom's arms, and even once on her face, and, with every fiber of her being, she wanted to kill him.

He scared her. The glare in his eyes when she had the audacity to question his authority, or wonder why her mother cried so often; and the hateful way he looked at her when he thought her mother wasn't watching. "Mommy, I don't like him."

"Anna, don't talk like that. He is the only reason I'm able to stay home and take care of you."

"But he hurts you."

"Nobody can hurt me, Anna. I'm invincible. And, tomorrow you and I are going to the museum. What do you think of that?"

"I love the museum, Mommy. But I love you more. Please promise me you won't let him hurt you anymore."

"I will try my best little one. But, sometimes things happen that we just can't control."

After a few more years of his anger and abuse, Anna found out the stark truth of that statement. She was told her mother had fallen while she was at school. She knew it was him, but who would listen to a ten year old girl? And, he had friends in the State Attorney's office. Friends who had other friends in the Coroner's office. Friends who were willing to risk their careers to fake the results of a death certificate. And, before you knew it, the death was deemed, 'Accidental'.

Her mother's funeral was a small affair. A few of his friends, and a couple of her ex co-workers. She had no living relatives, and had always been too busy to pal around with anyone but Anna.

"I hadn't even heard she was sick."

"Neither had I, but we really hadn't talked much since she got married."

"I feel especially bad for her little girl. They were so close."

"Well, at least she has him to take care of her now, with her mom gone."

"Yes, he must be a good man to take on a child that isn't even his."

"She's very lucky. It could have been much worse. Thank heaven she wasn't left completely alone. That would have been even more tragic."

A simple coffin of polished walnut, and her mother pale as pale could be, laying so very still in gathers and folds of pink satin. He'd picked her dress, but Anna was angry that it was one she never wore. And, in fact, one she genuinely disliked. That was how little he knew her. And whoever had done her hair and makeup, okayed by him, was way off, because the body in the casket hardly resembled the woman she loved. This time she knew better than to reach in to touch the face of her beloved. She knew from experience it would be cold and waxen. Her mother was laid to rest beside Anna's grandmother in the ancient cemetery behind the old church, in the shade of a hundred year old oak. Shadows whispered in the wind, secrets of the dead, and chills crept the length of Anna's spine. She stood in the shade of that old tree for as long as he would let her, wondering if her heart would ever beat again.

Now Anna was completely at his mercy. She tried her best to stay out of his way, and mostly succeeded. He ignored her most of the time, as he went about his life, unless he was in a mood. Mostly he yelled at her and called her names. Reminding her that she should be grateful he hadn't thrown her out on the streets after her mother died. Yes, he announced to empty rooms, he was something special for feeding her and putting a roof over her head, and she should be ever so thankful for his benevolent kindness.

Sometimes he beat her. Then she would scurry off and hide, licking her wounds and missing her mom. Sometimes he would go about the house shouting her name, especially if he'd had a couple of cocktails. She knew in those moments she'd be in for it if she allowed him to find her. But, she knew all the really good places to hide in the great big house, and how to move from one place to another without being detected.

Anna was in fifth grade. She loved her teacher, Mrs. Campbell, who often allowed her opportunities to do the special things essential to running a classroom effectively. Erasing white boards, passing out papers. She didn't even mind when other kids talked about her behind her back and called her teacher's pet. She'd always been a bit of an outcast, so it was just par for the course. Mrs. Campbell even let her clean out Mr. Wiggles' cage, after everyone else had left for home. Mr. Wiggles was the class guinea pig. When she held him she would bury her face in his soft fur and cry in the warmth of his small, trembling body. Mrs. Campbell knew things weren't right in Anna's home life. Knowing her mother had passed away, she could feel the tension between the girl and her step father. But, what could she do? So, she tried to be there for her in any way possible. The step father was a powerful man in town. Which left her very little recourse.

As noted, over the years Anna had discovered many places to hide from the yelling and the horrible arguments between her mom and her husband. And, now, more recently, from the always angry man who should have been her protector, but instead seemed to want only to hurt her. One such place was a large concrete drainage pipe on the end of the block, which emptied into the nearby river. The five foot tall cement pipe was meant to be sealed from entry by metal bars, to keep kids and animals out of danger. However, young people in the neighborhood, looking to explore the forbidden area, had pried one of the bars loose, and if you squeezed hard enough you could get through the small opening to the inside.

Everyone knew that the cement pipes were dry unless the floodgates, which appeared at intervals up the mountain, were opened to allow passage for accumulated snowmelt from Mount Shasta. Anna had watched on numerous occasions, mesmerized and covered with goose flesh, as the water rushed through the cement pipe with such force that it rattled the ground for hundreds of feet in every direction, leaving the foam, that flew through the air, to collect in small grey islands on the surface of the waterway and nearby earth.

She knew it was a dangerous place to be, but it was cool and quiet, and sometimes the desire to be alone, even if it meant danger, was stronger than the desire to be safe. Besides, she was confident he would never find her here. As long as she was careful, and listened for the accompanying pinging noises that preceded the freezing flow, she should be safe.

Walking through the cool pipe one day, thinking about her mom and grandmother, and ruminating on how much she missed their company and their unconditional love, she didn't realize how far she'd traveled. Suddenly, her thoughts were interrupted by a pinging noise, she stopped in her tracks. How long had the pinging been going on? She'd just noticed it herself, but that didn't mean it hadn't begun earlier while she was deep in thought. Anna spun on her heels and started to run back to the opening, at first far enough away that she could barely see the light from the gap. She ran until her lungs burned and felt ready to burst. She ran until the pinging became roaring. She got to the pipe's opening and squeezed her slight frame out between the loose bar and the concrete side, just in time to scramble up the side of the ditch and fall face first on the dry ground above. She turned around to witness the foaming flood bursting through the bars, where she surely would have lost her life, and began to cry. If she hadn't gotten out before the raging water hit the bars, she would certainly have been crushed by the force of the deluge. Shaking, she made her way to the house and changed out of her dirty clothing. He need not know about her near death experience, as she commonly did her own laundry.

Just two days after her close call, she heard people in town talking about a 'terrible accident in the drainage pipes'. It seemed a group of kids, looking for adventure, made their way into the pipe and didn't make it out before the flood waters overtook them in the concrete tunnel. Four crazy kids, between the ages of six and ten, who were crushed against the bars of their adventure, and who would never see the sun rise on another day. The town held a vigil for them. Lots of people crying and holding candles with little paper disks on the bottom, to keep the hot wax from burning their fingers. Prayers, poems and singing until far into the night. Anna snuck out and attended, knowing it might just as well have been her. And, wondering if anyone would have cared so much.

It was becoming harder to avoid the man. And his leering looks were becoming more uncomfortable as she grew.

One night as she slept he crept into her room. She woke, but stayed very still, peering through barely open eyes, to see what he was up to. He stood above her, watching her. Suddenly his phone rang and he stopped and turned to leave the room. He turned again and looked back long enough to see her watching him. An evil grin transformed his face into a caricature of everything that was wrong with the world. She knew in that moment she could no longer stay in his house.

Next morning Anna waited for him to leave for work, dressed in the warmest clothing she owned, packed her bag with a few essentials and what money she had in her secret hiding spot, and left. He didn't look for her. He wasn't particularly sorry she was gone. The only person who raised an alarm was her teacher. Human Services did a cursory investigation, chalked it up to a runaway situation, and in their over burdened, red tape choked world, went on to more pressing matters. Mrs. Campbell would always wonder what happened to the shy, troubled, young girl, but they never spoke again.

No, in all these things we are more than conquerors through Him who loved us. For I am sure that neither death nor life, nor angels nor rulers, nor things present nor things to come, nor powers, nor height nor depth, nor anything else in all creation, will be able to separate us from the love of God in Christ Jesus our Lord.

Romans 8:37-39

CHAPTER 3

Once free of the chopper's cracked cockpit, Gracie was thankful to see the craft was at the very least safely grounded. Grateful that the aircraft sat; though topsy-turvy; on somewhat flat terrain at the top of the mountain. Happily she wouldn't have to worry about Jason plummeting to his death down a ravine, or over a cliff, in her absence.

She would have to quit worrying. The worry was only causing more stress. There was just no other way to do this thing, but to leave her beloved alone as she ventured off for help. As much as she wanted to stay and care for him until he could walk and travel with her, time was not currently their friend. To sit here idle would mean their food and water would run out before Jason was able to move about effectively enough for them to gain freedom together. So, without a doubt, it was abundantly clear he couldn't go with her. She hated leaving him to fend for himself in his wounded state, but she also knew that Haiti wasn't as dangerous a place as some other locations in the world they could have been stranded. That was at least a blessing.

No large wild animals here, or poisonous snakes for that matter, even though the island boasted twenty seven varieties of the latter. True there were lots of venomous spiders, mosquitoes and poisonous centipedes, but he should be reasonably safe from insect invasion if he stayed inside the craft. And there was little chance he would be traipsing about the neighborhood in his current condition. Yes, there were certainly much more dangerous places to be marooned, and she was just thankful that they weren't in one of them. She was pretty sure she could take care of herself no matter what the island threw at her. She had always been very self sufficient.

She'd left all their food and water with her husband, but the island was rife with frogs, birds, fish and snakes, so she wasn't concerned about procuring food for her trip, and she had plenty of matches with which to start a fire. With purification tablets to treat her water; she'd be able to stay hydrated along the way; so there were no immediate worries.

Looking out over the mountain vista, on which the chopper had crash landed, she was struck by the amazing beauty of the land. Verdant rain forests, glorious native flowers and, now that the rain had abated, beautiful blue skies. She took a deep breath and then coughed deeply. The air was warm and muggy. So, there was that. But, things could have been much worse. Yes, things could have been much, much worse. She could do this. There was no doubt!

She could also see, from her vantage point, that she was quite far from the coast, or any city large enough to launch a rescue mission. It might very well take her many days to make her way to any real help. She could only hope and pray that Jason would be able to hold out long enough for that help to come. Heat and humidity, especially inside of the chopper's cabin was very high, and the opportunity for gangrene to set in was therefore very high as well. She'd left medical supplies within Jason's reach, so he could change the dressings on his wounds when necessary, and she would have to trust that he would have the strength to do that. He had plenty of food and water, if he rationed it appropriately, hopefully to last until she returned.

Again, it wasn't going to benefit anyone for her to worry, so she began her descent and prayed as she climbed down the damp face of the jagged cliff, clinging with all her might to the slippery rock.

While Gracie was still high enough on the face of the mountain to see over the tops of the trees, which would soon become her primary surroundings for the foreseeable future, she took account of the distance to the coast and the city which looked, at this moment, so very far away. Once she had her bearings and prayed again, Grace finished her descent to the next level leading to the forest floor. She navigated several such levels before achieving the base of the mountain, which took the better part of the day. There she would encounter abundant scampering fauna, copious flora, and streams, which would, by the Grace of God, always find their way to the ocean.

Just to the right of where Gracie descended the slippery cliff face a waterfall splashed down over the moss covered rock. Perhaps from an underground spring, but more likely created by the abundant recent rains. This particular fall emptied into a quickly rushing small stream at the base of the mountain. The whole area was positively soaking wet, so Grace retrieved her water bottle from the bag hanging on her back and dropped in a purification tablet. Filling the bottle, and fastening the cap, she shook the bottle to dissolve the pill. She'd wait a bit to be sure the water was fully treated. The last thing she needed was to pick up a parasite.

Before she settled down for the night she would make her way to a dryer location. Creatures in the area proved to be quicker than her amateurish attempts to pierce them with a quickly thrown knife. At one point she almost lost the knife in the stream. Perhaps some practice would help? For now, she was exhausted and figured it wouldn't hurt to go without supper this once. Drinking her fill of water, and replenishing the bottle while adding another purification tablet, she decided to set up a makeshift camp. Hanging the string hammock between two relatively sturdy trees, she lined it with the plastic sheeting, leaving enough extra, hanging over the side, to cover herself against any night-time rains, and then covered the inside with the light blanket from her bag. It took a bit to figure out how to climb into the hammock, without dumping herself out the other side. But, once she managed the logistics, she covered herself with the blanket, the plastic, and then the mosquito netting. Her sleep was fitful, as she spent much of her time concerned about Jason, and battling the muggy heat. But she managed to sleep for a short while. And, when she rose in the morning she washed her face in the nearby stream, smoothed her hair back, and drank a little water.

The plastic kept her mostly dry in the night, even when a light mist had begun in the wee hours of the morning, so she was grateful to have at least that much in her favor.

Her guardians were still in attendance, but at moments like these she almost resented their presence. It would be different if they were allowed to pick her up and carry her to the nearest source of help, or give her some kind of aid, but when all they did was watch her bumbling along, their company was most disconcerting.

And, yes, she was fully aware that it was probably these same angelic warriors who'd saved them and their chopper from a fiery death, but come on now, a little help getting back to the city would have been a huge blessing too. As much as she was grateful for their presence in times of emergency, when they were allowed to intervene in her favor; there was a part of her that felt it would be just fine if they would remain invisible the rest of the time. Well, she supposed it was like anything else, you take the good with the bad. And really, how bad was it to have visible heavenly warriors in your presence?

Back in the chopper Jason woke from a fitful night of mostly unsuccessful attempts at sleep. He'd seen the rain trickling down the wind screen in the wee hours of the morning, leaving rivulets of water on the outside of the

glass and tracks of condensation on the inside, and he began to pray for Gracie who was out in the foul weather. The
inside of the cabin felt like a sauna, and already stunk to
high heaven, but there was nothing he could do about the
discomfort. Sweat actively trickled down and through every crevice of his body, to be caught in the dampened piles
of clothing Grace had used to construct his makeshift bed.
Some of the perspiration was from the muggy heat, but
more was caused by the pulsing pain in his leg and chest.

Movement was agonizing. He supposed if he'd been
back in the states with a break so severe, his leg would be
in traction to stabilize the injury. Instead, he was forced to
move in order to use the chamber pot, and to reach food
and water. Even while splinted some movement of the leg
was inevitable and left him panting and moaning afterward. Grace had done her best to place everything in close
proximity to her injured husband, but there was only so
much room directly around him, so she'd also done her
best to improvise.

Jason was trying to control the pain in his leg using aspirin, throughout the day, with little success. He didn't want
to continue on morphine. It left him in a state of dazed
confusion for hours at a time, which he decided was not

a good state to be in when surrounded by Satan's hordes. Who knew what they might try if given half a chance. So, he slept fitfully and prayed unceasingly.

Thirsty, due to the heat and constant sweating, his throat was parched and he was beginning to cramp up from dehydration. But, he knew he must conserve his water. There was just no way to know how long the trek down the mountain would take for his wife. He had his Bible, and when there was enough light he read to comfort himself, and to fend off the boredom of sitting in a chopper in the middle of the rain forest, with no company and no other way to occupy his time. He knew God was on their side, and that they had been called to this mission field, so he trusted the Lord to get them out of the fix they were in. God is good. He had no doubt of that. It had been proven to him over and over, right through from his childhood until now.

He'd been a particularly quiet child. Mom was a single parent. He'd never met his father, and his mother flat out refused to speak of him. However, since some of the neighbor kids called him 'bastard', he guessed the union had not been highly approved of in the community. His mom lived with the frequent digs, of those who considered themselves morally superior to her, by putting her head down and averting her eyes. She worked hard and was bound and determined to make up to her son for the mistakes she'd made in bringing him into the world the way she did. The fact that she remained faith filled, and faithful, through it all was a miracle in itself, especially due to the way she'd been treated by the judgmental 'so called' Christians in their small town.

Yes there was trauma as a result of having no dad present in his life, but, due to that he remembered Uncle Tom being around quite a bit when he was small. He looked up to him and was always thrilled when his mother's funny, unpredictable brother showed up, seemingly like magic, usually when he was most desperate for some male bonding time and advice.

Uncle Tom taught him to fish, pitch a tent, start a camp fire, and play guitar (sort of). But, he also taught him how to spit, throw dice, and blow smoke rings. When his impulsive uncle was around, life was a laugh a minute; however, his mom didn't think much of it was very funny.

As he'd grown she approved less and less of the time he spent with Uncle Tom. And, when he was about fifteen years old, his uncle disappeared from his life. He didn't know, at the time, that his mother had sent the man away, as she believed him to be a terrible influence on her impressionable son. Thankfully, the cigarette smoking did not remain part of his future. And even better, he seemed to naturally gravitate, for some unknown reason, to a life centered around Christ.

His mother never told him about the cardboard village under a bridge, or any of the horrible crimes of which his uncle was accused. The only thing he knew was that his uncle was a guest of the state penitentiary. He didn't hear much about him after that, until Tom reached out to his sister in a letter to tell her of the radical conversion experience he'd undergone after meeting Grace.

Jason had also never shared his amazing gift with anyone. His ability to see into the spiritual realm. His mother knew, of course, but urged him to keep his gift to himself. She didn't want him to endure, what she was sure would be, ridicule and scorn. Therefore, even though he'd had this ability since he was a small boy, he'd never shared his secret, even with his Uncle Tom.

Kakos was inconsolable. He'd been called before the

big guy and read the riot act for several hours. And, when Kakos was upset, he made sure every one of his attending demons felt the building wrath as it trickled down to every single personnel level beneath. Keres knew every move she made upset her boss when she had to bring negative news from the front, but that didn't stop the unpleasant reports from coming in. So, once again she was standing before her superior with bad news. "Kakos, your Majesty. I'm sorry Sir. We've just received another report from those stationed on the front. And, I apologize Sir, but it isn't good news."

"Well, don't just stand there girl. Spit it out!"

"Sir, the girl has left the chopper."

"Explain to me how that is not good news? Doesn't that leave the injured one alone? We have a better chance of successful attack if they are separated, do we not?"

"Well, Sir, that would be true if they were not each surrounded by angel warriors. However....."

"Don't 'however' me. There has got to be a vulnerability. Find out what it is, and use it. I am not going to answer for this alone if these two are not taken out of the picture."

"Yes Sir. We will work on it. I will do my best."

"Well, so far your best hasn't been good enough, has it? So, I expect better than that. Just get it done and get back to me."

"Yes Kakos. Right away Sir."

"Keres."

"Has she figured it out yet?"

"Not that we have been able to tell, Sir."

"Keep it that way."

"Yes sir. With all in my power."

Keres walked out of the room relieved that Kakos hadn't thrown her across the room in a fit of rage this time, since she had expected as much or worse. But, how. How was she supposed to get to these two who were so entirely surrounded by heavenly host, and who could literally see every demon who would try to do them harm? It wouldn't be easy, but she was going to have to come up with something resembling a plan. She didn't even want to see what Kakos was capable of at his worst.

Her night in the hammock was still uncomfortable, even though she'd finally figured out a way to climb aboard without much hassle. She had to admit, though, that it was better than sleeping on the wet, bug infested ground. Hungry, but still ,sadly, a total klutz at using the hunting knife she'd brought for that purpose, she was on the lookout for anything that might be breakfast. Figuring that as long as she stayed on the path of the stream she would eventually wind up at the ocean, her direction was set. And, from what she'd been able to discern up on the mountain, Port au Prince was about as close to that general vicinity, as one could get; although still so very far away.

Suddenly, out of the corner of her eye, she saw something moving on a nearby tree. Slowly she removed the knife from its leather holster, and flung it in the direction of the movement as fast as she could. She completely missed the tree. And the snake that was supposed to be breakfast, slithered off into the forest. She would really need to practice her knife skills, or she might likely starve to death here in the woods. Loading her meager belongings in the pack she would carry on her back, she listened to her stomach grumble and growl. She drank a little more water and refilled the bottle, adding another purification tablet, and decided to be on her way. She'd keep her eyes open as she walked. And simply hope breakfast would happen.

It was light enough now that Jason could see the demons milling around outside the chopper. Grateful they couldn't get inside because of the protection afforded in the Name of Jesus and the presence of His angels, he went about his morning routine. A little granola and a ration of water. It wasn't much, but he was in so much pain he really wasn't very hungry anyway. And besides, he knew Grace didn't have any food at all with her, which made him feel pretty guilty about eating at all. So, he prayed she would be able to find nourishment out there somewhere. She'd been pretty confident that she wouldn't have any problems in that area. And, since he was always finding out something new about his lovely bride, perhaps excellent knife skills were one more thing he had to learn about this wonderful woman. After a couple of aspirin he pulled out his Bible. Reading might take his mind off some of the pain he was experiencing.

Hiking through wet vegetation near the brook Grace noticed the stream had calmed down a bit where the water was deeper, and she could see some small fish darting about. She didn't have any fishing equipment, but perhaps a spear. There were plenty of trees around, so she chose a branch about three feet long that was relatively straight. Removing the bark and sharpening one end she held it in her hand to test the feel of it. Standing on the stream's bank, as close to the water as she could get without falling in, she waited. Soon there was a school of small fish in front of her, so she thrust in her spear. Nothing. Again she waited and again she tried her luck with the spear. Praying, she asked the Lord to give her success. Once again she waited and another school of fish appeared. Once again she jabbed her weapon into the water, and once again she missed. Frustrated, angry, and in a fit of temper, she threw her spear. In so doing, she pierced a good sized fish as it and the spear quickly disappeared downstream. She sat down hard on the mossy bank and began to cry.

Once she was cried out she exclaimed, "Well, this isn't going to solve anything. I'm never going to get help for Jason if I don't keep moving. I'm sorry I got so angry Lord. Please forgive me. I know I can do this."

She stood up and made her way downstream, where as she walked, she saw her spear caught in the foliage on the stream's bank, still attached to the fish. She jumped up and down with glee and retrieved her weapon and her breakfast. "I knew I could do this if I just put my mind to it!" She was finally able to get a small fire started, though without a doubt the damp twigs produced as much smoke as they did heat. Once the fish was cooked through, though, she thought it the most delectable thing she'd ever eaten. She was feeling pretty proud of herself now. Cleaning up, and storing her cooking implements, she stood to stretch her legs. Downing the bottle of water from her bag, refilling it, and adding another pill, she tucked the whole thing back in her pack, readying herself to be off.

The ground was virtually alive with insects, and whether standing or sitting, she was forced to constantly brush herself free of ants, mosquitoes, spiders and the like. And, though Haiti's snake population was fairly innocuous, she knew the island contained several poisonous varieties of spider (tarantula, and banana to name a couple), as well as a certain breed of giant, poisonous centipede. So, not wanting to suffer the pain of a random bite, she stayed ever on the lookout.

Jason hummed to himself and sang old hymns. The demons who surrounded his resting place writhed in pain from the simple worship. Jason wasn't paying attention to them as he changed the dressing on his wounded leg. So far He'd been able to keep it mostly clean. And, he had plenty of supplies with which to change the bandages regularly, but he was detecting a subtle change in the smell emanating from his wound. If he could keep the area as sterile as possible and bound with clean gauze, he might have a shot at eliminating the possibility of gangrene. He prayed again. A couple more aspirin, and a few more hymns sung loudly were exactly the medicine he needed; and exactly the right form of torture to keep the enemy at bay.

Well, she certainly needed more practice throwing the hunting knife she'd brought with her. Frustrating to say the least, she was once again digging through damp, buggy vegetation to retrieve a wild throw. Suddenly, she saw a black snake looking back at her from the undergrowth. Knowing Haiti didn't have any snakes that were particularly venomous to humans, she reached in and grabbed the serpent by the tail. It came up to bite her hand, but she swung it hard, striking the nearest tree with its head. She was shaking almost uncontrollably when she finally stood up straight. If she'd thought at all about her recent action, supper would probably have been purified water again, but now, she could start a small smoky fire, skin her catch, and sit down to a hardy meal of roasted snake. Surprisingly, just as she'd often heard, it did taste a lot like chicken. And, she was finally beginning to think she just really might be able to do this.

As it grew dark she set up camp again. And, just as before, a hammock slung between two trees, covered first with plastic, then her blanket, was her bed for the night. It was easier to climb into the bedding tonight, now that she'd had a little practice. After covering up with the blanket, plastic, and mosquito netting, she settled down for the night. It was still dreadfully hot and muggy, but she was so exhausted she fell asleep saying her prayers. More light drizzle that night meant soggy ground again, but she woke up dry and fairly well rested in her sweaty, plastic cocoon.

Jason woke again in the night to bitter pain. He tried singing, humming and finally crying. Glad that his beautiful wife wasn't here to see him acting like such a baby, while she was being so brave. He gave himself an injection of morphine. As the drug took effect he prayed for

Gracie with all his might until he succumbed to the drug induced haze.

Blessed are those whose lawless deeds are forgiven, and whose sins are covered; blessed is the man against whom the Lord will not count his sin.

Romans 4:7-8

CHAPTER 4

The folks were getting pretty worried, aware they should have heard something more from the kids by now. They'd been in contact from the beginning; at least enough to know that the newly-weds had arrived in Port au Prince during some rather violent riots in the city. They also knew the young couple took, much to Gracie's avid protests, required medical certification classes before being allowed to continue on with their missions trip. Mom and Dad knew she was just anxious to get out there and get her hands dirty. Who could blame her for that. But, they were happy that the kids would be more prepared for any eventuality.

A call just prior to the ill-fated chopper flight had assured the loved ones back home that all was well. But they'd promised to call when they arrived at the mountain village, where they would be ministering to the locals, and no one had heard from them for days. When Mike finally broke down and called the satellite phone he'd purchased, purely to make Mom and himself feel better, all he got was static. This was the exact same satellite phone they'd communicated on just days ago. So, what was the problem now?

He called the missionary services office for Haiti to ask a few questions, and was told that it wasn't unusual to lose cell phone contact in that mountainous area, even with a satellite phone, so they decided to wait another day or two before raising any alarms.

As they talked quietly, Anna walked into the room and sat on a chair across from them. "Supper will be ready in a bit Dear. Is there anything you need?" Mom asked.

Anna smiled a strange smile that made all the adults in the room shiver and break out in goose flesh. And then she simply rose and walked back out of the room.

"I don't care what that doctor said, Nancy. There's something going on with that girl. She's not the same little girl who walked into the soup kitchen. And, she's not the same girl I brought home."

"Mike, please, she'll hear you."

"That's exactly my point, Nance. You're afraid she'll hear us. How is it okay for us to be afraid of our own daughter?"

"I've been meaning to talk to the two of you about that."

"Have you noticed something wrong too, Tom?"

"How could anyone not notice, Mike? I will agree that she is definitely not the same kid you brought home before

Grace and Jason got married, and it's been getting worse by the day. I don't want to hurt your feelings or anything, but she flat out gives me the creeps."

"Well, to be honest, we've been locking our bedroom door at night, Tom. So, I know what you mean. But, we can't just give up on her. The doctor seems to think she's going through some sort of adjustment period. I think we have to wait it out and see if it gets better. If things don't smooth out in a few weeks, we can seek further help."

"We'll do what you want for now, Nancy. But I agree with Tom. The whole thing has gotten pretty creepy."

"Fine Mike, but promise me you'll give her a chance. This is all a big change for her. We're her family now and we have to give her every opportunity. Please, tell me you guys agree. Can you just do this for me? Just for a while?"

"Agreed, but if things don't change, soon, we go get her some more help, understand?"

"Yes honey."

"Whatever you two want is fine with me, as long as you know how I feel. And, just so you are aware, I'm locking my door tonight too."

Anna was just outside the doorway as the adults quietly talked about her. Somewhere deep inside was a piece of her that was struggling to get away from the force holding her captive in her own body. But, the outer part, the part that was in control, was just waiting for orders from the boss. And the thought of the fun she'd have when he gave those orders, brought a small smile to her lips, as she slowly twisted the head off of the small teddy bear she held against her chest.

When Mom called her for the evening meal, and she didn't come right away, Nancy walked out the door of the dining room and saw the small teddy bear head laying on the floor. Picking it up, she looked around to see her daughter standing at the top of the stairs holding the small decapitated body. The look on her face was one of a malevolence so strong, it made Nancy take an unsteady step backward. "Come and eat your supper, Anna." She said as shivers ran the length of her spine.

"Kakos, I thought you might want to hear that we are getting reports back on the little girl we have stationed at the woman's parent's house."

"Go ahead. What report have you?"

"The watchers think she might be getting overwhelmed.

They don't know how much longer she can handle the in-filling without doing something which will get her noticed by the wrong people."

"Well, you know I don't want to empty her just yet. Unlike her new parents, she has never become part of the body of Christ. At least not yet. And we have to try to keep it that way. We may only have a certain amount of time to take advantage of that situation. There is a chance that after we use her we can also take possession of her eternal spirit. That is a reward I won't give up lightly.

My plan is to be rid of the ones in Haiti, once and for all. But, if that doesn't work out the way I want, I will use the girl. Perhaps in a glorious house fire of epic proportions. And, when we use her, she will rid us of the whole family at once, and then she will join us in hell forever."

" I will notify the watchers, Sir. You have my personal assurance. They will report back regularly, as ordered."

"Good, see that you take care of that immediately. And check back with me as soon as you hear anything."

That night, Nancy lay in bed listening to her new daughter wandering the house, up and down the stairs and bumping into walls. She hated the fact that she was terrified of the girl. When she'd glanced up the landing to see Anna standing at the top holding the small headless bear, she knew once and for all; no skirting the issue this time; that something evil was afoot. She'd gazed deep into her eyes, before the girl turned away, and saw an emptiness, an ugliness, that frightened her to the core. What could have happened to the shy little girl who'd come to live with them only weeks before? The little girl who'd longed to be part of their family? She felt like the worst mom in the world.

Mike was right of course. She absolutely needed help. But, the counselor they'd talked to seemed to think all was well. And, by all official accounts, she was doing fine in school. There were no reports of concern from teachers or other students. Maybe they were making more out of the situation than was warranted?

But, no. That wasn't true at all, was it? She knew deep in her heart that something was terribly, terribly wrong. She believed that the problem existed at a level beyond the mere physical, or mental. She knew in her soul that this was somehow a spiritual issue. That night, alone in their bedroom, she decided to broach the subject with Mike. "Honey?"

"Yeah Babe?"

"I wanted you to know I've been watching Anna, and I think you're right."

"How so?"

"Well, yesterday, when I walked out to the entryway, after we were all talking about what's going on with her, I saw Anna standing at the top of the stairs. She was holding her teddy, but his head was torn off and laying at my feet. The look in her eyes horrified me."

"I'll bet it did. So, what do you want to do?"

"I'm not sure, Mike. But, does it make sense to you if I say that I don't think this is an issue some lay-counselor can fix? I believe we are dealing with a problem that lives in the realm of the spiritual. One that involves the powers of darkness. I mean, doesn't it feel like something from our days of ministry in the prisons with Jason and Gracie?"

"Of course that makes sense to me. After all the things we witnessed in that prison ministry with the kids, that is the only thing that really makes sense at all. I don't know why I didn't see it sooner. What do you think we should do?"

"Well, I think we should sit down and talk to her. We need to gauge her reactions. Perhaps we should talk to her about Jesus, and see if issues arise at the mention of

His Name."

"I think you're absolutely right. Of course this couldn't have come at a worse time, since we are trying to figure out what's going on with the kids."

"Isn't that just exactly how the enemy works things out, Mike? Of course he would try to direct our gaze away from stopping anything that might harm those we love."

"Yeah, you're right. And that means there is probably something else going on in Haiti too; something more than what meets the eye. It would be just like Satan to misdirect our focus. We need to find out what's going on with Anna, while checking on Jason and Gracie too."

"I agree, Mike. And that means we can't take advice from Haiti's missionary council either. They wanted us to wait, but we can't do that, can we? Not when we know that the enemy is trying to take our focus off of intervening for the kids. That is pretty much a guarantee he's after them, isn't it?"

"Yes, it is, but we also know that Gracie is pretty good at taking care of herself, and she has an advantage. She and Jason can see the enemy where we can't, so we have to go about this the right way. I'm going to make some phone calls and try to find out what's going on. If there is anything to know, we will know it by the end of the day."

"Thank you. I know I can always count on you. Just sic 'em babe."

Sitting upstairs, on her white, lacey bed spread, in the lavender room she'd dreamt of living in for her whole life; Anna was consumed by hate. The small piece of her that could still identify as Anna didn't know where the hate was coming from, but it multiplied by the hour and had almost consumed her. She'd seen the look in her parents eyes. Especially her mom's. The abject fear. And it broke her heart, at the same time that it filled her with a sense of triumph. Tears trickled down her cheeks unchecked, though she was almost numb from the disgust which filled her whenever she thought of the love of her new family.

During brief moments of lucidity she longed for human touch. Hugs from her new mom. And smiles from the people who'd taken her into their home without a second thought. But then, like a rushing wind, the unexplained anger destroyed her resolve, and she was once again overtaken by the rage that couldn't be explained. It was tearing her apart from the inside out, and she didn't know how much longer she could hold on. She'd thought several times of throwing herself out the window of their lovely Victorian home. Perhaps that would quiet the voices. The voices that never stopped attacking her every thought. The only thing that stopped her was the hold 'he' had on her. It was very apparent that he wasn't done with her yet.

Mike made several calls, and finally located someone in authority who might be able to help. "I agree sir. And, you're probably right. We haven't heard from Jason and Grace here either. The afternoon of their departure from the base we saw a pretty bad storm hit the mountains, right in the vicinity of where they were headed, but we were experiencing storms here as well. Bad weather in this part of the world, especially at this time of year, does not necessarily constitute an emergency. We experience tropical storms in the region all the time, as I'm sure you are aware. However, there's no way they shouldn't have been able to land the chopper, since Jason is a very accomplished pilot. We didn't receive an S.O.S., so it couldn't be confirmed that they even needed any help. It didn't make sense then to send able bodied men on a wild goose chase if there wasn't an emergency. Not when those men are needed here. And, let's face it. The satellite phone could simply be out of commission."

"Captain, I get what you're saying, but these are our kids. I know that something is wrong. I can feel it in my gut."

"Mr. O'Sullivan, I can hear how worried you are. But, a gut feeling is not really a good reason to take men who are needed here, and redirect them to unknown locations for no apparent reason. We have been very short handed and simply cannot spare the manpower."

"Okay, okay, I understand. I'll take care of it myself."

"What's going on Mike? What did you mean you'll take care of it yourself?"

"Nance, they don't have the manpower to hunt for the kids. And, the more time that passes, the more sure I am that something is wrong. I'm going to Haiti to look for Gracie and Jason."

"But, how? I don't understand how you think you're going to find them on that big island, in the middle of a rain forest?"

"I'm going to take Tom with me, if he'll go, and we will bring them home. The missionary office has a last filed flight plan for the kids and that should at least get us going in the right direction. Please don't try to stop me, Babe. I have to do this, and that's all there is to it. The holidays are almost here. We'll call Lilly and have her come home early, to stay with you and Anna, so you won't be alone. I'll take a satellite phone with me, so we can stay in touch, and I will figure it out. Do you trust me?"

"Of course I trust you Babe. I'll call Lilly. You go talk to Tom, and call the airline about tickets. Things with Anna are just going to have to wait a little longer."

Lilly headed home to stay with Mom. They would share the master bedroom while Mike was away, and they would try to keep an eye on Anna together. Mike had to dig into their savings, as last minute airline tickets were pricey. But he and Tom would leave the next morning, as soon as they were sure Lilly had arrived safely to help Mom. They didn't know exactly what they might find when they arrived in Haiti, but they were resigned to doing whatever was needed to get the kids back home safe and sound.

With the men gone, Nancy and Lilly would be constant companions. They decided to get some fall decorating done, and invited Anna to help them. She stood in the living room and stared at them for a full five minutes before turning on her heels and heading back upstairs to her room.

"I don't get it Mom. What is going on with Anna?"

"That's why we asked you to come home for a while, Lilly. We don't know what's going on with your little sister, and Dad didn't want me here alone with her until we find out."

"Well, I can tell you right now that she's acting just like the men in the prisons. The ones who were filled with demons. Don't you remember?"

"I guess you're right, Lilly. I think I just didn't want to see it. I'm glad you're here."

"We were going to be home in a couple of weeks for the holidays anyway, Mom. All my professors were willing to work with me via computer, since my grades are so good."

"I don't know if I've told you lately, how proud I am of you young lady?"

"Only every time we talk, Mom. Thank you. I could never have done any of this without you and Dad. I'm so grateful to you, and I would do anything to help."

"Thank you sweetheart. God is good."

"All the time, Mom. All the time."

Anna laid back on her bed, a cacophony of sounds exploding in her head, confusing her and making her long for an end to it all. Warm tears seeped from the corners of her eyes, emanating from a deep, deep place that she could barely remember, and ran down the sides of her face to drop on the clean white bedspread. Flashes of her former life with mom and grandma, before their untimely deaths, played in her mind and caused her heart to feel as though it had turned to lead in her chest. Swallowing tears until her stomach was bitter with the taste of them, she turned on to her side and sobbed until sleep took her.

When she woke, still filled with grief, she wondered. How had she survived without them for so long? And, perhaps a better question was, why had she survived without them? If she had her way right now, that would be quickly resolved. She truly had no desire to be alive even one minute longer, but couldn't seem to do anything about it. Whatever entity was in control simply would not let her end her life until her task was complete.

Laying on her bed now, with her eyelids shut tight, she could see her mom in her mind's eye as clear as if she were right there in the room with her. So lovely and delicate. The exhaustion on her face, as she tried to work three jobs to keep them in groceries, was painful to see. The smile in her eyes, when she looked at her daughter, made Anna's heart sing. Yes, she knew her mom had loved her. The bruises on her face and arms after she married 'him', and the sorrow in her face after, first, the loss of Grandma; and then the loss of her self-respect, as she dealt with abuse trying to keep a roof over her daughter's head, were proof of that.

Anna had been taught not to wish harm on anyone. Her mom and grandmother were decent people, who would help a stranger at the drop of a hat. They'd taught her to go the extra mile for someone in need. They'd just never explained to her the reason why she should be good to people. And, as she'd watched her beloved mother deteriorate more and more, by the day, at the hands of that awful man, her desire to do him harm grew. The enemy was using that hatred now, to turn her into the tool he would need, to do his despicable work.

With her eyes closed to her current situation, she could smell the distant ocean breeze and feel the sand between her toes. Her skin tingled at the rush of wind from the giant redwoods. And, the beautiful paintings and sculptures brought a smile to her lips. She could imagine the fragrance of her mother's perfume and feel the warmth of her hand. Until Satan grabbed hold of her heart and she was once again filled to the brim with a white hot hatred she couldn't explain.

"I love you Mike. You guys be careful. We will be praying for you day and night. Please keep us posted, and bring our kids home safe. I don't want to have to send the cavalry in after you too!"

"I love you too Babe. Take care of yourself. And Lilly, help your mom with Anna. She's going to have her hands full. I promise we will keep in touch, but we don't know what we're going to run into, so be patient."

"I will Dad. God bless you both. Be safe and come home soon. I love you."

Mike and Tom loaded the gear they would take on their flight and drove off into the pre-dawn darkness. Not aware of the challenges awaiting them, they boarded a flight to Miami where they would change planes for their final destination.

For we know that if the tent that is our earthly home is destroyed, we have a building from God, a house not made with hands, eternal in the heavens. For in this tent we groan, longing to put on our heavenly dwelling, if indeed by putting it on we may not be found naked. For while we are still in this tent, we groan, being burdened-not that we would be unclothed, but that we would be further clothed, so that what is mortal may be swallowed by life. He who has prepared us for this very thing is God, who has given us the Spirit as a guarantee.

2 Corinthians 5:1-5

CHAPTER 5

With no shortage of demons hiding behind trees and in every possible nook and cranny, Grace knew she must be on the lookout for peril every step of the way. There are those things in nature that can be innately dangerous, but, she must also be wary of various traps set by the enemy. And, though it was true, she had winged protectors guarding her, she was also abundantly aware they would only interfere if the Gospel message was in clear danger.

She'd been made aware of that stipulation on a number of occasions lately when she was, in what she considered imminent danger, and thought it would be nice to be rescued from this or that difficulty. Perhaps she'd just been too full of herself for way too long, once she'd first been made aware of the heavenly guard surrounding her. It's not as though she was the only one encircled with mighty warriors after all. Every human being on earth was surrounded by either angels or demons, as fulfilled by their own eternal choice. The only difference was in that she and Jason could see them.

However, aware of the spiritual realm surrounding them, she'd gotten a bit used to that protection. Now, she was finding more and more that the job of the heavenly host in her presence was not merely to answer her every whim, but to assure the safety and purity of the Gospel message. And to guarantee that the inerrant Word would be passed down from generation to generation. Grace was discovering that she was but a tiny piece of that puzzle, with no guarantees other than the eternal love of God through her salvation in Jesus.

Knowing all of this, she was becoming more aware that her angels were less her own personal servants, and instead, entirely the servants of God and His message, answerable only to Him. It was a humbling thought, and might even help her stay on her toes. She decided to ignore her heavenly escort for now, with the full expectation that they would leap in to help if the situation warranted. After all, she'd pretty much always been able to handle things on her own.

Packing up for the day she sighed. The heat, and humidity, ever present, sapped her of strength before she could even begin that day's trek. But, she had to push on. Her goal, to rescue her husband, became a more pressing matter with each passing minute. Every hour which passed without the proper medical attention, made it more likely that gangrene would take his leg, and even his life. Grace said a quick prayer for the safety of her husband, and slung her bag over her shoulder.

Her water bottle was empty. Dropping in another purification tablet from the front pouch of her pack she leaned over the bank of the nearby stream to fill the container. At precisely that moment, a tarantula the size of a baseball dropped from above, and into her hair. She lurched forward, arms flailing, and fell headlong into the rushing water. Her bag left her shoulder and bobbed downstream, soon sinking into a deep pool, and filling with water. At the same time she struggled to keep her head up as she crashed full bore into every jagged rock and embedded branch along the way.

Gratefully the hands of her heavenly guardians, those that she was questioning a short while before, kept her head from smashing into boulders that would surely have knocked her unconscious, had she connected directly with a single one of them. About two miles downstream, from where she'd launched ungracefully from shore, the water began to slow ever so slightly and she was able to make her way to the slimy, mossy bank. Hauling her wet and battered body from the water she groaned, rolled on to her back, and attempted to take stock of her injuries.

Mostly bruises and bad scrapes. But her right wrist was already swelling. She wasn't sure if it was a break or a severe sprain. There was no doubt about her ankle though. It was most definitely broken, as she could see a piece of stark white bone poking through torn skin and noticed the odd angle of her foot. The pain was searing and she was doing all she could to keep her wits about her through the throbbing ache.

Without her bag she didn't have any supplies. No way to make a fire. Not even minimal first aid with which to treat her wounds. No hammock, blanket, or plastic. And, worst of all, no water bottle or purification tablets. Somehow, the hunting knife she wore strapped to her thigh had survived the trip, but without cooking implements and fire, she didn't have a lot of use for that either. Suddenly her situation had gone from serious to life threatening. Now, she prayed for herself. Lost and alone, she closed her eyes for a moment and imagined Jason, her mom and dad, Lilly and Anna. Would anyone ever find her dead body? Would Jason ever get the help he needed? She broke down and began to sob. Then she shook her head. "Stop it you ninny! Quit your whining and whimpering." She said out loud. "Just get up and keep going. You've been taking care of yourself for years, so this isn't any different than all the things that the world has thrown at you your whole life!"

The knife came in handy after all. She cut strips of bark from various trees, and several small branches. Next she pulled large leaves from a nearby tree. Placing the branches strategically around her ankle, she adjusted the bone as best she could through lots of tears, packed leaves for padding and wrapped several layers of bark strips around the surface, tucking the ends into the exterior layers of 'bandage'. She cut a longer branch, to use as a makeshift cane. Not ideal, but with leaves for padding it just might work well enough to get her by. Using the cane was difficult, to say the least, because of her injured wrist. But, concentrating on that might take her mind off of her current untenable situation.

At the exact moment Grace fell in the water, Jason had an urging in his spirit to pray. He knew he was praying for Grace again. He wasn't sure what had befallen her, but the demons outside were certainly excited about something, whooping and hollering with vigor.

He began to entreat the Lord in earnest for the only woman he'd ever loved. And, he knew he couldn't stop. Something told him she would need every one of his most urgent prayers. "Father God, I trust you to keep us safe. I implore you Lord to keep your hand on Gracie, and walk her through whatever might lie ahead. Thank you Lord for your direction, your protection, your provision and your Grace. In Jesus' Name. Amen."

"Kakos, Sir, I have news!"

"Speak! What news have you?"

"It's about the ones in Haiti!"

"Good news?"

"Great news Sir!"

"Spit it out Keres. What have you heard?"

"Sir, the girl fell in the water, just as you planned, and her supplies are washed away! She's even managed to break her ankle and her wrist! We have her now, Sir. There is no way she can survive without clean water and medical supplies."

"Wonderful news, Keres! This is the break I've been waiting for! I finally have something worth telling the boss.

Stay on top of this. I want to know every new development, do you understand?"

"Yes Sir. Absolutely Sir. You will know the moment I know."

"Make it so. And, Keres, is she still ignorant of her other situation?"

"Yes sir, as far as we can tell."

"Good."

"Mike, I see the runway below. Wake up buddy."

"Thanks Tom. Hey, did you get any shut eye?"

"Yes Sir. I just woke up about twenty minutes ago. It looks like a nice day down there."

"Good, that will make it easier to find a pilot who's willing to take on passengers." What he didn't know was that the available pilots in the area were so desperate for the few extra dollars they might make piloting a customer, that they would have flown rain or shine. But, stories were rife of pilots who'd gone down in those mountains, never to be seen again. So, it wasn't going to be easy to convince anyone to champion their cause.

"Do you still have those numbers?"

"Yep, and they should begin to lead us in the right direction. Are you ready for this?"

"Yes I am."

"You know it's going to be rough, right?"

"Yes I do. But, we've got gear. And that's probably more than Jason and Gracie have."

"I'm sure you're right, but we are still going into uncharted territory and we don't have any idea what we're going to find."

"I'm not worried about it. What do you always tell me Mike? 'God's got our backs'."

"Thanks for reminding me, Tom. And you're right, buddy. God does have our backs. Let's go get our kids."

After checking with the local missionary office and getting Jason's flight itinerary; It was a bit harder than they'd thought it would be to find a local pilot willing to ferry the men to their kid's last known location. It seemed the locals were all too familiar with the difficulty involved in trying to put a craft down in the mountainous rain forest, and most of them actually didn't want to risk their lives for a few bucks.

Wanting to be ready once they could find a willing pilot, they took some time and checked their gear. Medical supplies; protein bars, jerky and nuts; hiking boots and a change of clothes; light weapons and flashlights; fire making and cooking equipment; hammocks with rain cover and mosquito netting; flares; and the most important of all, water filters for their drinking water. The ceramic/carbon element in their units would remove all bacteria and protozoa, including giardia and cryptosporidium; an absolute necessity in most of the world, but even more so here in the midst of so much heat and humidity where bacteria are an abundant factor. The mission's office had been an invaluable resource for the guys, to sufficiently ready them for their expedition into the rain forest.

"What do you think we're going to find out there, Mike?"

"Well, we wouldn't be out here unless we thought there was a way we could help, Tom. I believe we're going to find the kids and take them home, that's all."

"Good. I just wanted to be sure we were on the same page. I sure hope they were able to scrape together some provisions. I know the missionary council said they had lots of supplies on board the chopper when they left the city. But, if the aircraft went down in the storm, who knows what they were left with?"

"One thing I've learned along the way, Tom, and you just reminded me of it recently, is that God is good and He is faithful. I'm sure that Jason and Gracie are more resilient than we've ever realized. We're going to find them, and everything will be fine."

"From your lips to God's ears my friend. From your lips to God's ears."

Sun warm on her head and damp sand oozing between her toes, as the ocean's tide rose slowly to wash gently over her feet, she looked up to see her mother's smile. Her heart sang at the sight. Could this be? She'd almost forgotten how beautiful she was. The sunlight framed her lovely face and hair in an aura of gold. Anna leaned in hungrily for a long awaited hug and fell to the floor from her queen-sized bed, in the lavender room. Shocked by the hardness of the cold, wood floor, she looked around dazed, as a single tear traced her cheek. For a few moments, almost as if her mom was directing her thoughts back to reason, she entertained the idea of running to her new mother's room and telling her about the evil which currently held her hostage. Then, just as quickly, that evil grabbed her heart again and squeezed.

While she'd slept, but shortly before the dream of her mom that left her laying on the floor, she'd experienced another dream. That one haunted her now, from deep in her subconscious. She dreamt of a man with the kindest eyes she'd ever seen. Even kinder than Mike's, or Tom's. His hair was like white clouds around His face and when He spoke the world stood still. She didn't think she'd ever met this man before, but He seemed familiar somehow. Could this be the man, Jesus, that her new family spoke of? The God man that the pastor at her new church preached about? The moment this thought entered her mind, a migraine filled her head that was so severe she thought she might die. And, as quick as that, evil had control again.

The chopper, a modified Bell AH-1 Cobra, and its pilot were both Viet Nam era antiques. Ace had removed the armaments and replaced them with additional fuel carriers, so he could stay in the air for much longer periods of time. His exceptional mechanical skills had kept the chopper functional, if barely, for over fifty years. Since he'd purchased it from salvage. Mike and Tom respected the older man's talent, and it was obvious he could use the money he would make transporting them to the rain forest, but they questioned the fitness of both pilot and machine. A cloud of alcohol vapors surrounded their new friend, and his chopper made more noise than they thought sounded entirely normal, with the clangs and clunks, various knocks and odd vibrations. On several occasions during their trip, the shuddering progressed to degrees that caused the men to think they might soon have to abandon ship, however, the parachutes strapped to their backs; for use in case of emergency; looked to be in worse condition than either the man or the machine in question.

Once they were over the approximate crash location; as deduced by examining flight itineraries and calculated storm times on the day of the accident; the three men conducted a visual search that lasted for over two hours. Frustrated and wondering if they had figured incorrectly, they were about to head back to the city and endeavor to launch out again tomorrow, when lo and behold they spotted what appeared to be an area of broken branches large enough to hide a chopper. Filled with a sense of hope they went in lower to check things out.

As the chopper ventured nearer the crash site they saw flashes of metal through rustling leaves and knew they'd finally found their target. However, they couldn't land there. With no clearing in the vicinity a search was in order. So, they marked the longitude and latitude of the spot, and flew off to find a place to set down. It was evident why no other pilot had taken them up on their offer. Only the most experienced of chopper pilots would have dared to try a landing on the mountain; what with the unpredictable wind shears and limited clearings.

Suddenly, as if the chopper was grabbed in the air by flying demons, which was exactly the situation, they were tossed about like no body's business. If any pilot, besides Ace, had been in control of that flight, they would have certainly crashed into the trees below. As it was, he quickly regained control of the aircraft and set about on the prearranged route. It appeared that God had sent this man to these two anxious men for such a time as this.

Mike was excited. He had no doubt now, that the hand of God was covering them and keeping them safe. He knew positively, that they would find the kids, and was counting the minutes until he could hug his daughter again. It had been mere weeks since he'd last seen her, but after the drama of the past week or so, it felt more like years.

Jason thought he heard the sound of an engine, even over the howling of the demons outside his door. Relief washed over him. He hadn't wanted to admit it, even to himself, but the pain in his leg had been growing worse instead of better, and he was convinced an infection had set in. The smells in the cabin of the aircraft had gotten so bad he couldn't separate them from the way he assumed gangrene might smell, but the grayish yellow colored puss oozing from the wound was a pretty sound indicator of worse things to come. Not sure he'd have the strength to hold out for Gracie's return, he'd been doing a tremendous amount of praying for both of them. If this was indeed someone who'd come to rescue them, he was grateful to God for the intervention.

After some scouting the men found the closest and safest place to land, which was about five miles from the downed chopper. They would have to hoof it from there. Not knowing what they might find there, by way of inju-ries, they toted a collapsible stretcher. It was the toughest five miles any of them had ever hiked. Wet ground covered by downed trees and thick vegetation, rocks and rises, uphill and downhill through streams and obstacles.

Darkness was slowly ascending by the time they reached the location of the chopper. Jason heard them coming and hollered from the craft until his father-in-law opened the door of the cabin.

Mike was forced to take a step back and shake his head. The stench emanating from the inside was gut wrenching, and he thought he might lose it. Human waste was the least of it. The cabin was permeated with the smell of rotting flesh. Then, taking a deep breath he stuck his head in and saw Jason. He motioned Tom and Ace forward to enlist their help. It would most assuredly take all three of them to move the young man. "Mike, I'm so glad to see you. How did you know where to find us?"

"Good old fashioned ingenuity son. We didn't hear from you, and the authorities couldn't prove there was a need, since they didn't receive a distress call, so we had to take it upon ourselves. Did you think we would just sit at home and wait? No, we are a much more stubborn family than that. I would have thought you'd have figured that out by now. You are married to my daughter after all."

"Thank the Lord for this stubborn family! The storm came on us so quickly, and the lightening strike was so sudden, we didn't have time to do much of anything."

"I'm so glad to see you, boy."

"Uncle Tom, thank you for coming. I didn't know if I'd ever see you, any of you, again."

"Jason, this is Ace. He piloted us in here to find you. We're parked about five miles from here, so we brought a stretcher."

"Now, I'm going to calmly state the obvious. I don't see my daughter. Where is Gracie, Jason?"

"She went for help, Dad. The radio is broken, and we didn't get a distress call out, so we knew no one would know where to find us."

"How long has she been gone?"

"She's been gone at least three days now. I've been kind of in and out of it I guess. The demons surrounding the chopper have been laughing it up, so I've been worried about her. I've been doing a lot of praying, that's for sure."

"Demons around the chopper? What do you mean, demons around the chopper?"

"That's right, I almost forgot you can see them too, just like Grace. That must have been hard. Don't worry about it, Ace. I'll explain it all later. It looks like she tried to use her newly acquired medical skills on you, Jason."

"Actually, she did an emergency surgery. I had a collapsed lung. That seems to be doing okay. But, my leg is the thing giving me some problems. I'm sure it's all the heat and humidity. Couldn't get it sterile enough in here I guess. I'm thinking an infection has set in. My fever is up, and there's a lot of puss, no matter how clean I try to keep things."

"Yeah, don't want to over state the obvious, Jason, but we can smell it from here. We're going to get you help son. But, tell me, was she hurt? I'm going to need to know what's going on."

"No, other than some cuts, bumps and bruises. I believe she's probably tougher than all of us put together."

"I would have to agree with you on that one. The things that young lady has survived are remarkable. That's why I know I'll be able to find her. God kept her around for a purpose, and I don't have any reason to believe He's done with her yet. Here's what's going on guys. I'm going to help you two get Jason loaded up for transport. And then I'm going to head out to find my girl."

"Mike, I don't like the idea of leaving you out here alone."

"I won't be alone, Tom. Not after I find Gracie. Jason needs medical aid, and we can't give him the kind of help he needs out here. A hospital is the only place where they are going to be able to care for that leg. Jason, what kind of supplies did Gracie take with her?"

"She left most everything with me, Mike. She didn't take any water, just a bottle and some purification tablets. Let's see, a knife, a hammock and bedding. Mostly she was going to kill her food and cook it. Oh, and some fire starting tools and cooking equipment. She wanted to travel light, and she was sure she'd be able to find what she needed along the way."

"I'm getting a bad feeling about this already. I know Grace has been through a lot, but camp fire girls wasn't part of it. I need to get on the road. Especially if she has a three day head start on me. I already know I don't have a signal out here for the Sat phone, but I do have a dozen flares. When we get to the edge of the rain forest, I will start shooting off those flares every half hour until you come get me. Does that sound like a plan, Tom? Ace?"

"I'll be looking for those flares, Mike. Be careful and God bless you. And remember that Nancy will kill me if anything happens to you, so come back safely."

"I will be on my best behavior, Tom. Stay in touch with Ace here when you get Jason back to the city, so the two of you can come get us after I find Gracie. And, be careful getting that young man back to safety."

"Thank you again, Dad. Please find her, and when you do, please tell her I love her. I will be praying for you both. I love you."

"Love you too, Son. Don't worry. We've got angels, remember?"

For I know the plans I have for you, declares the Lord, plans for welfare and not for evil, to give you a future and a hope.

Jeremiah 29:11

CHAPTER 6

"What was that?"

"I don't know. I'm going to go check on Anna."

"Not without me you're not."

Nancy and Lilly raced up the stairs. The thump on the floor above them was loud, loud enough to worry them. And they didn't know if Anna was hurt, or was just in the process of destroying another room in the house as she'd taken to doing the day before. They entered her room and saw her on the floor. For just a second Nancy saw a clarity in her eyes that hadn't been present for weeks. However, just as quickly, it was replaced by the look of malevolence to which she'd become accustomed. "Are you okay, Anna?" A flicker of recognition, and then the look of hatred.

Anna glared at her again, got up from the floor, and pushed past the ladies to leave the room. "Well, I guess she's fine then."

"Mom, you know she's not okay."

"Yeah, Lilly. I just don't know what to do about it."

"Have you thought about praying over her like Grace and Jason did with the prisoners?"

"I'm not sure I would know what to say. They could see when the demons came out. We wouldn't have any assurance that they were gone, would we?"

"Mom, what have you always told us? The Name of Jesus is the most powerful Name in the world! The demons have to flee when they hear His Name. We could do it together, if you're afraid."

"You're right. God hears our prayers just the same as He hears Gracie and Jason's prayers. Let's go find her."

The ladies searched the house, but Anna had vanished. Demons overheard their conversation and reported back to Kakos with the plans the two women had for his hostage. He in turn reported to Satan, and, as a result Anna had been prompted to take off into the local woods. The evil one wasn't about to lose an asset like this. Not if he could help it. He would keep her hidden until she could be of most use to him.

Her thirst had become unbearable and she just didn't have another choice. Without the purification tablets, she knew she'd be drinking contaminated water. But, she was already in so much pain, she could barely think. If she didn't do something she might just as easily die of thirst, and, only a few feet away from a cold rushing stream.

The story of God narrowing down Gideon's army came to mind as she tried to decide how to drink from the flow. It didn't take long to figure out she couldn't squat, due to her ankle. And she couldn't cup her hands together, because of her wrist. So, she made her way gingerly to the edge of the water, laid down in the moss, put her face in the stream and drank.

The going was getting rougher by the hour. Swelling in her wrist and ankle made her extremities resemble cartoon drawings of body parts, except the pain was anything but funny. She was hungry, but without fire starting equipment and cooking utensils, there wasn't much she could do about it, even if she did manage to catch anything for supper. She'd spotted a few snakes that might have made an excellent meal, but didn't have the ability to capture them in her current condition. "I just need to get going. Food, or no food, I need to get to Port au Prince to get help for Jason. If food happens along the way, then it happens. I can do this. I know I can."

Sleep would be almost impossible. With no hammock she was forced to lay on the wet ground with every manner of small creature; spiders, lizards, snakes and the like; crawling over her. She hadn't felt this vulnerable for a very long time. But, nothing was going to make her admit she couldn't do this. Jason needed her.

It was fully dark now. Tom and Ace struggled to get the stretcher, with Jason aboard, back to Ace's chopper. They'd tripped over roots and limbs several times, and Jason was dumped from his ride at least once. He screamed from the excruciating pain of the fall onto his injured leg, a scream that echoed through the mountain. Tom was worried about him. The fever was higher and the leg smelled even worse than when they'd arrived at the crash site. Finally, they made it to the clearing where their chopper was parked and waiting. Jason was unconscious as they got him on board, which was a good thing, considering the maneuvering they had to do to accomplish the task. It would be a long ride back to the city, and the first thing they must do after arriving would be to get Jason much needed medical attention. Tom would also be searching the darkness, ever on the alert for flares in the night sky.

Once Mike made it down the slippery side of the mountain next to the waterfall, using the same path Gracie used several days ago, it was almost completely dark. Trees shut out what little light might be available from the moon and stars. The wet conditions made the idea of sleeping on the ground very unappealing, so he took the time to set up a makeshift camp and attach his hammock to a couple of sturdy looking trees. He had no way of knowing that a mere three days ago his daughter's hammock had hung from those very same trees.

He would find her. He had to. He ate a granola bar and drank his fill of cold clean water. Just as he laid down and covered up, a distant scream echoed through the rain forest. All he could do was shake his head and pray. "Father God, I don't know what that was, but I am claiming your promises here. Please get Jason, Tom and Ace safely back to the city; and please help me find Gracie. I need you Lord. Thank you for watching over us all. In Jesus' Name."

Police and neighborhood volunteers had been searching the woods for hours. But, it was getting dark and they hadn't found a trail. So, they were packing up for the night. The lead officer told her they'd be back at first light, but Nancy knew if Anna didn't want to be found she wouldn't be found. She'd taken a jacket with her. That was the first thing Mom checked. It was chilly, even for fall, but at least the temperatures weren't freezing yet. Now she was kicking herself that she hadn't thought to pray over her before. Why had she not been the one to think of that? Thank the Lord for Lilly. And, the moment they could get their hands on Anna again, they would be praying for her whether she liked it or not.

Nancy was so grateful to have Lilly home. She guessed she was even more terrified of her new daughter than she'd been able to admit to herself. It was good to have company. And, it was good to have someone here who understood what they were dealing with.

The cramping in her stomach began in the middle of the night. At first she thrashed about, trying to get comfortable. A mighty feat with a broken ankle and a fractured wrist. But, after a while she knew she would need to relieve herself. She was certain the cramps, and diarrhea, were from the contaminated water, but what was she to do? She had to drink to stay alive. Only now she was being forced to do her business every fifteen minutes or so, throughout the night, and no amount of water could keep her from becoming desiccated. As the forest became light enough to travel the next morning, she packed more leaves around her injuries, twisted more bark around her broken ankle, relieved herself for the umpteenth time, grabbed her makeshift cane, and headed out.

Watery stools had grown exponentially worse throughout the night, and the accompanying spasms were downright agonizing. On several occasions she'd barely gotten her jeans down in time for the ensuing flood. But, each time she relieved herself, she felt so dehydrated, she was forced to drink more of the impure water. Thus perpetuating a never ending cycle of sickness. There were moments when she wondered if she was going to die, and other moments where she just flat out wished she would.

Terrible headaches and constant dizziness left her barely able to clearly see the path she must take, and soon she was so ill she was wandering around in the trees, no longer sure in which direction she should be traveling. It was then that her guardian angels began to lead, instead of follow. They had protected her from breaking her neck on the many boulders in the rushing stream after she fell, and now they were leading her to the help she would need. Obviously she'd been too hard on them before, as she assured herself she could do it all alone.

Mike woke at first light, wondering if the guys had gotten Jason back to the city safely, and if Gracie was doing okay. He'd been plagued by nightmares and felt something was amiss. Family was connected that way. She was his little girl, and his gut was telling him she was in very big trouble. He packed up his gear, ate a protein bar and drank some more water.

When he set off he found himself walking at a quicker pace than the day before. He was absolutely sure Gracie needed him right now. The question was, how to find her? Assuming she was headed to the city, he was pointed in the right direction. But, if she was hurt or sick, would she still be in her right mind? She had a three day head start on him, and depending on the circumstances, that could mean almost anything. He found himself praying as he walked. Praying for Gracie, for Jason, for Nancy, Lilly and Anna, and for Tom and Ace. Prayer eased his worry, but didn't take away the sense of urgency propelling him on.

Ace had set the chopper down on the hospital roof when they arrived in Port au Prince. Immediately he had hospital staff telling him he couldn't land there, but he stubbornly refused to move until they took Jason to the emergency room directly from the chopper. "Thank you my friend."

"You are most welcome, Tom. I haven't felt this useful in a very long time. You have my number, so call me when you see Mike's flares, and I'll pick you up for the rescue."

"You've been a great help, and I couldn't have done any of this without you. Hopefully, you will be hearing from me very soon. God bless you."

Jason was rushed to surgery. He was conscious when the doctors came in to examine him, so he was able to fill them in on all the particulars of his injuries. The familiar doctor took one look at his leg and his eyes grew huge at the sight. Tom waited until a nurse came through the waiting area to ask questions. "Nurse, can you tell me about Jason? The young man who arrived with the chest wound and the infection in his leg?"

"I will have the doctor talk to you as soon as he knows more, Sir. I know they were worried about the young man's leg. It looked as if the infection had gotten pretty bad before he was brought in."

"Yes, I know. He and his wife were in a helicopter crash. We just found him a few hours ago. We got him here as quickly as we could."

"Is his wife with you?"

"No, her dad is out there in the wilderness looking for her now."

"Oh my. Well, Jason has consented to surgery on his own. I hope she's okay. Bring her in as soon as you are able to locate her. I'm sure she'll need some medical attention, or at the very least to be checked over for exposure."

"We will. Nurse, I want you to know that Jason is my nephew. Please let me know how things are progressing."

"I will, as soon as I know anything. And, I will have the doctor come and speak to you as soon as he gets a better idea of what he's dealing with."

"Thank you. I appreciate all your help." Tom was humbled by how much his life had changed since Gracie came on the scene. He recognized how lovingly God had dealt with him, after all the evil he'd perpetrated over the years of his life, and was grateful beyond words. The one bad thing about all this family stuff, was that now he had people in his life he truly cared about. People he loved. And when you love people, sometimes you ache for them. That was what he was feeling now, and it was a terrifying, gut wrenching feeling.

Anna wandered. She wasn't cold. As a matter of fact, she really didn't feel anything at all. She'd heard people yelling her name until after dark, but was compelled to stay out of sight. Intermittent thoughts of doing harm to herself, and the pain she would soon be allowed to inflict on others, fought for dominance and flickered through her mind.

When hunger struck, she picked up spiders, worms, and other insects. Tossing them into her mouth, she bit down on each one until she heard a pop, and felt the wet stickiness fill her mouth. When she was thirsty she sucked on damp moss. And, eventually she was led to a small cave hidden by an overgrowth of trees and vines. While inside the earthen fissure she stared, unmoving, at the pitted dirt walls of her enclosure. It was as if the enemy was keeping her in cold storage for future use.

"Kakos, Sir, you will be happy to know the girl is secure."

"Good. What about the situation in Haiti?"

"Well, the family has come, Sir."

"What do you mean the family has come?"

"The young woman's father, and the young man's uncle hired a helicopter to take them out to the crash site."

"Are you kidding me? What did you do to stop them?"

"We did our best, Sir. There wasn't a whole lot we could do. The chopper pilot is a Vietnam war VET, and his skills were just too well honed. He was unshakable, no matter what we threw at him. The uncle and the pilot have gotten the young man out, though we threw plenty of obstacles at them, and he's currently having surgery at the hospital in Port au Prince."

"Why am I only now hearing of this?"

"I'm sorry, Kakos. We were hoping we could cause some kind of event in surgery that might take him out. You will be happy to hear though, that the young woman is not doing well at all. Dumping her in the stream and washing her bag away has been very effective. She's been forced to drink contaminated water and is quite sick."

"I thought you said her father has shown up as well? I didn't hear his name in with those who carried the young man to the hospital."

"Well, no, he's in the forest looking for his daughter."

"Then how is any of this good news?"

"Well, Sir, we believe we can cause enough distraction and havoc that we can take them both out while they are most vulnerable."

"See that you do. I will be watching. I don't want any more mistakes. Do you understand, Keres?"

"Yes Kakos. You have my word."

"And, Keres, please tell me that she still hasn't figured anything out yet."

"No sir, not as far as we can tell."

"Good, we can't let her find out. We must stop her for good, and if she knew her current situation, she would fight all the harder."

"Yes sir, we will do our best."

Gracie gained consciousness while laying half on and half off of the mossy stream bank. Not remembering where she was upon opening her eyes, she tried to move and was wrenched to a state of full wakefulness by the jarring pain in her ankle and wrist. Now she remembered. With no way to know how long she'd been out of it, she couldn't know that a full twenty four hours had passed. And, more thirsty than she'd ever been in her life, she drank again from the contaminated water flowing quickly by her head.

The cramps were worse than ever. Doubled over in pain, she now had a third handicap to deal with. Again she struggled with her jeans and just in time relieved herself, but was so thirsty afterward she had to drink more of the parasite infested water. "Lord, I need to get help. Please give me the strength, Jesus, to get the help I need for Jason. I don't care about myself. Just let me help him. I don't want him to be alone."

Gracie wasn't aware of how close her dad was to her present location, or that her husband had already been rescued. Her hours of aimless wandering and unconsciousness on the streams edge, added together with the rapid pace of her father's rescue attempt, were bringing them close together much faster than Mike had anticipated. If only she'd known his location, perhaps she wouldn't have ingested so much more of the water that was making her sick.

Her ankle hurt worse now than before. Sure that an infection had set in, she unwrapped the conglomeration of leaves and bark around her leg to expose the wound. The smell that assailed her was that of rotten meat. With no first aid supplies there wasn't much she could do. So, with tears streaming down her face she washed the site as effectively as possible and rewrapped the injury with new leaves and bark. She knew she couldn't just sit around and mope. She had to get up and get going. So, she pulled herself upright with the aid of a tree and her handmade cane and stumbled off.

Hungry and in unimaginable pain, she hobbled along beside the stream that was proving to be her biggest help, and her worst foe. Now, as she limped slowly along, she hummed her favorite hymns. Trying to keep her mind focused on the task at hand, she would ultimately make it farther this day than in the previous two days combined. And, because the enemy didn't want her to connect with her father, he would give her every advantage along her path, so that she could make plenty of ground. While her dad would run into one obstacle after another throughout the whole of the day. By the time it was getting too dark to travel, Mike found himself exhausted from the past sixteen hours of endless trials. And, knowing how much trouble he'd had trying to traverse the rain forest during the day, he figured it would be fruitless to attempt any further progress in the night.

Mike had done plenty of camping with his dad and grandpa when he was a kid, and then later in the military. He knew how to start a fire, how to fish and hunt, and how to take care of himself. He'd had an ideal childhood. Grampa was a preacher, and Dad was an accountant. They'd both been Marines, and Mike carried on the family tradition, with time served in 'Desert Storm'.

He'd had the love of good parents, and many fond memories of growing up in a small town. He played high school football, and was class president during his senior year. Lots of girls chased him, but he never found one he was interested in until he met the new girl in town. Sweet Nancy.

After his stint in the service, he used his veteran's benefits to pay for culinary school. And, when he and Nance married, they planned a huge family. A family that never happened, until God brought young Gracie, and her brother and sisters into their lives. Sure, his restaurants were successful. And, yes they made a good living. But, nothing can fill the void of childlessness. He wouldn't let Satan take his daughter. Not now or ever. Not over his dead body.

Mike set up camp and climbed into his hammock. Covering up with plastic and mosquito netting, he pulled out his Bible, a flashlight, a protein bar and his water bottle, and began to read.

Gracie, on the other hand, got her second wind. Whether out of desperation to be out of the trees, or because she was so very famished and desperately wanted to get somewhere that she could find food and clean water, it didn't matter. Even badly wounded and sick, she was making headway

and widening the gap between them before she would settle down for the night on a mossy patch beside the rushing stream.

Many more emergency stops throughout the day had left her so weakened and dehydrated she could barely think, but still she'd trudged on. Now, stopping because she didn't have anything at all left in her, she laid down and as soon as her head hit the moss, she was asleep.

Nancy and Lilly searched all day, along with police and dozens of volunteers from town. The sheriff wasn't offering much hope, not after so much time had elapsed since the disappearance. But they would continue to search for awhile longer. "Do you think we're going to find her, Mom?"

"No, I think she's holed up somewhere waiting for instructions."

"Instructions from who?"

"Well, I've been thinking about what you said. About how she's acting like the men in the prisons where we were ministering with Jason and Grace. Those men were possessed by demons, because they didn't know Jesus. And, they were obviously getting directions from some entity somewhere. Don't you think?"

"Yes, you're right. Someone had to be telling them what to do. Just like the angels that Gracie and Jason see get their instructions from the Lord."

"Exactly! Well, the way I see it, Anna hasn't come to know Jesus yet. I believe she's been taken over by demons. And those demons are getting instructions from Satan.

What do you suppose they might use her for? Do you think it's a coincidence that she has made her way into our house and our family, where Jason and Grace are able see the spiritual realm? Your sister and brother in law have been thwarting Satan's plans at every turn? Do you think that maybe Satan and his minions would like to get rid of Gracie and Jason, right along with their gift and their ministry? This would be the perfect way to destroy the whole family at once, don't you think?"

"You're right, Mom. He's got her hidden somewhere. He's planning to use her like a secret weapon. But, what can we do?"

"Well, obviously we have to find her. We can't let her lurk around out there. Especially after the kids get back. We wouldn't have any idea when she might strike. And, she wouldn't have to be inside the house to set it on fire in the middle of the night. We need to find her before everyone else gets home. It's the only way to protect them."

"Should we say something to the sheriff? Maybe if he knows what is going on he can think of a better way to help."

"No, Lilly, I think we have to keep that part to ourselves. What would you think if you were him and two women came to you with this kind of story?"

"Yeah, I guess you're right. We don't want him to call off the search because he thinks we're crazy or something. Just know I'm right here with you, Mom. I'm not going anywhere."

"Thank you sweet girl. It's so good to have you here. And, it's good to know that God is still on the throne, isn't it? We can trust Him to get us through this."

"Yes Mom, and He will, I know He will."

"How's he doing Doc?"

"He's stable for now, Tom. We were forced to remove some tissue from his leg, so we borrowed a bit from his upper thigh to graft into the wound site. The leg is set now, but it will take some time to heal. The break was very severe, crushing both the tibia and the fibula, and we had to use a series of pins and rods to stabilize the bones. We are giving him very high doses of an antibacterial mix, in an attempt to clear up the gangrene which had already begun to set in, and in an effort to keep his body from going into septic shock. Something that I'm frankly surprised hadn't happened already under these circumstances. I'm also surprised that his chest wound is doing as well as it is. I've been told that Gracie did the surgery?"

"He's a strong kid, Doc. And, yes, Gracie did the surgery. She didn't have much choice considering the situation she was in."

"That young woman never ceases to amaze me. I don't know why I thought I wouldn't be seeing any of you folks until we returned stateside. But, God evidently had different plans."

"It seems God always has different plans where these kids are concerned. I'm very grateful that He had you here."

"Yeah, Jason was pretty surprised when he saw my face."

"When can I see him, Doc?"

"He's in recovery now. But he should be waking soon, and I'll let you have a short visit. He's going to need his rest."

"No problem. thanks Doc."

"Keres! Get in here!"

"Yes Sir. Right away Sir."

"What news have you? You must know something by now."

"Kakos, Sir, I haven't heard much. Only that the young

man has come out of surgery. They are saying he will be fine, and will make a full recovery."

"What? You weren't able to complicate the surgery? Give me answers. I want answers, now. And what of the other situation in Haiti?"

"So far we have been able to keep the young woman and her father apart. She is doing worse by the hour, Sir, and we aren't finished there yet. As for the young man, an American doctor named Phillips did the surgery and he is one of theirs. He is there in Haiti with a Christian doctor's outreach program. Evidently he knew the young man. They are involved in the prison ministry together."

"I can't believe my miserable luck! Alright, we may be forced to put the girl into action when they get him home. For now, concentrate on the young woman and her father. There must be ways to keep them apart, so that we can attack her from all sides. If she is weakening, then we must strike before she's rescued."

"Yes Sir. I'm on it."

Mike woke to a light drizzle, thankful he had utilized the sheet of plastic over his bedding during the night. His jacket was water proof and had a nice hood, so that would make his journey a little less damp throughout the day, but he couldn't help thinking about Grace wandering around out here somewhere. Jason had told them she didn't take any food or water. Only a knife, water purification tablets and fire starting tools. But he'd been moving at a pretty quick pace since leaving the crash site, and so far the only evidence of a campfire he'd seen was on the first leg of the journey. Wondering why he'd seen only slight evidence of two campsites, and no other remains of prepared meals, he was concerned. What was she eating? Where was she sleeping? Was something going on that he didn't know about? He had to find her.

"Mom, come look at this." Lilly had been straightening up in Anna's room. Well, more like looking for evidence that might help them understand her better. She hoped she might come up with some answers. The girl had been acting odd since Grace and Jason left for their trip. She went to bed one night, normal, as far as everyone could tell. And she woke up the next day, what, possessed? The whole thing was just too crazy.

"What did you find Lilly?"

Lilly held up the edge of Anna's bedspread. Under the bed was a veritable storehouse of food. Anna had been stealing supplies and storing them under her bed. "Why do you suppose she was keeping food under her bed, Mom?"

"I guess she had more problems than we knew about. She'd been living on the streets for quite some time you know. It looks like she didn't quite trust us to take care of her the way we promised. That just might have left her more vulnerable to the wiles of the enemy. She was exactly the confused sort of young person Satan is always looking for. Someone who didn't feel that they belonged, and thought they might be back on their own at any moment. I really hate that she felt that way."

"I know, Mom, but it wasn't because of you. You have always been the best mom ever to all of us. Grace, David, Bella, Me and Anna."

"Then why do all of my babies end up hurt, or even dead?"

"I don't know, Mom. I guess we're all a threat to Satan, so he wants to take us out. And I would much rather know I'm a threat, than to be just like the rest of the world. I'm glad he's afraid of us. And remember, we know we have angels surrounding us."

"Anna doesn't have angels, Lilly. So, I failed. All I ever wanted to be was a nurse and a mom, and I've failed at the most important job God gave me."

"No, Mom. You were showing her the love of Christ. You were teaching her Jesus. But, the turning her life over to Jesus part, that has to be her choice. She didn't come to us when she was a baby. She already had some pre conceived notions. She has free will, and she has to invite the Lord in, all by herself. You are not to blame. Please don't worry. We are going to get her back. And when we do, we will cast those nasty old demons out and help her to know the Savior."

"I hope you're right, sweetheart."

"I know I'm right, Mom. God is good."

"Yep. All the time baby girl. All the time."

That night Nancy had a hard time falling asleep. Even with beautiful, successful Lilly beside her, she felt like a failure. Gracie was lost in the rain forest, and Anna wandered the woods possessed by demons. And, what was more, David and Bella were both lost to them forever. That didn't say much for her skills as a mother.

She'd never wanted anything more in her life, than she

wanted to be a mom. Her own mother had been a beautiful, soft spoken woman of faith, who passed down many loving, life lessons to her only daughter. Slight and delicate, she was often sickly, and always seemed just one step away from a terrible ending. Nancy had grown up with a fear that her mother would be taken from her by one disease or another. A fear that was recognized when the girl was only fifteen.

Her mom was diagnosed with stage four ovarian cancer in the summer of her junior year, and Nancy spent the whole of that season caring for her, then watching her worsen and die; as first her hair fell out in clumps, then her skin became thin and grey, and finally the sparkle that had always drawn people in finally grew dim. She just knew if she'd been more knowledgeable she might have made a bigger difference. She made up her mind then and there she would become a nurse. The memorial service was filled with people Nancy didn't know, as well as friends and the few family members still alive at that time. It seemed her mother had made quite an impact on many people, despite her quiet and unassuming demeanor.

Nancy's grandmother was prepared to stay for a while to help her and her dad get back on track, before heading back home to her own life. However, her father, broken and despondent, took his own life shortly after the loss of his wife.

He had taken to sitting alone in the garage, looking at family albums and drinking a few beers. Soon a few beers turned into many more, and Nancy could hear him crying by himself. She wasn't sure how to help, because when she'd tried to comfort him, he'd only pushed her away.

One night he drove off after supper. Where alone in the woods, with a hose carrying carbon monoxide from his tailpipe through a crack in the window to the interior of the car, he took an irreversible grief stricken step and passed quietly away. He left a note for Nancy, apologizing for his cowardly act and lamenting again the loss of his wife. Obviously forgetting that his daughter was suffering from the same great tragedy. And seemingly oblivious to the fact that now she would be grieving for two.

Nancy and her grandmother stayed in town just long enough to close up the house. Then, they went together to live in the small town, and in fact the very same house, where Nancy's mom had been raised. Nancy would occupy her mother's childhood bedroom, surrounded by her mother's beloved memories, and register for her senior year in the same high school from whence her own mother had graduated twenty two years before.

She was deeply saddened by her parent's passing, and didn't smile for a very long time. Not until one day when a dashing young football player, who was also the senior class president, invited her to attend an evening service at his church. From that moment on, they were inseparable, at least until his military service took him from her for a very lengthy and frightening year.

During his absence, she began college, with a nursing degree as her goal. In the beginning of her second year of school, her grandmother suddenly passed away, and she was left alone in the big, rambling, Victorian home of her mother's birth.

When Mike returned from war, they were anxious to get on with their lives, and put the sad memories of the past few years firmly away. They were married in a small service in the church where they had spent their first date. The same church they attended to this very day.

He worked doing odd jobs, until he attained his culinary degree. Then he used the money he had accumulated for hazardous duty pay during his deployment, to put a down payment on his very first restaurant.

Slowly, they began renovating the huge Victorian home, little by little and bit by precious bit, to hold all the children they planned to have some day. But, sometimes the best laid plans don't work out quite the way we would like, and those children never came. Nancy lamented their childlessness, and Mike tried everything he could over the years to convince her that he didn't blame her and was every bit as happy with only the two of them rattling around in the big empty house.

Since then, much had happened. Their small town had grown, they now owned two very successful restaurants, and Mike volunteered two days a week at the soup kitchen where he met Gracie and then young Anna. Nancy achieved much success in the medical arena, had played a big part in saving many lives, and trained many fine young nurses. Best of all, now, they were slowly filling their house with the children they'd always longed for.

Looking at her life from this perspective, she supposed they had done the best they could with what they were given. She prayed again for the safe return of her husband and daughter and drifted off to sleep.

"Hey, Uncle Tom."

"Hey, how ya doing, Jason?"

"Well, the old adage about feeling like I've been run over by a dump truck might fit. But, I'm breathing, so it could be worse. Did you see Dr. Phillips?"

"Yes I did. What a miracle that he was here when you needed him, huh?"

"Well, I would certainly call that a God thing, wouldn't you?"

"Absolutely."

"Have you heard anything from Mike?"

"No, not yet. I've been checking the sky for flares."

"I know I shouldn't be, but I'm worried about Gracie. I had some pretty terrible dreams, and I feel like she is in trouble. I've been praying for her nonstop."

"Well, that's the best thing you can do. We know prayer works. She's a fighter, Jason. No matter what the enemy throws at her, you know she's going to come out swinging, and smelling like a rose."

"I know, but this feeling just doesn't want to go away. I'm angry with myself anyway, you know, that she's out there alone."

"But, she's not alone son. She's got Jesus on her side, a whole pack of angels surrounding her, and soon, one very protective dad who, guaranteed, is going to find her and bring her home."

"Thanks for reminding me. I just love her so much Uncle Tom, and I don't know what I would do without her."

"Well, You're not going to have to find that out. Not for a very long time. God is good son."

"Yes He is, Uncle Tom. Yes He is."

Blessed are those whose strength is in you, in whose heart are the highways to Zion. As they go through the valley of Baca they make it a place of springs; the early rain also covers it with pools. They go from strength to strength; each one appears before God in Zion.

Psalm 84:5-7

CHAPTER 7

Gracie woke to the distinct sensation of something large and smooth slithering over her neck and shoulder. She kept her eyes closed and resisted the urge to bolt. Knowing it might be one of the island's twenty seven different varieties of snake, she didn't want to frighten the creature, causing it to strike. Instead, she waited for it to slink away before trying to rise. Though Haiti didn't have any snake varieties that were particularly deadly to humans, they could still bite. She certainly didn't need that right now. Besides, her sleeping on the ground was not their fault. In so doing, she had left herself vulnerable to all sorts of critters wandering about the rain forest floor.

Her mossy bed was damp and not nearly so comfortable as her lost hammock. But she'd been exhausted when she laid down the evening before, and had no problem dropping off. Rising painfully only to relieve herself several times during the night and drink a little more water, she'd slept though any number of visitors; including a few of the eight legged variety who'd made their way through her ever loosening clothing and out again.

Aware that her guardian angels surrounded her as she slept, she was also conscious of the fact that demons lurked behind every tree waiting to pounce at the first opportunity.

Puzzled, as to why her travels went so smoothly the day before, when she knew Satan's plans from the very beginning had been to destroy her and the ministry God had given her; she wondered why in the world he would stand down now? What kind of trick was this?

Rolling over, Grace tried to rise for the day, and was stopped by searing pain in her wrist and ankle. Looking down toward her feet, she was shocked at how much worse the color in her leg appeared after this past night. The skin there was a mottled grey and black, which certainly couldn't be good. Gritting her teeth, and mounting all the resolve she had in her, she rolled to the edge of the water. However, this time she just moistened her lips and washed her face. She knew she needed water, but the parasites in her gut were already ripping her apart, so she decided to see how long she could go without the life sustaining fluid today. Unwrapping the injured ankle and wrist, she washed them again and rewrapped with more damp leaves and bark.

Hunger didn't seem to be an issue any longer; though the need in her body would vehemently disagree. It seemed, due to the sad state of her digestive tract, she'd gone past the desire for food. However, thirst haunted her throughout the morning, until she could stand it no more. Finally, with tears streaming down her face, she drank again from the waters that were causing so much pain. Praying, she said, "I'm so sorry, Lord. I know the Bible says You are the living water. I should be strong enough to survive without this filthy water that's making me so sick, but it continues to draw me back in. What is wrong with me? I know I am stronger than this. I've always been strong!"

Lack of food; and struggling with severe dehydration, just a few feet from a rushing water source; was causing a fogginess that left her vulnerable to unwise decisions. And, with infected, painful injuries, and a gut full of parasites, she found herself stumbling along much too close to the stream that was currently her key to life and ultimately her path to ruin.

Just an hour into her morning trek Gracie lost her footing and fell headfirst into the water's rapids. Once again her winged warriors protected her from plowing headlong into the myriad of boulders in her path. However, the rapids also flipped and twisted her damaged body until she thought she would be ripped in two. She thought about giving in, giving up, and letting the stream win. It would be so much easier than fighting the current. She also knew death would mean the end of suffering as she entered the presence of the Lord. But, something inside her was urgently reminded that Jason still needed her help. He would keep going for her, she was sure of it, so she had to survive to save him, her shining knight and the love of her life. She was strong. She always had been. And, she could do this. She could save Jason all by herself.

Miles downstream from where she'd started, she saw a large root jutting out from shore and grabbed at its hooked end as the rushing water tried to rip her hands from their prize. Holding on with all her might, injured wrist and all, she braced herself against the water's pull. Then, hand over hand, in pain so searing she could barely breathe, she inched her way up the root until she was close enough to dig her fingers into the bank. Flopping her drenched body onto the mossy shore, she rolled onto her back and pulled her mangled leg out of the pounding current.

In her clumsiness she'd managed to put even more space between herself and her dad's location. Still not aware of his presence in the forest, and still believing she was the only thing standing between Jason and certain death, she willed herself to go on.

Dragging her useless leg behind her, and in so much pain she had to force herself not to scream out with every step, while lightning bolts of pain flashed in her brain, she looked for something that might make her journey less challenging. Searching the trees, Grace found a branch that could make a functional crutch, so she wrapped the 'v' opening at the top in layers of moss. Tucking it under her arm she set out downstream. Stops along the way to relieve herself were still using more than their share of her valuable time, and depleting her body of every last drop of moisture, but without fluids she would die. So, she drank again of the contaminated water, and the cycle continued.

Attacks against him, from the enemy, multiplied. One obstacle after another presented itself all throughout that day. He knew Satan was behind the onslaught, but the result was exhaustion on all levels. As Mike searched for a place to set up a light camp for the night, he practically tripped over a pile of makeshift bloody bandages prepared from leaves, moss and tree bark. He picked up the leaves and held them to his nose. "Wow! So she is hurt. It must have happened after she left Jason. And, from the smell of those bandages, the wound is badly infected. Where are you Gracie? Don't worry baby girl, Dad's coming to take you home."

"Uncle Tom, I'm worried. If you haven't seen any flares, then he hasn't found her yet. What if she's hurt?"

"Jason, you can't do that to yourself. We don't know that he hasn't found her. He can't light the flares until he's out of the forest. Gracie is pretty tough, and your father in law knows what he's doing. Trust the Lord to bring them out safely, son."

"Thanks again Uncle Tom. Thanks for coming all the way out here to find us. And, thank you for reminding me that God is capable. The way I've been acting, you'd never know I was the one who can see angels."

"Don't beat yourself up about it kid. It's easy to lose your confidence when things around you are squirrely. No one would fault you for that. But, remember, the Lord is the one who sent you out here, and He's not done with you yet."

"Did you ever think that you'd be the one to give me

godly insight Uncle Tom? I mean two years ago things were pretty different for you."

"Yep, that wife of yours is pretty special. Without her forgiveness at a crucial time in my life; and then the way she reached out to me, even after all the terrible things I did to her; I can assure you my path would have been much different. She helped me to see how much Jesus loves me. The sacrifice He made for me. And, the plans He had for me. I owe her my life. And, I would do anything in the world to see that the two of you are okay. The way Mike and Nancy took me in, a convict of the worst order, and made me part of their family. I couldn't ask for better friends. Just to be a part of your life again, Jason, I, I don't know where I would be....."

"Now, don't get all emotional Uncle Tom. You're going to make me cry. You know what? God knew the man you were deep down inside. Who you could be with His help. He had faith in you even before you had faith in Him."

"Well, there you go, son. God did know the man I was deep down inside, and He died for me anyway. I don't try to fool myself into thinking that I deserved the sacrifice He made for me. I know full well I didn't deserve it. But you see, that makes it all the more wonderful. That He would suffer and die for a useless old criminal like me, and put me in a position to draw others to Him, is the greatest gift He could have ever given me. I will happily serve Him for the rest of my days."

"Yeah, I see what you mean. Wow, Uncle Tom. What a testimony you have. I'm so glad I've been able to see the transformation. It just proves to me again that God is good."

"That He is Jason. That He is."

"I'm so sorry ma'am. I'm afraid that headquarters has downgraded the search from rescue to recovery."

"What exactly does that mean?"

"It means that, in their expert opinion, they no longer believe we will find your daughter alive. We will continue to search, but with fewer eyes. Considering the lower temperatures we've been experiencing at night, the experts don't believe she could have survived this long out in the open."

"I see. I hope you don't mind if I disagree."

"No ma'am. We expect a certain amount of resistance from the family, and I certainly understand. I just wanted you to know what my orders are, in case you wondered why there seemed to be fewer in the search parties."

"No, I get that you have your orders. But, I'm not going to give up that easily. I believe God can deliver her, no matter what your experts predict."

"Yes ma'am."

Quietly, and away from prying eyes and ears, "That might actually be a good thing, Mom."

"I thought so too. I don't think for one moment that Anna is dead. I believe she is out there somewhere, waiting for orders, just like we figured. Satan is saving her for his last ditch effort to destroy this family. But, he'd better think again. Because, we are going to stop his evil plan and cast the demons from that little girl. She will belong to Jesus once and for all, before this whole thing is said and done."

"Now, that's what I wanted to hear, Mom. There is no force in the world stronger than a praying mom. You proved that when you took all of us on after what we'd been through at the hands of the Russians. I've been waiting to see that old spark come back to life again. If you ask me, Satan hasn't got a chance."

"Kakos, Kakos, I have great news!"

"Speak, Keres. I could use some good news."

"Well, first of all, the search parties have decided the little girl is probably dead, and they have downgraded their search. We are in the clear. So, when you need to bring her out of hiding, she will be ready and much more effective."

"Before you go further, I want you to know that we cannot underestimate this family. Their ties to the other side are strong and they will be on the lookout for anything out of the ordinary. But, what other news have you?"

"The young woman in Haiti. She took another swim, without any help from us this time. She is getting weaker by the minute. I think we've got her on the ropes."

"Good, good. Keep pushing. She must have a breaking point and we need to find it. Does she still not know?"

"No sir, we're quite sure she's unaware."

"Good, we can't let her know. This kind of revelation would keep her fighting no matter the situation or circumstances. Human women are funny that way. And, the boss has already tasked us with making sure this 'blessed' event never takes place. With the extreme gifts possessed by each of the parents, a child like that would be extraordinarily powerful. We can't ever let them have that kind of advantage. God already has way too many effective tools on His side."

"Understood sir. We will keep pushing. If we're lucky we can stop her before she ever makes it out of the forest. And, we can do our best to take out her dad as well."

"Well, be off then. You have much work to do."

Mike was up and off again. After another miserable night trying to sleep in the awful heat and humidity, he'd packed up camp and downed a protein bar and a quart of water. Washing up a bit in the nearby stream, he thought he saw something caught on a root, bobbing up and down with the rushing current.

Stepping out over several large stones and on to a big boulder in the middle of the stream, balancing carefully, he used a long tree branch to retrieve the tangled item. After pulling it to shore, he saw it was a rather beat up and partially shredded backpack. Inside were a couple of boxes of wet matches, some cooking implements, water purification tablets, and a couple of other odds and ends. He knew it was Gracie's backpack. She must have fallen in the water and lost her meager supplies. Without her water purification tablets, she would be forced to drink water contaminated by parasites. and, with no matches or cooking implements, she was probably starving. He had to find her, and fast.

Now an urgency; stronger even than that which had propelled him at the beginning of his mission; drove him. He couldn't see them, but his angels were clearing a path to Gracie as fast as the demons were throwing obstacles in his way. Like a steamroller, plowing its way through the forest, Mike opened his heart wide to let the Holy Spirit lead him to his little girl.

Completely overwhelmed, Gracie finally broke down, and petitioned her God. "Father, I know you love me. And, I know you love Jason. I need to get help back to him, Lord, and I have finally realized I can't do this on my own. We both know how stubborn I can be, always thinking I can do things by myself; and that I don't need anyone, including You. I don't mean to do that Father. You know it's the way I lived my life for a very long time, and it's an easy pattern to fall back into. Lord, thank you for reminding me that I can do nothing without you. And that because of your holy sacrifice, I can do all things through Christ who strengthens me. I need you now more than I've ever needed you before, Jesus. Please help me." And the Father smiled.

For quite some time now Gracie had been counting entirely too much on her own strength and not that of her Heavenly Father. I mean, let's face it, she was the one who could 'see angels' after all. Throughout it all, she'd slowly fallen back into the habit of depending on herself, and not on the Lord. An easy thing to do, when you've grown up the way she had. And, while we serve a God who is patient and loving; He will not allow us to steal His glory for ourselves forever. By counting on her own meager and temporal strength, instead of the strength of the God she serves, she had slowly but surely become weak on her own and her ministry began to suffer as a result. Now, because she was once again recognizing the true source of her power in the Lord, the Holy Spirit was activated anew. Nothing would be able to stand in her way!

Tucked away, like a top secret weapon, in a small forest cave; Anna opened her eyes. Her body was telling her she was hungry. She rose stiffly and made her way outside. There she dug in the damp soil, until she found several large earth worms. She popped them into her mouth and chewed mindlessly. Next, she found a patch of damp moss and sucked the moisture until her thirst was quenched. Lastly she relieved herself, before climbing back into her holding place. Her final instructions had not yet come, so she must wait for 'his' prompting. Closing her eyes, she drifted back off into dreamless sleep.

Mike's urgency was electric. He wouldn't stop again to sleep or make camp. He knew it was imperative he find his daughter.

"Kakos, Sir, I've come for your advice Sir. The young woman has slowed down and her father is getting very close. If we are going to stop him it will have to be soon."

"Throw everything that we have at him, Keres. We can't let him reach his daughter."

Suddenly, the daytime sky grew dark as night. The light breeze started to pick up and trees began to sway. Rain, which commenced as a light sprinkle at first, turned quickly into a pounding monsoon. Then, in the blink of an eye the landscape changed. The wind picked up speed until trees whipped and bent low. Various pieces of debris swept up in the surprise storm took flight and barely missed Mike's head, being kept at bay only by the protective hands of his heavenly sentinels. Gracie, not much ahead of her dad now, was being shielded by her own angelic guard.

The winds grew stronger until trees were uprooted, and all manner of projectiles flew through the air like the weapons of the enemy that they indeed were.

Grace, in her wounded state, couldn't stand up to the violent winds. So, hobbling over to a large boulder near the stream, she hid against the onslaught; golden warriors protecting her on every side.

Mike powered on through the storm. Determined to ignore everything the enemy directed at him. He would find Gracie, no matter what!

If he'd had any doubt about the origin of the sudden storm, his suspicions were put to rest when a large boulder flew through the air, coming at him from behind and barely missing him. It was clear that the powers of evil were working overtime to achieve their wicked plans. Once again, due to the protection afforded him by God's golden guard, he was saved. But, now he was angry! "Satan, you can throw everything you want to at me, but you will not keep me from my daughter! Don't you think I know this is you?" He shouted in a booming and defiant voice. A voice that his daughter would have been able to pick out anywhere.

"Dad? Dad, is that you?"

"Yes, Gracie. Where are you? Stay right where you are. I'm coming to get you sweetheart!" There is no 'earthly' way Mike and Grace could have heard each other over the clamor of the storm, especially with a mile of distance still between them, but God!

Mike covered that expanse in record time, with the help of his winged sentries clearing the way before him. And when he found Gracie in a heap beside a giant boulder, he bent down and scooped her up in his arms. She cried out in distress, almost passing out from the soreness of his embrace. But gasping, she asked, "Dad, how did you get here? How did you know where to find me?"

"I'm sure it was the angels directing me, Gracie. I've been looking for you for days now. We got worried when we didn't hear anything."

"Dad, we have to save Jason. He's at the crash site on the mountain, and he's badly hurt."

"It's okay honey. Jason is safe. We found him first, days ago. Tom and Ace have taken him back to Port au Prince to the hospital there."

"So Tom is here too? Wait, who is Ace?"

"He's a pilot, and now a very good friend. He flew us around for hours, until we found the location of the chopper. We had to hike in about five miles from the clearing where we landed."

"Thank you Dad. For coming all the way out here to rescue me, and for not giving up."

"I wouldn't have had it any other way baby girl."

The wind continued to howl, and every manner of vegetation and likely or unlikely projectile filled the space around them. Like spears, the objects flew through the air, attempting to connect with their targets from every direction. But, angelic warriors, powerful and alert, were on guard, and threw up a barrier so strong the enemy hordes could not penetrate.

"I'm afraid I'm not in very good shape, Dad. You might have to go on without me."

"Don't be ridiculous, baby girl. I am not leaving you anywhere. Ace is waiting to see flares in the sky, and that is what we are going to give him! I need to get you out of here as soon as possible. Your wounds are infected."

"How did you know?"

"I found bandages along the way. I also found your backpack, so I know you have been drinking contaminated water and going without food. There is no way you can survive out here much longer, and no reason you should have to."

"So, how do you propose we manage that, Dad? I can't walk fast enough to keep up with you, and you certainly can't carry me all the way home."

"Then I'll make a travois and pull you."

"Dad, now you're the one being ridiculous. I'll just slow you down. It's better if you go on alone. When you get to help you can send someone back for me."

"Don't argue with me, Daughter. This is the way it is, and you don't have a choice in the matter. But, first I'm going to get some food and clean water into you. We also need to clean your wounds and change your bandages." Protein bars never tasted so good. And, it felt great to be drinking water that wouldn't perpetuate her intestinal problems. Mike shook his head as he cleaned her injured ankle and wrist. Both wounds were badly infected, but the ankle was worse by far. He had gauze and bandages with him, as well as antibiotic creams, so at least they were headed in the right direction.

"Have I said thank you Dad? I mean for coming all this way to rescue me?"

"What did you think I was going to do Gracie? I couldn't just leave you out here."

The two laid low, avoiding the many projectiles flying through the air; until the storm created by pure evil quieted; and then Mike went to work. He cut branches for a frame and others for supports. Using long strips of bark he wove a mat, attaching it to the long poles and supporting it by the cross braces. Once he was finished with the basic design, he covered the whole thing in strips of bark, large leaves and layers of moss to cushion the ride. Leaving enough of the long poles exposed to act as handles, and wrapping them in moss and leaves for his own comfort, he loaded Gracie on board and headed out. "You comfortable baby girl?"

"Dad, I can't believe you. I'm sure I'm a lot more comfortable than you are. And, I feel pretty guilty getting the royal treatment over here while you're doing all the work. Have I told you thank you yet? I mean for coming all this way to rescue me?"

"You just behave. Lay back and relax, honey. We're going to have you out of here in no time."

"Whatever you say, Dad. Behaving now." Mike grabbed the long poles and began pulling Gracie behind him. He wasn't a young man anymore, or as fit as he'd been in his youth. And frankly, this whole rescue trip had been hard on him, but he would never let his daughter know that. So, even when his muscles began to burn with the strain of pulling extra weight behind him, he endured with a smile. He had found Grace, and all was well with the world.

As they made their way along the stream and through the trees, the enemy mounted attack after attack, to which heaven's guardian host countered with expert tactical precision. Gracie, much sicker than she'd let on to her dad, laid back into the relative comfort of her transport, and faded in and out of consciousness. During lucid moments she witnessed angelic warriors battling demon hordes, and knew she and her dad were securely in God's hands. Confident that everything would be fine, she gave herself up to the rest her body had craved for so many days. She was heartily sorry she had ever said a critical word about her protectors, and would never question them or their purpose again.

Mike plowed stubbornly on until the day's light began

to dim. Then he found a small clearing in which to set up camp for the night. Grace woke to the smell of fresh caught fish cooking over an open fire. Dad saw her eyes flutter open and offered her fresh water. She drank of the clean, refreshing liquid, and then asked for help to rise, needing to relieve herself. He was immediately concerned; because upon their skin touching he noticed her fever had spiked tremendously. A sure sign that the infection was turning critically worse. Struggling off, into the trees, using her crutch to steady her steps; Grace found herself undeterred by their circumstances and humming her favorite hymns as she had done before acquiring her recent injuries. She was just so happy for the presence of her dad.

It was true, she thought. God had never given up on her. He had never stopped protecting her, watching over her and being on her side. He surely was good and worthy to be praised. She took care of her business, turned, and thumped her way back to the light of the campfire.

Mike heard her coming and smiled when she made her way into the clearing. "Come on over here baby girl. I want to check your bandages before we eat." He shook his head again once her wounds were revealed. "I'm hoping we will be out of these trees soon. Once we're clear of the forest I'm to set off flares to alert Tom and Ace that we are ready to be picked up. I want to get you straight to the hospital, so we can get your injuries tended to. There's only so much I can do out here, and so far it isn't nearly enough."

"Do you think I'm going to lose my leg, Dad?"

"I don't know Gracie. The infection is pretty bad. But, they can do a lot with medicine these days. And, I've seen things a lot worse than this healed. We're going to leave that up to God, and ask for favor in all these things. I know the Master has plans for you yet, so we will trust Him for every good thing and figure that it will all work out for His glory in the end."

"I love you Dad. Have I told you thank you yet? I mean for coming all this way to rescue me?"

"Yes, baby girl. about a hundred times."

Steadfast love and faithfulness meet; righteousness and peace kiss each other. Faithfulness springs up from the ground, and righteousness looks down from the sky. Yes, the Lord will give what is good, and our land will yield its increase. Righteousness will go before him and make his footsteps a way.

Psalm 85:10-13

CHAPTER 8

Tom had actually begun to give up hope a little when he thought he saw a flash of light in the distant, ebony sky. Then, another burst of brightness high in the night's abyss at the edge of the trees assured him he was not merely imagining the brilliant glow. It was the signal he'd been awaiting. Mike's flares, were igniting the darkened horizon like fireworks on the Fourth of July. Praise God, his good friend had finally made it to safety with Grace! He dialed Ace's number. "I just saw flares in the sky, at the edge of the forest. Are you ready to go?"

"I saw the flares too, Tom. But, the weather channel says there's another big storm headed this way. We can leave at dawn; right after the worst of it has passed; but I wouldn't dare try to fly so close to the tree line in the dark. Especially with all this wind. Don't worry, we'll get them home safely. But tonight, they're going to have to wait it out, and we're just going to have to be patient a little bit longer."

"Keres! Get in here right now!"

"Yes Kakos, Sir!"

"What's going on in Haiti? I haven't heard any more news, and you were to keep me posted on all developments."

"Sir, I'm sorry. I didn't want to come to you with information until I had better news to tell. I knew you would be displeased, and I thought I could get things turned around before it all went sideways." Keres saw the look on Kakos' face and took a step back.

"What do you mean sideways? Speak up girl!"

"Sir, the girl's father made it past our most recent onslaught, with the help of their heavenly guard of course, and he has managed to get his daughter all the way to the edge of the forest. They've already signaled for help from the others. We've launched another storm, using help from the atmospheric services department. Sir, we're still hoping we can stop them in their tracks before anyone can get her to the hospital."

"Keres, I am telling you right now, we cannot allow them to get her to the hospital. Satan has given orders that she must not receive medical help under any circumstances. And, that she cannot find out about the child she carries. Drop a tree, or a boulder, on her if you have to. Throw her into another river if that doesn't work. We have to eliminate this threat to our very futures. If she is allowed to give birth, this child will have more power through the infernal indwelling of the 'Holy Spirit', than the two of them could have ever imagined even put together. We have to stop this. Do you understand Me?"

"Kakos, Sir, it isn't as though we haven't been trying all along. Nothing would give me more pleasure than to do away with this damnable threat. I will put my best teams on it right away, Kakos. We will do our best, Sir."

"Your best hasn't been good enough yet. Do better than your best, Keres, or you will be sent to the deepest pit in the kingdom of Hell. I assure you of that. Now go!"

"I just wanted to let you know we saw flares tonight, Jason."

"Praise God, Uncle Tom. So, are you going out to get them now?"

"There's a big storm on the way, son. Ace says we can't take off in this wind. The rescue is going to have to wait till the morning. But, they've made it out of the forest, through only God knows what, so I know they can hang on till then. Just promise me you'll keep praying."

"I haven't stopped yet, Uncle. It's just that she's been through so much already. I hate the thought of her spending another night out there in the rain. I just want it to end."

"I know, kid. I want it to be over too. But, God is watching over them and they have angels, remember? Don't worry, we're going to get them home."

As Mike and Gracie parked themselves on the edge of the forest, to await rescue, the winds began again in earnest. And, for the second time in as many days they found themselves taking shelter at the rear of a large boulder. That is, until the huge rock suddenly lifted right off the ground. Like a spacecraft taking flight, it hovered for a few seconds, and then launched at them as if shot from an enormous cannon. Only the quick action of their warrior sentries, deflecting the colossal projectile, protected them from certain death.

Gracie could see the war being waged around and against them from every direction and by every manner of grotesque demon imaginable, and then in contrast, the excellent defense being strategized by those golden soldiers of the Most High. She would have loved to pass that vision along to her dad, to remove the look of abject fear from his face. She knew, without doubt, his biggest worry was that something might happen to her, after all he'd already done to save her. She was also sure he'd promised Mom that he would bring her home safe and sound. And he would hate to ever break a promise to his beloved wife.

The battle continued throughout the night, amidst pelting rain and hurricane force winds; until finally, through much prayer from all quarters and by the power of God, the tide was turned in their favor. When Grace saw that her heavenly host at last prevailed, she breathed a sigh of relief and curled up in her dad's arms, surrounded by a wall of angels, to fall fast asleep.

Mike couldn't have slept a wink if he'd been paid to do so. He knew deep inside, and without a doubt, that they were protected under the Savior's wings, as Gracie had assured him over and over. But, without his daughter's powerful sight all he'd been able to see throughout the night were trees and rocks, and all sorts of foreign objects flying through the air. And, these things being used as weapons to harm them. His chest was pounding so hard he thought there might be a stroke in his near future. Then, suddenly, his hammering heart remembered. Because they were children of the King, "No weapon formed against us can prosper". Suddenly things around them began to quiet. God would absolutely keep them safe, he was sure of it. All he had to do now was convince his racing mind.

Pulling plastic sheeting from his backpack, he unfolded the length and width of it. And though the sun was already slowly beginning to rise in the East, he covered himself and his sleeping daughter against the still misting rain. Her face was hot as a furnace, and he was scared for the young woman who had filled his life with so much joy in these past years. So, he rocked her and prayed.

Mike knew full well the reason Grace had succumbed so easily to slumber. She was horribly, terribly sick. Her fever raged, her wounds stunk, and she was frighteningly dehydrated from fighting the parasites which invaded her body. Infections and debilitating diarrhea had drained her of the ability to fight any longer. "Lord, please touch her. I know you've saved her many times in the past. But, I also know that the reason you save her over and over is because she is a fighter, and she is willing. Willing to serve you, willing to put herself on the line, willing to go the extra mile. Just give her the strength to fight this, please. I place her in your hands sweet Jesus. Amen."

As quickly as those words left his mouth, his heart calmed and he felt at peace. Perhaps he would close his eyes and rest a little after all, while they waited for their friends.

"Kakos, I'm sorry, but the hedge around her is too strong. We can't break through, and dawn is fast approaching. Their rescue will no doubt be arriving soon."

"No! This can't be. I am going with you this time. We are taking one more shot at this. I will not give up. Satan will have me skinned and banished to the deep. Come on, grab a team of your most experienced demons and let's go."

"Yes Sir."

The mist subsided and Mike pulled the plastic, which had been draped over them while they rested, off to the side. He would shake it out and fold it in a minute. Gracie was out of it, mumbling incoherently. He shook her gently and felt her face. She was literally burning up from within. "Gracie, honey, it's Dad. Honey, wake up. Help will be coming soon baby girl. You have to hang on a little longer sweet girl. Please Grace. Wake up. Mom and Lilly and Anna are all waiting at home for us; and Jason is at the hospital waiting for me to bring you back to him. You have to wake up sweetheart."

But, Grace wasn't available just now. Opening her eyes once again in an 'oh so familiar place', she found herself, as she had when she was a child, smack dab in the arms of Jesus.

"Oh Lord, I don't want to go back there. Please don't make me go back. I was in so much pain, and I don't think I can stand it anymore. Please, Jesus, can't I just stay with you?"

"Grace. You must go back. There is more for you to do. And your daughter will need the best teacher we can provide for her. There is much yet to accomplish."

"My daughter? Lord, I don't have a daughter."

"But you will. You are carrying her in your womb as we speak. This is one of the many reasons Satan is trying so very hard to kill you. He knows that your daughter will have spiritual sight even stronger than that of you and Jason combined. Your daughter will help to thwart many future plans of the enemy, and help to lead many souls home to me. She is an essential piece of the never ending puzzle in these last important days."

"But I've been so sick. Won't that sickness have harmed her?"

"I have had my hand on her from the beginning, Grace. Just as I have had my hand on you, your entire life. Now, you must go back beloved. Your earthly father is waiting, and his heart is heavy indeed, believing he may have lost you for good."

As Grace's eyes fluttered opened she saw the tears in her dad's eyes, and the relief on his face at her sudden consciousness. At that precise second, she saw the most hideous, giant demon she'd ever witnessed storming toward them, over her dad's shoulder. His face was contorted by a rage she couldn't begin to fathom.

His rock filled fists were raised high in the air, and he flew with fury in the direction of his enemies. But, just as those evil weapons were about to come down full force on the back of her father's head she remembered her place in the Grace of God and yelled, "Demons be gone in the Name of Jesus, be gone!"

As simple as that, every demon was forced to flee from sight, sucked into a spinning void. Gracie and Mike held each other. Then taking a collective deep breath, they looked up as they heard the wonderful sound of an approaching chopper.

Inside a small dirt cave, deep in the woods; behind the beautiful, Victorian house where she'd recently come to live; the girl's red hued eyes opened with a jolt, and a small smile slowly curved her blue tinged lips. Only a while longer now. She already had her instructions. When the rest of her new family arrived home, she would be ready for them all.

Good to his word, Ace came first thing in the morning to carry Tom out to the forest's edge to retrieve Mike and Grace. Tom was shocked at Gracie's deteriorated condition. Jason had told them she'd not taken any supplies with her, but he'd also said that she was sure she could gather provisions along the way. Looking at her now it was obvious things had not gone as planned. Tom could see she was half starved, very dehydrated, and sported what appeared to be a badly broken ankle and an injured wrist.

When the chopper landed, whipping trees and grasses into a frenzy around them, Mike gently lifted his daughter and held her close in his arms, waiting to safely board. Gracie's eyes had once again closed and he didn't want to disturb her any more than necessary. She was easy to carry, especially after being nearly starved to death during her days in the forest. She was so tiny to begin with, weighing next to nothing, and he was deeply concerned for her health.

Mumbling something he couldn't quite make out, she rested uneasily against his chest. Something about taking care of the little one. He assumed she was talking about Anna, so far away, and he smiled. It was so like Grace to be concerned about everyone else before herself. They would get her straight to the hospital and get her checked out. His greatest concerns were the wrist and ankle injuries that had obviously become infected, and getting the parasites cleared from her system as they tried to get her hydrated once again.

When Grace opened her eyes two days later, she was covered in fresh, clean sheets. In a room with mist green walls and a large window filled with sunshine just to her right. She guessed she was probably not on the first floor of the building, as all she could see was blue, cloudless sky, and the tops of a few tropical trees. When she gently, and carefully, turned her head to the left, she was pleasantly surprised to see the bed next to her was occupied by her sleeping husband. As if on cue, he turned to look at her. And, when their eyes met they both smiled. "I've been waiting for you to wake up, so I could tell you that I love you."

"I love you too, Jason. I'm so happy they found you. And, I'm so sorry I didn't bring help back for you sooner."

"No, Gracie, I should never have let you go out on your own like that. You could have been killed."

"Well, here I am alive. Though, I do have to say that Satan and his gang sure made a stab at the whole 'killing me' thing."

"I know. Your dad told us all about it. Or, at least the parts he knew about. I'm sure you saw things that would have terrified him. I'm so sorry you went through all of that. Did you know?"

"Know what?"

"About the baby?"

"Not until we were out of the forest. I passed out and spent a little time with Jesus. He told me that I was going to have a daughter. That was the biggest reason I knew I needed to keep fighting."

"So, we're having a baby girl?"

"Yes, and He told me she will have spiritual sight twice that of what we have, Jason. I'm not even sure how to prepare her for that. But, the Lord also told me that she would help to take down many plans of the enemy, and lead many to know Him, so we have to help her get ready, and make sure she grows up knowing Him. She will definitely need His strength and understanding, in order to serve Him properly."

"That is a lot to ask of anyone. A great honor, but also a great burden. And, one that she didn't ask for. Do you think it's fair that we ask so much of her?"

"It isn't we that are doing the asking, Jason. She is coming into the world for such a time as this, at His bidding. And, God will make sure she is equipped for the job. She will know much younger than either of us did, what her purpose on earth is to be. So she will have an advantage we never had. But, first we have to heal. We have time to figure the rest of this out later. Satan does not want this child born, so we will have to be prepared for his attacks along the way. How is your leg? Did I mess it up badly when I tried to set it?"

"Actually, Dr. Phillips said you did an excellent job re-

lieving the pressure on my lung, and a pretty good job setting the leg. There was a lot of infection, due to the wet
and humid conditions, but they think they caught it in
time, and they've had me on some pretty heavy antibiotics.
I think I'm in the clear. Now, your ankle is another matter. Your dad said you fell in the water, but he wasn't clear
about exactly what happened to your wrist and ankle."

"Well, I had a bit of a tangle with a very large spider. I
fell into the rapids and lost my pack. I believe I hit every
rock and boulder for two miles on the way down the stream.
The angels protected my head and the baby I didn't know I
was carrying. I haven't given the Lord nearly enough credit
for taking care of me over these past years. His angel warriors have had quite a job on their hands watching over me,
and I don't think I ever fully realized what a blessing that is.
I think I was getting a little full of myself, and this whole
experience has made me see a few things more clearly."

"Like what?"

"Well, when I was a kid I had to take care of everyone
else. No one ever gave me a choice. I learned I couldn't depend on anybody else for anything. I assumed that meant
God too. And I guess it's easy for me to fall back into that
same mind set when I start getting too caught up in things.

You know, thinking I can do it on my own and not letting go so God can do what He does best. I was kind of; no, not kind of; I was getting settled into a fake place of self-sufficiency again, and not remembering where our abilities come from. Or, for that matter, who we are supposed to be using them for. This trip has really cleared up a few things for me. I'm ready; when we get healed up a bit; to get back out there and start winning souls for the Kingdom again. In Jesus' Name. I haven't felt this recharged for a long time."

"I'm happy about that, Gracie. I've missed our revivals."

"Remember that when you've got a roomful of demons screaming in your face."

"I will. I love you wife."

"And, I love you husband."

"Is everyone ready?"

"Yes Dad, we are ready. This is the third time you've asked, remember?"

"I just want to make sure we have everything we need before we go, Lilly."

"I know, Dad. I'm anxious to see them too. I can't believe it's been fourteen weeks since they left!"

191

"Well, after Dr. Phillips said we should wait to fly them home until their injuries were better stabilized, I figured God had put him in Port au Prince for a reason, so we should heed his advice."

"Are we all ready?"

"Yes, Mom. Dad has already made quite sure we are all ready to go."

"Are you sure we're going to be able to fit both wheelchairs in the back of the van, Mike?"

"Yes, Babe. I've already moved the seats."

"Oh, I just can't wait to see them. I can't believe my baby girl is going to have a baby girl!"

"Nance, that's quite a way down the road. Doc figured her due date for about another five and a half months out yet."

"I know. I just can't wait to be a grandma I guess. And, I've missed those two kids so much! I can't believe they are going to be here where I can take care of them and watch over them every day. And now they will be here for Christmas too. Isn't that wonderful? Just in time for Christmas!"

"Well, try not to smother them, Mama. Give them a little breathing room."

"Mike, you know Anna is still out there. The authorities are sure she's dead, because of the cold, and all the time that's passed. But, we know Satan has her in cold storage somewhere, just waiting for the opportunity to use her in whatever evil plan he has designed. I'm sure he has been waiting for the whole family to be together again. We will have to keep our eyes open."

"Nance, I know you're concerned. But, do you really think she could have survived these freezing temperatures, especially after all this time, and with no food? As much as it breaks my heart, the authorities might be right about her being dead."

"No. First of all, I refuse to believe she's gone. She absolutely can't be gone, not without knowing Jesus as Lord. I won't accept that. We have to reach her before it's too late. Mike, Lilly and I are both sure that she is just waiting for instructions. That she is out there somewhere, ready to strike."

"I agree with Mom. Dad, if you had seen her face that last day, before she ran off. You would know that Satan has got her pretty tightly wound. Just waiting for the right time to do whatever he has programmed her to do. I know she's out there in the cold somewhere, and that might make you think she won't be prepared. But, he's got her tucked away somewhere waiting for his signal to strike. I'm sure of it."

"Well, we will keep our eyes and ears open. No one is going to get anywhere near this family. And we are going to keep Grace and Jason safe. Don't you worry about that."

"Oh, Mom, Dad, Lilly, I've missed you all so much! I'm so glad to be back, and I can't wait to get home!"

"I can't wait for you to see the house, Gracie. Lilly helped me decorate and it looks wonderful! Her professors are letting her study from home these days. She's been able to keep her grades up so well that this can be permanent if she wants it, unless she has a week of labs. And she will only have to check in for grades and counseling if it is warranted."

"I'm sure you've gone all out, Mom. We always did say the only thing in the world you own more of than garden gnomes is Christmas decorations. I can't wait to see it. And, Lilly, I'm so glad you could be there with Mom. Thank you for helping her out so much. I'm really proud of you. Bella and David would be proud of you too."

"We're all so excited about the baby, Grace. But, you don't even look like you're carrying a baby. I guess I was expecting you to look more, well, pregnant. Mom is practically bursting at the seams waiting to be a grandmother. She stops people at the grocery store to tell them. It's quite embarrassing, really, but, pretty sweet too."

"Aw, Mom, I knew you would be excited. I'm glad you're happy about this."

"For heaven's sake, Gracie, of course I'm excited. My baby girl is having a baby girl. I get to be a grandma! But, I have to agree with Lilly. Shouldn't you be showing a little by now? I wouldn't even know you were pregnant if the doctor hadn't confirmed it for us."

"I'm only about fourteen weeks along, Mom. I probably won't even really begin to show until I'm about five or six months. At least with a first baby. That's what Dr. Phillips said anyway. And that's just fine with me. I want this leg all fixed up before we have to put extra weight on it."

"Hey all, I'm going to go home myself. I just wanted to be here to see these kids picked up. I promised the little woman I would head straight to the house from the airport."

"I was hoping you'd stop by and have supper with us, Doc."

"No, not tonight, Nancy. My wife is waiting. I've been gone for more than three months, remember?"

"Yes we do. And we so appreciate everything you've done for all of us, Doc. How can we ever repay you?"

"Don't be ridiculous. You know that isn't necessary. I will be in touch. I have to check on my patients. And, Gracie wants me to take care of her during her pregnancy as well, even though that isn't within my usual purview. I told her I would be fine with that, as long as we have an OB/GYN on board, for any extraordinary eventualities."

"Good, I'm so glad you agreed to that. She will feel much more comfortable in your hands than anyone else I can think of."

"I don't know, Nancy. With your connections, you could have called anyone."

"I can't imagine anyone I would trust more."

"Well, with the things I'm hearing about 'double sight' for the baby. If there are any unusual aspects to the delivery, another doctor might be confused or even 'freaked out'. And, we certainly don't want anything like that going on."

"Well, call us when you have a minute and we will figure out another night for you and your wife to share a meal with us. Does that sound good?"

"Yep, sounds like a plan to me. You all have a great evening. I'm glad everyone is together again. I will talk to you soon." After the doctor drove away, Mike began to load the back of the van.

"I've got the luggage on board. Now, let's get these two in the van, so I can stow the wheelchairs."

"Good idea, Dad. If you and Tom can help them in, I'll fold the chairs."

"Thanks, Lilly. Doc says that the wheelchairs will only be necessary for another week or two, and then they can go to crutches. Things seem to be healing just fine for both of them. And, just so you know, Jason and Gracie, we've made up a bedroom for you downstairs in the den, until you are out of these wheelchairs. Trying to get you up and down the stairs would have been quite an ordeal. Is that okay for now?"

"That will work out great, Dad. I was wondering how we were going to work that out. Thanks for thinking ahead. I will be happy to be back in my old room afterward though."

"What do you say we hurry up and get everybody home. I've got beef stew in the crock pot, and I made bread this morning. Oh, and there's apple pie for dessert!"

"Sounds good to me, Nancy. I've missed your cooking!"

"Oh, Jason, you do know all the right words to say, to

flatter your old mother in law."

"So, nobody has mentioned the elephant in the room yet."

"Yeah, Lilly, we're all thinking about Anna."

"I know we're all thinking about her, Mom. But, shouldn't we be making a plan? You know he has been saving her for when we would all be together. It would be foolish not to be prepared."

"We are prepared, Lilly. Dad has already filled us in on the change in Anna after we left for our honeymoon. Wow, saying it out loud is strange. That seems like such a long time ago, doesn't it? Anyway, Jason and I will be able to see her coming a mile away. You know, don't you, that you would have been just as capable of calling out the demons, in Jesus' Name, as we are, right? I forget sometimes how powerful a gift it is to be able to see. But, anyone who knows and trusts the Lord can use the Name of Jesus to cast out demons, heal the sick, and do any manner of miracles in His Name. I want to make sure you all remember that. It's easy to start assigning those miracles to the humans who are being used by Him, instead of Him alone. I think I got a little caught up in that myself for a while, and perhaps forgot momentarily where that power was coming from. I don't believe I will be doing that again."

"We know that His power extends to us as well, Gracie, and if we'd put two and two together for ourselves sooner, things wouldn't have gotten this far."

"It's not your fault, Mom. You always want to see the best in every one and that is most assuredly not a bad thing. If only the whole world were more like you, there would be a lot less division in this country. We will get this figured out. I promise."

Sitting on a decaying fir carcass, just past the tree line and behind the huge Victorian house, the girl waited. She'd stayed alive these past months by eating worms and bugs, animal droppings, and pine bark. And, recently, she'd hydrated herself with one mouthful of snow after another. It was cold outside, but she didn't feel the frigid temperatures. Her mind was twisted beyond recognition. Matted hair and filthy beyond imagining, she was covered in her own urine and feces. Just the smell of her would have sent brave men running for cover. The look in her eyes had grown so venomous that no mere mortal could have withstood it's penetration, without the very blood of Jesus for protection.

She plopped a beetle into her mouth and crunched down on its hard exterior, until she felt a satisfying pop between her teeth; then she lifted up one cheek and passed gas in a long uninterrupted blast. Settling down to wait, she knew that tonight would be the night. Tingling with anticipation, she had her instructions, and those directions played slowly through her mind in a continuous loop, leaving no room for error.

"Keres, what report have you? Are they home? What can you tell me? Out with it!"

"Yes, Kakos. The couple is home. The whole family is together for the first time in over three months. The girl is stationed outside the home, simply waiting for the 'go' sign. All is set commander. All we need is your signal to advance."

"We will wait. They are likely expecting a strike, and will be prepared for anything we attempt. We shall be patient and once they are sleeping, we will hit them with all we have. Does she have everything she needs? I don't want any mistakes made for lack of preparation. Do you understand me?"

"Yes, Kakos. She knows which valves to open to release gas into the house. And, we have made sure that she has plenty of fire starting materials. They won't know what hit them. Also, she will be burning alive with them, so no witnesses will be left behind."

"You know she will fight, right? Grace I mean. Now that she knows there is a child, she won't go silently into the night. And her husband will try to protect her at all costs. We must get through their defenses first, and quickly, before they realize we are in their midst. If they spot us before the deed is done, it will be too late."

"Yes sir, all the squad leaders have their orders. We will block their view of the girl for as long as we can. But, you know we can't keep the couple from seeing us, Kakos."

"Don't remind me, Keres. They have been one step ahead of us from the very beginning. But, this will be our last chance to use the girl we have prepared and I plan to use every bit of life left in her to take the lives of those interfering usurpers. I will have good news to report to the boss this time, and nothing will stop me."

"Oh, Mom, it is beautiful!"

"I'm so glad you like it. It does help that we drove up as the sun was going down, so you could see the exterior lights come on as well. And, it also helps that the design of the house lends itself to this sort of thing, but I'd like to think we worked within those classic designs to create something really special this year."

"Over and above, Mom. Over and above. This should be on the cover of a magazine. And you too, Lilly. It looks great. It feels so good to be home. I can't tell you how much I've been looking forward to this moment. It seems as though God wanted to bless us too. The snow, lightly falling all around really adds to the Christmas mood. It couldn't be more perfect."

"Hey, if you and Tom will help the kids into the house, Mike, Lilly and I can get the bags."

"It's a deal. but please be careful, it's a bit slick out here. I'll have to come out later and salt the sidewalks. I can't wait to dig into that beef stew you've been slow cooking. I swear I can smell it out here." Once inside, with the door closed behind them, Nancy surveyed her crew with tears shining in her eyes. It felt good to have almost the whole family together again, and just in time for Christmas. She felt so very blessed. And, to think, by next Christmas she would have a tiny new granddaughter to spoil. All she could think was, God is very, very good.

"Okay, everyone get out of your wet things. We can put the kid's things away later. If anyone else is as hungry as I am, we should make quick work of this meal. I'll cut the bread if you'll grab the butter, Lilly. And Tom, would you take the lemonade out of the fridge, and gather some glasses to put it in? Mike, honey, hit the button on the coffee maker. We can have coffee with our pie later, unless you'd rather do hot chocolate?"

"Yes ma'am. Boy, she is quite the organizer, isn't she kids?"

"Yes she is Dad. That's one of the things we love about her."

"So, you are sure everything is set up for tonight? I mean nothing can go wrong, Keres, so you have to be absolutely sure."

"Yes Kakos, we know. But we are more confident about this attack than we have ever been before. The girl will be a huge asset. I know that this time we will get the job done."

"Good, Keres. I have waited a long time for this. I can't

wait to be able to smear this in his highnesses face. A victory for once. Perhaps this will finally get the old serpent off my back once and for all."

"I hope so, sir." Keres knew this plan had as little chance of working as any before it, and she was pretty sure they would be thwarted, as usual, due to the ever vigilant winged warriors posted throughout the woman's home. But, she hoped for her own sake, if it didn't work out perhaps Satan would quickly destroy her boss, so she wouldn't have to deal with the horrors of his resulting mood due to the outcome of this mission.

Working with Kakos had been her worst nightmare, and it only continued to get worse all the time. She had only herself to blame for her position. Stupid decisions made millennia ago had set her on a course that would cause her to be cast from the heavens, and the presence of God Almighty, with Satan and a third of the angels. Regrets couldn't help her now. Angels who have been thrown from heaven can never go back. She would remain a fallen angel, a demon forever. And would be judged with all those who had not been content to serve the Creator on His terms.

Quietly, while the entire household was asleep, the girl crept in through the basement window on the North side of the house. Lowering herself silently to the stack of wooden crates below the window, she climbed down and walked toward the gas valves on the furnace system. All she would need to do is turn off the valves, extinguish the existing fire in the burner, and turn the valves back on.

Once there was enough gas built up in the basement, she was directed to light a fire on the stack of wooden crates, with the paper and matches supplied to her. Those were her instructions. As the fire reached the accumulated gas, the entire house should go up with an explosion rivaling any fourth of July celebration, and would be heard for miles around. And, actually, that kind of detonation would level not only the entire house, but probably half the neighborhood with it.

She reached for the valve......"Anna?" She recognized the voice. But the inner instructions were stronger than this voice from her memory. So, she reached again......"Anna, it's me, Gracie. I missed you my sweet little sister." Grace could tell that something inside the girl wanted to acknowledge her, but the evil invading her mind was currently too great. "Anna, look at me." The demons attached to the girl were huge, and holding on to the youngster at her shoulders with their long yellowing talons. Devils were actively keeping her head turned away from Grace and preventing her from turning back around to look at her sister. But, they, themselves, were looking right at her, full in the face, with their red eyes focused, pointed teeth bared, and rigid frames ready to wrap themselves quickly around their captive. This exchange would be quick, very quick.

Grace had gone to bed with the family that evening, but as soon as she heard the house settle she began to get an uneasy feeling, she hoisted herself back into her wheelchair and made her way to the kitchen. From there, she wasn't entirely sure how she'd gotten down the basement stairs, but here she was, without her chair or crutches. She'd felt an urging in her spirit, and knew that God was telling her Anna was near. Satan was out to kill her entire family. But, for some reason he continued to forget he had no real power over those who belong to the Son of God.

Her angel protectors were near, as always. And Grace suspected it was they who had ferried her the distance from the kitchen to the furnace room. There was no other earthly explanation. And when they stepped from the shadows to reveal themselves to the demons holding Anna, unfurling their powerful wings, those demonic creatures began to visibly shake. "I command you, to come out from her, in the NAME OF JESUS." Upon those words being spoken, those two demons were swept into a vortex of black and smoke, and the girl collapsed in a heap on the cold cement floor.

Grace approached and knelt beside the girl. Her own leg no longer hurting. Then, sitting on the smooth concrete, she placed the girl's head in her lap, and stroked her brow. "Anna, wake up child."

"Grace? What, how, where am I? Why are you here? I thought you were with Jason in Haiti? Why are we in the basement?"

"We have much to talk about, Anna. But, first I want to introduce you to my very best friend. His name is Jesus. And, He did something very special for you and me. Can I tell you about it?" In those next moments Grace shared the beauty of the Gospel message with her young sister. Who, after hearing of God's magnificent Grace, love and forgiveness, asked Jesus into her heart. Now, Satan could never again use her for his evil devices.

Kakos' screams could be heard far and wide through the corridors of hell.

"Mom, it's time. Gracie is calling for you."

"Okay, I'm coming. Mike, call Doctor Phillips. And Anna, please get the stack of clean towels we set aside. Tell her I'll be right there."

"Can I do anything, Nancy?"

"No, Tom, just be in prayer. So far everything has gone well, so I don't foresee any complications. But, additional prayer is always good."

"So, why are we doing this at home again, Nancy?"

"I told you before, Tom. Grace felt an urging from the Holy Spirit. She knew it wouldn't be safe to give birth at the hospital. Satan must have managed to get some of those that he controls into the staff there. You know he has been out to kill this child from the beginning. Everything will be fine. Doc is on his way, and I am a nurse, remember?"

"Well, if Satan can get his minions into the hospital, then he can get them into every place this child will be for the rest of her life, can't he?"

"Yes Tom. So, we will deal with that one day at a time. For today, we are delivering a baby. Please go watch for the doctor, and send him upstairs the minute he arrives."

"I'm on it, Nance." Within moments the sound of a crying infant filled the air. And, by the time Dr. Phillips made his way up the stairs, Mommy and baby were quietly bonding. He checked things over, and pronounced the delivery a success; and the beautiful baby girl in her mother's arms healthy and whole.

"She is a tiny little thing, just like her mommy. Only five pounds and two ounces, and seventeen and a half inches long, but healthy and strong. And, with the set of lungs she has on her, I would say she's going to be a preacher like her mama."

"Thanks for coming out, Doc. Sorry we stole your thunder. She was obviously in a big hurry to make her way into the world."

"That's fine, Mike. She came much quicker than any first baby I've ever seen."

"I wanted to thank you too, Dr. Phillips. We appreciate you coming so soon."

"No problem, Jason. Glad to do it. So, how do you like

this whole idea of being a dad?"

"I think I'm going to like it. It's all a bit overwhelming. You know, the idea that another human being is depending on us. But, we've got lots of support. And, God is certainly keeping us informed when danger is near. She already has guardian angels."

"I'll never get used to that. The idea that you two can see angels and demons. But, I think it's wonderful."

"Well, it's three now."

"What?"

"Three. It's three now. Three of us who can see angels and demons. We have a lot to teach her, and a lot to learn, I'm sure."

"Yes, a lot to learn. If you three need anything at all, don't hesitate to ask."

"We won't. It's nice to know that we have people to depend on. God is good."

"Can I come in now?"

"Yes, Anna. Come in and meet your new niece."

"Oh, Gracie, she's beautiful. But she's so tiny. May I hold her?"

"Tiny, but mighty. And yes, you may hold her. She will need you as she is growing up. She will need us all to keep her safe, as she grows into the mighty woman of God that He intends her to be. We will have to share the Gospel with her, and help her to know of His eternal love and Grace. And, most of all, she will need to learn the most powerful Name of all. The Name above all names. The Name of Jesus."

PART TWO

But do not overlook this one fact, beloved, that with the Lord one day is as a thousand years, and a thousand years as one day. The Lord is not slow to fulfill His promise as some count slowness, but is patient toward you, not wishing that any should perish, but that all should reach repentance.

2 Peter 3:8-9

"I will plant them on their land, and they shall never again be uprooted out of the land that I have given them," says the Lord your God.

Amos 9:15

CHAPTER 1

"Mom", said in a whisper, "Here, come over here. You can see the soldiers from this vantage point. Duck down, quick, so they can't see you. I think I see the girls in there too. Can you see them?"

"Yes", answered back in a whisper, "I can see them too, barely. But, how are we supposed to get in there to get them out with all those guards around?"

"We will likely have to wait till dark, when the night shadows will cover most of our movements. We can settle in right here. There's enough vegetation to shield us for now. Our angel warriors aren't going anywhere either, so there's that."

"Well, I guess you won't hear me complaining about any of it anyway. Not after what I know these girls have gone through. Poor things. Look at them all crammed into that tiny hut."

"I can't wait to see their faces when they see that God has answered their prayers. I always love seeing the faces. It's my favorite part of the job. Well, that and the time I get to spend with the Lord."

"You know I could always tell when you were spending time with Jesus. Even as a tiny little thing, before you could speak in intelligible English, you were always yakking away to someone in your dreams. Later it carried over into your waking hours as well, and I knew you had a very special relationship with Jesus going on. But, you've also been blessed in other things, Gabrielle. The way you pick up languages is amazing. All you have to do is be in close proximity to someone speaking a new language, even for just a short while, and in no time at all you are conversing with the natives."

"You do know that's God, Mom, right? I did just fine when you and Grandma home schooled me, but I was no genius, that's for sure. It has to be the Lord. There's no other explanation for that much talent."

"Yes, I have no doubt. He does not call the equipped, He equips the called. And, He has certainly equipped you, Gabby."

"Well, I know I couldn't do what we do without Him. That's for sure. Or without you and Dad. But, I love what we do. Don't you?"

"Yes, I do. I've always loved this, though I think I got a little lost for a while before you were born. A little too caught up in myself and my God given abilities. I stopped giving Him the glory for a while, and got pretty cocky. Not a good place to be, but a real good reminder for me, not to ever let it happen again. Now, though, since you've been old enough to come with us, and help out in all the ways you do every day, our trips have been an even bigger adventure. Much more action than your dad and I ever experienced on our own, that's for sure."

"Oh, I don't know. Grampa and Gramma have told me a few stories about the prison ministry, and a certain trip to Haiti when you were pregnant with me. I think you had your share of excitement before I officially started coming along with you. I love being part of the Lord's army and helping all these lost souls find their way home. It's the best feeling in the world. God is good!"

"Yes He is, baby girl. All the time."

"Dad is probably getting worried. You should call, and leave him a message. Tell him we had to hunker down till dark. I don't want him to come looking for us and walk in on the middle of anything."

"I'll do that. But, I'm sure he will stay with the vehicles. He knows he's our way out, once we get the girls, so he won't jeopardize that. Uncle Tom and Grampa have headed over to the missionary outpost to clear civilians out of possible harm's way, in case the soldiers decide to follow us and shooting begins, but they will be back later."

"Good. I wouldn't want anyone to get hurt in the exchange. Wait, I think that's the guy in charge. I want to hear what he's saying."

"Saman 'yan mata. Ina son su fita a nan yanzu."

"What's he saying, Gabby?"

"He's telling the men to get the girls. He wants them out where he can see them, right now."

"That's good. We can get a better idea of how many girls they have, and what kind of shape they're in."

"Sanya su. Dole mu bar gobe, kuma ina so in ga wanda zai iya tafiya, kuma wajibi ne a kashe shi kafin tafiya."

"Well, that confirms it, Mom. We most certainly need to get these girls out of here tonight. He plans to march them out in the morning. And, any that don't look like they can make the trip will be killed before they leave."

"Do you have a plan, Gabby?"

"God always has a plan, Mom. You know that. And He will unveil it to us when the time is right. We just have to be ready to act the minute He does. Things are about to get interesting!"

"I'm ready when you are. What are you seeing right now? Is it the same thing I'm seeing?"

"Yep, legions of demons surrounding the girls. But the girls have angel guardians too, and that will be a big help when the plan is revealed."

"So, the rumors were true then. The girls weren't just taken to be sex slaves among the Boko Haram soldiers. They were taken because it was discovered they had converted to Christianity."

"I think both parts are relevant. When they were taken from their village, there were rumors that their teacher had succeeded in converting them from Islam to Christ. The teacher was killed during the kidnapping, which was supposed to play out as partial retribution for their apostasy. But, the whole plan was that the girls were also going to be trafficked among the Muslim tribes. I'm sure that's why I got this call from the Lord. Their families wouldn't have thought the punishment fit the crime unless they also found out about the conversion. After that, they couldn't speak out for fear of being targeted as apostates themselves. They simply couldn't condone the conversion from Islam to Christianity, not without paying a price they weren't prepared to pay. It seems we have arrived just in the nick of time. Which, as usual, is in God's perfect timing."

"Isn't that just the way? God has a knack for that doesn't He? I will be forever amazed how He works things out. And yet, wouldn't you think I would have stopped being amazed long ago, since I have seen so many miraculous things?"

"Oh, I don't know. I think I will always be amazed by Him. Just like I will always be amazed by you and Dad. You never stop surprising me. And, I find that to be pretty exciting too."

"We are the ones surprised by you, Gabby. God has blessed us so much."

"Wait, look. You can see that two of the girls are having a hard time walking. Let's see. Thirteen total. I'm going to have to get in there and talk to them. But, we'll have to wait till dark before I can do that. The two who are limping will have to be our priority. I don't think any of the girls speak Hausa, which is what the soldiers are speaking right now. I'm sure it is making this whole thing that much more frightening for them. Poor things. I'm sure the troops know English. It is the cultural language of Nigeria after all. My guess would be that they are speaking Hausa, on purpose, to keep the girls in the dark. That is why I'll need to get in there and fill them in on the escape plan before it can be executed."

"Okay, so as soon as we know what the plan is, we will move in closer and I'll cover you while you make contact. This whole thing will likely go down very quickly, so be careful."

"I will, Mom. Careful is my middle name."

"No. Reckless is your middle name. That's why I told you to be careful."

"Okay, okay. I know you're right. I promise I'll be as careful as I can under the circumstances."

Reflecting, Grace had to admit that the past twenty one years had been packed with Spirit filled, hair raising adventures around the globe, in one broken and hurting country after another. This trip to Nigeria, to take on Boko Haram in the jungles; was just one more example of the way their family had been used mightily of God, over and over, to defeat Satan's plans. Nothing surprised her anymore.

After Gabrielle was born in 2019, the family took up their former prison ministry again in earnest, with a plan to see many more know and come to the Lord. But, sadly, times changed, and the American government began taking on a larger role in the lives of its people, whether those people liked it or not.

After all the years the family had spent in that successful prison venue, and all the conversions they'd witnessed; most prisons, and government run or funded entities, began to clamp down on Christian pastors or Evangelists sharing Christ in their facilities. Now, that didn't mean they clamped down on the activities of all religions. It appeared Christianity was the only real threat they detected on their "separation of church and state" radar. As ridiculous as that was, with crime rates and prison populations rising at an equal and exponential rate, the family was forced to curtail their prison visits.

When faced with this challenge they shifted their focus, and soon felt called to other, urgent, mission fields. They knew God desired that no one should be without the Gospel message. So, whether stateside, or around the world, they would take the message of God's Grace to humanity, wherever they found it.

Fast forward twenty one years, to 2040, and the world was clearly a bigger mess than ever in the past. The Name of Jesus had been completely eliminated from schools, and then wiped out of public places and forums of all kinds. So, the correlation seemed oddly appropriate. Could it be that the more Jesus was removed from the mix, the more evil prevailed? Counting back twenty years, when political correctness took over the country in such a huge and devastating way; there had been a distinct and obvious shift in the sanity of their culture then, that permeated the whole of society to this day.

It was no longer safe to speak the truth, and no longer safe to be a Christian. Even in America. A country where its citizens were once covered by constitutional rights. But whose people were being systematically stripped of those constitutional rights, one by one. Rights that brave Americans had fought and died to protect for centuries. Their country had slowly but surely begun to embrace collectivism, until it was so completely immersed in the quick sand of socialism it might never rise again.

People, everywhere around the world, were in urgent need of salvation and in danger from many totalitarian regimes and ideologies. So, the family's entire focus had changed direction to what the Lord was currently putting on young Gabby's heart.

And, now that warriors for the Kingdom were in

short supply, every place where anti Christian sentiment and hatred reigned, this evangelical family never seemed to run out of missions around the globe requiring their unique expertise.

Grace remembered that, even as a baby, Gabby had not been particularly afraid of the rooms full of demons that her family regularly encountered. As a tiny child, she seemed wholly unaffected by evil threats and horrid, hissing creatures. It was second nature for her to call upon the Name of Jesus, to cause Satan's minions to flee. She loved seeing the bad guys being sucked into the swirling vortex to hell. And whenever that exchange happened she laughed her sweet baby laugh and clapped her chubby little hands with glee. That joyful response only grew as she got older, and her delight at defeating the enemy and sharing the Word multiplied.

Gabby was an enormous source of happiness for the whole family. And, it was clear she had a very special relationship with the Lord. She confessed Jesus as Savior and Lord at only two years old. And, at that tender age, she began to demonstrate some other rather remarkable gifts. As she learned to speak English proficiently, she also learned any and every other language she was exposed to for even a short period of time. She now spoke over thirty languages. That number grew with each new mission, and each new people group she encountered.

She could also become invisible, when circumstances warranted. Oh, I know that sounds crazy. The way she explained it was, her heavenly guard stood between her and her enemy, becoming kind of opaque and creating a barrier of sorts, which made it almost impossible for her foes to see her. It worked best at night, when the distraction of darkness was already in her favor. So, where she wasn't actually invisible, for all practical intents and purposes, she may as well have been.

Jason and Gracie could both still see clearly into the spirit realm, and took advantage of that gift on their various missions; but they were both in awe of their daughter's extraordinary abilities. When Gabby confronted the enemies of the Lord, it was as if she was bullet proof. And, where the angelic guard often wouldn't step in the way of natural consequences for the rest of the world. With Gabby, they would fend off bullets and other projectiles that could have proved fatal for other mere mortals. She was truly special. But, the best part about this remarkable young woman was her humble nature. She never took credit for herself, and gave all glory to God, thereby not creating for herself those same issues her mom had encountered over the years.

In taking on this new ministry mantle, they also knew they were taking on some brand new, very huge responsibilities. Therefore, the family began to train, not only mentally, but physically as well. And, after years of extreme instruction, all three of them: Jason, Gracie and Gabby; were proficient in the use of all manner of firearms and explosives. Additionally, they had learned an assortment of fighting techniques, including several martial arts skills. Gracie knew she and Jason were easily in the best shape of their lives, and she felt better, stronger and more confident at forty than she'd ever been in her twenties or thirties.

Now, Gabby had acquired quite a reputation around the world, in her short twenty one years of life. An enduring reputation of invulnerability that frightened those who encountered her. Bad guys who witnessed her fighting prowess were dumbfounded, and awed, by her strength and agility. Most thought her either an avenging angel sent from heaven, or an American super hero.

When she showed up, grown men were known to beg and cry, or wet their pants and run away. That reputation certainly didn't hurt when confronting many of the evil thugs they dealt with on a regular basis.

Boko Haram, labeled a radical terrorist organization for the past twenty five years in a row, was particularly extreme and violent. And their fundamentalist Islamic views had only grown worse over the past two and a half decades. They operated for the most part in Nigeria, Chad, Niger and Cameroon, but had a number of cells in Europe and The United States as well. And, like many fundamentalist Muslim groups, they were particularly upset about the idea of government schools educating girls. In part because when young women discover there is a life that doesn't define them as forced cooks and sex slaves, they often opt out of that stringent Muslim lifestyle to pursue their own dreams.

This terrorist group had taken to attacking schools and killing teachers, for the past twenty five years, to keep the government from educating women. Another aspect of life, among others, the Qur'an and other Islamic teachings specifically warns against.

For what it was worth, those terrorists were essentially right. When taught that they have a choice, most young women choose life instead of slavery. And, most who encounter the living Christ choose Christianity instead of Islam. So, these Muslim extremists were up against some pretty stiff competition, and they were correct to be scared.

When Gabby heard about the latest kidnapping, and was led to believe this group of girls had recently given their lives to Jesus, which of course would cause the terrorists to be harsher with them than usual, she felt that oh so familiar urging in her spirit. Immediately she told her parents. And, well, they knew they had to help in some way. So, here they were in the jungles of Nigeria, once again about ready to go into full combat mode.

So far, the demon hordes surrounding the girls had not been alerted to their presence. But, as evening approached, Gabby knew she would need to warn the girls and make them aware help had arrived. She'd received a plan she knew was from the Lord, and she quietly filled her mom in on the particulars. It was almost dark enough now to make contact.

Just as she'd been alerted they would be, the soldiers were called and made their way to a makeshift mess tent for their evening meal. With only one guard watching the girls, contact would be much easier. Though the demons were still in full force, their angels were also there in great numbers. The girls, sitting out in the open; in front of the tiny hut where they'd been kept prisoners for the past week and a half; were visibly frightened. Wrists tied behind their backs, and ankles connected one to another like prisoners on a chain gang, they were filthy and exhausted. Their discomfort could be felt, even from a distance. And, several of the girls were quietly crying. As the guard moved to one side of the opening, Gabby moved to the other side of the hut, her warrior guard moving with her to block the line of sight of the human guard and that of those hideous creatures surrounding the group.

Once she was within quiet earshot of the girls, the angelic guard moved just enough for her to gain the sight of the one girl who seemed to be the oldest and most capable of following directions. "We are here to help you escape. But, you must listen and do exactly what I say. God has heard your prayers, and has sent us to rescue you from the grip of these monsters, before they kill your two injured friends and sell the rest of you into sex slavery."

The girl listened, and said, "Tell me what we must do." After full instructions, and a nod from the young woman, Gabby made her way back to her mother and the weapons that were stashed there for quick access.

First, Gabby and Gracie made their way slowly, and deliberately, in the dark, around the entire outer circumference of the enemy camp, setting booby traps as they'd been instructed by the Spirit. Then they found their way back to their original position, where they would create a distraction big enough and loud enough to cause the men to run frantically into the jungle.

Whether they were running from fright, or in an attempt to capture those they feared might arrest them, it didn't matter. The only thing that mattered was that they run out into the trees, where the snares had been set. This would eliminate most of the enemy's fire power, and cut their remaining man power down to a small fraction of its current numbers.

God had given Gabby a plan. As in all things He simply wants there to be no doubt that He is the victor. So, He generally causes us to win by His might, and not through our own meager human capacity. When that happens, there can be no doubt He has prevailed.

Knowing this, Grace and Gabby followed instructions to the letter, and set up more than two dozen large snares in that outer ring. In accessible areas where the enemy had previously scouted and would think it safe to set foot. Frankly, stepping there now would leave men dangling upside down in the trees, from those well executed and well positioned traps.

This should also give the two women plenty of time to take out any soldiers who lingered back in the camp guarding the prisoners; and time to get the young ladies unbound and out of sight before their captors might find release, rally, and take pursuit. It was a good plan. It was God's plan. And it would work perfectly. Now, all that remained was to create the illusion that the camp was surrounded, so the soldiers would run into the jungle in all directions attempting to capture their supposed attackers if they were brave, or attempt escape if they were cowards.

Gabby's other instructions were to attach a wire lead to noise makers that would surround the camp. Luckily, in this case, the soldiers were filthy pigs and simply threw their garbage into the jungle in various places outside the main campsite. Thus leaving plenty of cans and bottles available to be used for this purpose. The women quietly attached wire to the tin cans and glass bottles all around the perimeter of the camp. Positioning that wire on the far side of a ring of trees that encircled the camp, they stooped low as they walked, and brought the lead pieces back to their staging point from either side of the tree line, waiting for the exact moment in which to execute their plan.

Satan's hordes were as clueless as the human soldiers, since the angel guard had shielded their view while the women worked, and they were completely unprepared for all the upcoming events.

After the soldiers were fed, of course completely ignoring the needs of the girls they held captive, the camp began to settle down in the quiet of the night. Troops congregated around the main fire and engaged in a game of chance that kept them sufficiently distracted. Others were smoking, drinking, picking their teeth with their knives, and scratching their unwashed butts. A number of them had peeled off from the main group, and talked quietly in various clusters around the clearing, huddled around smaller fires. All was well in their terrorist circle.

At that time shall arise Michael, the great prince who has charge of your people. And there shall be a time of trouble, such as never has been since there was a nation till that time. But at that time your people shall be delivered, everyone whose name shall be found written in the Book.

Daniel 12:1

CHAPTER 2

"Keres!" Kakos yelled through the halls of hell. Causing Keres to run full tilt to the main hall.

"Yes, Kakos." Sadly, Kakos had not been thrown into the deepest pits of hell when Gabby was born, as Keres had hoped would happen. And, yes, he was still Keres' superior. She'd grown more and more resentful about the abuse she endured every day, and woefully, it had actually become exponentially worse over the past couple of decades. If she was honest, she was probably almost as anxious for the soon coming of the Lord, as many Christians were, simply to escape her current plight. Oh, yeah, she knew the old story, and knew that when the Lord came back she would be thrown into the lake of fire with Satan. However, in her mind, anything would be more desirable than being answerable to Kakos for the rest of eternity. Yes, even burning.

"What have you heard from the troops in Nigeria?"

"Sir, there has been no further action from the young woman and her family. The soldiers are currently sitting tight. But, the kidnapped girls are surrounded by angels,

Sir, and our demons can't penetrate that circle, as you well know."

"Don't tell me what I know and don't know you idiot. And, that's impossible. Our U.S operatives said she flew out with her family. They must be in country by now. Send out a couple of scouts. See if they can be located. I don't want them to succeed in rescuing those girls. Hourly reports. I want hourly reports."

"Yes Sir. I will send out the scouts, and I will see that you get your reports." Then, under her breath. "Though it won't do you a bit of good."

"What did you say?"

"Nothing, Sir. Nothing at all."

Anna loved the soup kitchen. The smell of it, the simple experience of it, made her feel wonderful, useful, productive and safe. It was the same soup kitchen she'd come to for help as a kid, and the same place she'd met Dad, Gracie, Lilly and Uncle Tom. And then, through them, mom, who was now her very best friend in the world. After the tragic loss of her own mother, when she was a little girl, she'd imagined she would never have another relationship like the one she shared with this great woman. The only connection she found even more rewarding these days, was her relationship with Jesus. His presence in her life was the best thing she'd ever known.

From the 'FREE' table, where she tried to keep fresh stacks of coats, hats, gloves, scarves, and other articles of clothing; as the seasons necessitated; for her clients. To murals on the walls, created by school children; certainly grown with children and possibly grand children of their own by now; decades ago. To the shiny clean serving line; with its sparkling carts; stacks of clean trays, plates, bowls, coffee cups, water glasses, and bins of assorted eating utensils; stainless steel, ridged sliding surface; glass shields, through which one could view that day's tasty selections; and table decorations, matching the nearest season or holiday; the place was just about exactly as she remembered it to be all those years ago. And, that gave her a sense of history and pride, that she'd been able to provide that same feeling of welcoming family, and safety, that had drawn her in so long ago.

She kept the property impeccably clean, with special attention given to the food areas. And, on the days she wasn't there, her wonderful volunteers were just as fastidious. Anna didn't believe in treating those who were less fortunate than she was, as second class citizens. She thought everyone should be respected and loved. After all, she'd once been that little girl reaching out for a hand up. With every fiber of her being, and every tool at her disposal, she blessed all those who graced her doors. Due to that, and, of course, her famous cuisine, she was universally loved, as her dad had always been, in this very same place.

With situations in the nation declining daily, places like the food kitchen were becoming more essential to the survival of the teeming masses being so badly hurt by burgeoning socialism. But, she didn't know exactly how long she would be able to hold out, as supplies were becoming harder to obtain by the day, and her own personal resources were starting to run out. It would break her heart to close the place down, so she'd try to keep it going as long as possible, but without supplies that might be sooner than later.

Anna didn't remember anything from the terrible months she'd spent possessed by demons and living in a cave in the forest behind her family's home. Her last solid memory was of the day Grace and Jason left for their honeymoon. She'd gone upstairs, happy as you please, that evening. Feeling kind of special, like a princess, in her pretty bride's maid dress. She twirled and twirled, watching herself dance in the full length mirror, as fragrant bubbles filled the steaming tub, then she undressed and slipped into the warm water.

With great plans of snuggling under her fluffy, white comforter. Surrounded by soft, purple pillows, in her cozy, queen sized bed. She slid down till the sweet-smelling bubbles burst in her nose, and the hot water covered her chin. The next thing she knew, she was waking up in the family's basement; filthy dirty, stinking to high heaven, with matted hair, and cricket legs stuck in her teeth. Looking up, scared witless, she saw Gracie holding her head in her lap, stroking her hair and rocking her in that special way she had. That was over twenty one years ago.

Those months were ones she would never get back. But gratefully, Satan's plan of using her to destroy her family had not been achieved. And, Jesus, who clearly had other designs for her, now commonly used her to thwart the devil's evil plans, by the access He gave her to those hurting people who entered the food kitchen for help.

That night in the basement, so long ago; with Gabby still safe in her mother's womb, gently moving and kicking against her new aunt's matted hair; Gracie led Anna to the

Lord, and the weight of the world lifted from her shoulders. She had not been the same since that night. And the joy she felt was immeasurable.

Thirty two years old now. With a culinary degree, just like her dad, a love of cooking, and a desire to help people in need, she cherished her peace. In Dad's absence; as he was off saving the world with Gabby, Gracie, Jason and Uncle Tom; she ran the two restaurants, and cooked at the soup kitchen two days a week. While she was at it, and much to the dismay of local authorities, she shared Jesus with everyone she met. Her life might not have been as exciting as the life Gabby, Grace, Jason and the rest of her family led on a day to day basis, but it was rewarding and fulfilling for her.

She liked the fact that she could remain here in the states to help mom. After that terrible fall a year and a half ago; when Nancy tumbled all the way to the bottom of the basement stairs and broke her hip. An injury which required three extensive surgeries. Her mom had been forced to retire early. If not for Anna, she would have been left to rattle around in the big old house alone, trying to do for herself. But, in the process of this latest trial, the two had become inseparable. Anna could no longer imagine her life without this loving, kind, wonderful mother God had given her.

Lilly dropped by pretty often to check in on them; which worked out great for taking care of Mom. But, she was pretty busy with her medical practice, which seemed to be extra hectic these days. She regularly took care of many who were falling through the cracks of the gravely decimated social medicine system. It seemed that even though they'd been told that socialized medicine would give everyone equal health care, it turned out the elites were still at the top of the food chain, even there.

Many people died waiting months, or even years, for an appointment to see a doctor, or to undergo an important procedure. Lilly wasn't making any money helping those less fortunate. But, due to the chain of command in their current government system, she was forced to keep her extra activities secret, or suffer retribution for her good deeds. So, she happily treated these people for free. She hadn't entered the field of medicine to get rich after all. She'd become a doctor to help people, so that was a non-issue for her.

Lilly had helped some in the work of the ministry when the family was still all stateside, but since she wasn't living at home anymore, even that had slowly tapered off. And, now that public meetings had to be approved by the state, and Christian meetings were all but prohibited, she only saw Grace, Jason, Dad and Tom occasionally. Therefore, she was aware that Anna's presence was essential to Mom's present and future health, and she counted on her to keep their mother safe.

One would think Dad might have stayed home with his wife, especially after the fall, but Nancy wouldn't hear of it. She knew how important the work they did was, and wouldn't have deprived her husband of that feeling of usefulness for anything. Especially after the excited way he sounded when he arrived home from his most recent missions. Going on and on about all the good they were doing around the world, and the difference they were making. No, she would never deprive him of that. She sure missed him though. Now that the travelers were often gone for many months at a time.

Anna was engaged to a wonderful guy named Luke; had been for three years now; who was not only a member of their church, but a really nice guy too. Mom loved him, and the three of them ate supper together almost nightly. He taught fifth grade at the local Christian school. Well, he had taught there until a new law recently passed by Congress, made Christian schools, and home schooling, illegal in all fifty of the United States of America. Seemed they were going, like it or not, the way of most of the secular world. Luke was currently in the process of interviewing for a position as principal of a large grammar school in a nearby town.

He was hopeful, even if most of his recent interviewers had turned up evidence that he was an outspoken Christian. That one fact seemed to be putting a damper on any hiring possibilities for him so far. But, he'd been called back for a second interview on this one, and that was usually a good sign.

Luke missed his students, and the opportunities he had to share the Gospel with those great kids. They were like sponges, wanting to be filled with knowledge about the Lord. It was an opportunity he wouldn't have if hired by a secular school system, but the work was essential to his independence and financial security. Something that was rare in today's ever crumbling America.

Life in the United States had changed tremendously in the past twenty five years. So much so that it would have left one walking into this new situation dumbfounded. Plainly, if an average person had magically left the earth two and a half decades ago, and then arrived back in the country in 2040, they would necessarily be appalled at the current state of affairs in America.

More and more socialists had wormed their way into the fabric of the American political structure. And slowly but surely many of their ideas had permeated the value system of this once free country.

Guns were banned by congress in 2024. First came the seemingly innocuous required registration of all firearms. Strangely, even those, such as rifles, that had never required registration before. Government receiving stations were set up around the country to claim these illegal arms, and once received they were promptly destroyed. Of course, not all citizens complied with this new demand. Knowing they might have to protect themselves against their own crooked government someday, many patriots kept back essential protection for such a time as might be needed in the future. After all, if those guns never made it into the 'registered' database, there was essentially no proof they'd ever existed.

Those persons, who the government suspected, were actively watched. And, if they gave indication that they were armed, or hiding weapons, their properties were searched and their weapons seized. Then they were quickly imprisoned as enemies of the state.

Of course, as was fully expected by the masses, bad guys had not relinquished any of their weapons, so crime rates around the nation rose exponentially, and now regular citizens had no way of protecting themselves.

According to the new socialist state, it was okay to kill babies at all stages of pregnancy, and further. If a child's parents felt, for any reason, that he or she was not fit, or living up to their potential, they could kill that child up to the age of four years old, without suffering any legal repercussions.

Parents, in today's socialist state, were not allowed to have more than two children, as that was considered a negative strain on resources. But, even then, some would ignore the state's demand to come in for sterilization, hoping they would not be discovered. When government officials realized this discrepancy they 'put down' the 'excess' child, like an unwanted animal, and forcefully sterilized the parents. If it happened more than once, the parents were 'put down' as well.

Euthanizing of people with disabilities and the elderly, when their consumption of products outweighed their productivity, was not only acceptable, but encouraged; and withholding of all medical treatment in case of disease or emergency, such as cancer, Parkinson's, ALS, or any number of illnesses; for people over the age of seventy; was not just encouraged, but expected from all government sanctioned medical personnel.

Social Security had become defunct years ago. Elderly and Veterans were often seen digging through garbage bins for food and necessities, and sleeping on the streets. 'FREE' programs for non-citizens and those unable or unwilling to work, plus FREE healthcare for all, caused the nation's debt to skyrocket exponentially. Over ninety trillion at last count, which was far past anything remotely sustainable, and it grew larger from interest alone by the day.

This once admired nation, had become a pariah, and those few solvent countries, that still had power to help if they dared, wouldn't take any more chances on her. The greatest country in the world had gone the way of all nations who turn their backs on God.

American people suffered miserably, well, at least the average American suffered. Those politicians, the ones who had placed themselves in positions of higher echelon in the new government structure; and those working with the U.N. to bring the country in line with the perceived 'logic' of a 'One World Order' and 'One World Religion' seemed to be doing just fine; as is always the case in the face and practice of Socialism.

What the left considered measures that might save the country in 2020; or so they falsely claimed then; were destroying it bit by bit and day by day. It seemed almost as if the stripping of our rights as American citizens, and the destruction of our country as we knew it, had been planned from the beginning. And, very likely it had.

Anna noticed more and more people availing themselves of free food and clothing at the food kitchen these days, as government help dried up, and she helped wherever she could. But her personal resources were now dangerously depleted, and would soon give out. Numbers at her two restaurants had declined over the past couple of years, due to the fact that even well placed people had less discretionary money these days, and she would soon be closing down. A sad fact, due to this being her father's legacy and her own dream. She knew the moment she was forced to close down the restaurants, the food kitchen would follow in short order. It was a sad fact, but a fact nevertheless.

As is the usual pattern in socialist societies, many things were no longer available in the U.S. Due to massive shortages, various food and clothing items were simply no longer attainable. And those things that were available on grocery store shelves, were completely unaffordable. The land of plenty had become, for all intents and purposes, the land of lack.

Food lines, over the past months, had grown long; and individuals were required to register with the government for a citizen ID number to enter those lines. Which ultimately meant you had a number tattooed on your arm to give you access to those very same food lines. The tattoo was similar to the tattoos Anna had seen on the arms of Holocaust survivors. Every day saw men and women going to jail, or being shot by U.N. officers, for stealing a loaf of bread, or a bag of beans, to feed their starving families. Gasoline was also severely rationed, so even if you still owned a car it was difficult to fuel it in these circumstances. Most people depended on public transit, but that required walking great distances to get to those few transfer points;

and for the elderly and disabled was a near impossibility.

United States military, and local police, had been slowly but surely replaced by U.N. appointed troops, leaving men and women who had much pride in their country, and a strong desire to work, without gainful employment. What those government officials didn't fathom was that this was creating more dissent among people with the power to fight back when the time became right to do so.

Laws were passed, due to so called 'climate change', that allowed each family only so much electricity or natural gas usage, before their carbon footprint for the month was maxed out. At that time they were shut off until a new carbon cycle began. Even if that happened in the dead of winter. When the time came, candles, and fires in the fireplace, were options for Nancy and Anna, but not everyone had those same alternatives.

The ladies made out okay, with most of the family gone much of the time, off to save the world and all. Because of that, they only fed two or three at a time. It also helped that their property held a large greenhouse in back, on this side of the woods, rife with a variety of vegetables and fruits, at all times of year. This was Anna's personal project and she took great pride in the number of people her garden helped. She also raised more than a dozen chickens, and two miniature goats. Meaning they had access to eggs, milk, and all sorts of variables thereof. So far those personal items had not been confiscated, and they'd helped her to feed many more people at the food kitchen for far longer than she'd expected before being forced to close. She knew, though, that troops could come at any moment to seize her property, in the name of the socialist state.

With this current available abundance, they often invited others who had less to share in their bounty. Community suppers were a great way to distribute help, without embarrassing others, and a great way to check in on the elderly who weren't doing well. Nancy couldn't get around like she used to in order to prepare meals, but, Anna was there to fill in where she couldn't manage, and because of her amazing culinary talent they shared many tasty meals with dozens and dozens of neighbors, friends, and even total strangers in their time of need.

As was her custom on Wednesday nights, Nancy hosted a meal and Bible study. But, in the past year or so she'd received threatening letters from government entities ordering her to curtail her 'religious' activities; since she wasn't a recognized, state licensed and certified place of worship. Many churches around the country had been forced to close their doors, if they weren't in line with what those in charge considered acceptable lines of doctrine. So far she had ignored those orders to 'cease and desist', and continued in her ministry, but was trying to keep the meetings more low key, so as not to attract much attention. After all, there were still many who did not know the Lord, and in these times He was their only hope. She determined that the law of man was meaningless in comparison to the Law of God. So, her ministry would continue.

She had to admit though, she'd seen this coming. Clear back in her childhood, when she'd seen the pope, and the highest ranking Muslim Imam in the world, came together to sign an agreement for unity; one that was supposed to lead to world peace, but actually seemed to push harder toward a one world religion, the signs were abundantly clear.

Shortly after that meeting the U.S. signed a treaty that put the country under the further 'guidance' of the U.N. Council. Americans had seen the results of that treaty destroying their nation ever since. Now that same U.N. entity took 'dues' from hard working Americans to give in over abundance to other countries around the world. This, in an effort to 'equalize' life style worldwide.

It was almost amusing, really, the way many people who'd thought they were in favor of socialism when politicians posited how 'fair' and 'just' it was for all members of the world community. You know, when those people thought it was going to mean all those nasty rich people had to give up everything in order to pass it along to them. Especially those young college students who thought socialism would give them everything they wanted for FREE. Instead, all those grasping, greedy individuals saw it ravage their own dreams, their lives and their country.

Now, they could clearly see those politicians had lied. That the upper class, those liars, were living in the lap of luxury, and that they'd been duped. It was too late now. And, all those people who had rushed en mass to elections around the country, to vote for socialist leaders, were paying the price. Right along with everyone else.

Along with that change, and in part because of it, came the slow, but deliberate changes in their collective rights to worship as they chose. Churches closed around the country by the thousands, because they didn't project the only 'inclusive' message the government decided was acceptable.

Religious programming on television and the internet was limited to U.N. approved and sanctioned broadcasts. And, local governments were coming down harder and harder on those who chose to worship in their homes, especially if they were inviting others in to worship with them.

When those same government arms began reaching deep into the private sector and the lives of citizens, total control was obviously their absolute goal. Decades ago Nancy had begun to witness a creeping, but definite, decline in the country's morals. Once Jesus was outlawed in the city square, society started to crumble and suffer significantly for those rash and wrong decisions to sell out to the despots who abhorred even the very Name of Jesus.

From a country founded upon Christian values, to a nation that would not abide the Name of the very Jesus who had blessed it so abundantly. And just look at the destruction and devastation that resulted. If she could only make those government officials see the damage their foolish and greedy decisions had made. But they would remain blinded by their own interests, as long as they lived in their mansions on the nation's hills. Never noticing the suffering of the lowly citizens around them.

At the exact moment she was prompted in the spirit, Gabby turned to her mom and said, "Now". Both women picked up their ends of the wire and pulled hard, causing immediate tension, which made bottles and cans all along the prepared line rattle and clang. The awful ruckus this simple action caused, terrified everyone within earshot, except for those captive girls who had been warned by Gabby about what was to come.

Men in the camp, not knowing what was going on, grabbed their guns and rifles and ran from the clearing into the surrounding jungle, in directions all around the perimeter of the encampment. As they stepped unwittingly into the snares prepared by the women, they were whisked instantly high into the air. Before they knew what had happened, they were hanging upside down in the trees. In every case, they had been so entirely surprised they dropped their precious weapons, and those arms were now eight feet or more beneath them. With no way of reaching their rifles, and no way to get down from their embarrassing traps, they were shouting for help from their comrades back in camp. Gabby and Gracie were doing all they could not to burst into laughter, for the fiasco playing out in front of them. And, almost as humorous were the demons scrambling, knowing the wrath they would face from Kakos and Satan for missing so large and obvious an attack.

The ladies knew they still had work to do. There were enemy combatants to neutralize, and thirteen frightened girls to lead to safety. God's plan was working; as it always did, as long as they were faithful to follow His lead; even when His lead sometimes seemed outlandish.

Their deeds do not permit them to return to their God. For the spirit of whoredom is within them, and they know not the Lord.

Hosea 5:4

CHAPTER 3

"They what?"

"Now, Sir, calm down."

"Don't tell me to calm down you insolent wench! How dare you presume to command me!"

"Kakos, Sir, I'm not trying to tell you what to do Sir, I just know how out of proportion you tend to blow things."

"How, what? How out of proportion.....Leave this room immediately!"

"No, no sir. You have misunderstood me."

"Oh, I have misunderstood you? No, Keres, you have presumed far too much for far too long. Guards, take this feckless wench out of my sight."

"Kakos, Sir, I beg of you. Please don't do this. I am only trying to do my job. I'm very sorry, Sir. I misspoke. The entire thing was my fault, Sir, and it won't happen again."

Agitated and angrier than she'd ever seen him in all the centuries they'd worked together, Kakos sat down hard in his captain's chair. She should have known he'd be touchier than usual, given that he'd just come back from a trip downstairs to see the boss. "Then tell me, Keres. What hear you from the jungle?"

"Sir, the news from the front will not be pleasing to you."

"Keres, nothing seems to be pleasing anymore. We just never seem to get a break where this family is concerned. And, it's only gotten worse since the brat was born. This has been the worst twenty one years of my existence. What can we do to defeat them?" He suddenly sounded entirely defeated himself.

"I assure you, Sir, I don't have a clue. What I do know, is that the troops sent to the jungle to keep watch on the thirteen girls were fooled."

"How can that be? We sent our best demons. I thought no one knew where the girl was?"

"Well Sir, I know this isn't what you'd like to hear, but it seems she was there all along. You know that thing she does, where she becomes invisible to us. Well, understandably, the troops were taken completely by surprise." As she watched him turn several different shades of red, purple and black, she took two steps back, and contemplated what existence would be like in Hades' deepest pit. Then, oddly, as if his entire grotesque being sagged with defeat, he leaned over, and looked, for all the world, like the kingdom of hell rested upon his shoulders.

"We simply must figure this out Keres. Satan told me just today that more rests on our ability to take this family out than we could ever know. They are reaching people around the world that we thought couldn't be reached by anyone. He is counting on us to bring our very best to this fight."

She was more confused than ever. If she'd been put on the spot, she might have to say she almost preferred the old screaming, angry Kakos, to this seemingly tired and defeated one. "Yes Sir. I promise. We will do our very best to see them taken down, Kakos. I know they will be heading back to America soon. And, when they get there, they will find a surprise waiting for them.

"The human government of their country has acted very much like an extension of the arm of hell for quite some time now, whether they realize it or not. Over the past five months of human time, while the woman and her family have been in Africa, their American politicians have accomplished great things in our favor."

"Fine. That does sound like some good news for once. Please keep me apprised of the situation."

"Yes sir. Will do sir."

"Hey, Mom, I'm leaving now to go get Luke."

"Okay Anna. Try not to be long. People will be arriving soon for supper. It smells wonderful, by the way. What did you make this week?"

"Lasagna, with homemade noodles. I used goat's milk ricotta and mozzarella, that I made fresh today; and some of my famous marinara sauce, with ingredients from our garden. I didn't have any meat rations left, so I hope that's okay. I also tossed together a nice salad with all sorts of things from the greenhouse and baked several loaves of homemade bread. I left the Lasagna pans on the counter to cool. The salad is in the fridge, but it isn't dressed yet. You can do that if you'd like. The vinaigrette is in the jar next to the Lasagna. Shake it up a bit before you pour it on the greens, and then give it all a good toss, if you would."

"Yes dear. I have actually dressed a salad or two in my time."

"Sorry Mom. Of course you have. I didn't mean to imply."

"I know honey. You have run a couple of restaurants for a while now, so you're used to managing things. And,

I have been married to your dad for a long time. So, I'm aware it comes with the territory."

"Hey, you know I didn't mean anything by that. You are a great cook and I've learned easily as much from you over the years as I've learned from dad."

"Well, thank you for that, sweetheart. I wasn't insulted, much. No, I'm just kidding."

"Well, funny lady, if you're finished cracking jokes, the bread is wrapped in foil to keep it warm. I set it on the back of the stove. It needs to be sliced, but we have some of that honey butter I made the other day to go with it. I also made a couple of nice apple pies too. Those are on the window sill cooling."

"You did? Where in heaven's name did you get apples for pie?"

"I made a trade with one of our suppliers. A supplier I probably won't see anymore, now that the restaurants are shut down. You know I can grow all the vegetables I want in the greenhouse, but an apple tree, that's something special. I never see apples anymore. The gentleman said he hasn't had lettuce, tomatoes, carrots, cucumbers or onions in a while. So, I traded a small basket of vegetables for a basket of apples."

"That was an excellent trade! Apple pie, I can't believe it!"

"I used the last of the cinnamon today. I hope that's okay. I saved some of the apples, so we can have fresh for a few days, they're in the fridge."

"Wonderful. That will be lovely. And, don't worry about the cinnamon. We don't have much call for it these days. You know what else would be super yummy?"

"Well, I can think of lots of things, Mom. But, what do you think would be super yummy?"

"Oranges. Doesn't that sound great? Sweet, juicy oranges. So succulent that the sticky juice just runs down your chin. Oh, it gives me the chills thinking about it."

"Well, if I run into anyone with oranges, I will keep that in mind. For now we have apples."

"And, apples sound terrific. Yummy, I can't wait!"

"I don't know exactly how long I'll be. When Luke called he said the shop didn't know what was wrong with his car. The mechanic wasn't even sure he could get parts anymore, so he's going to check it out and let Luke know. For now, and the foreseeable future, I will be his wheels."

"That will be inconvenient, for both of you, when he has to get back and forth from work."

"No, actually, I just found out when he called. The principal's position didn't work out. The minute they did some investigating, the offer was pulled. Evidently we are not the friends you want to have if your new employer hates Christians."

"That's too bad. Tell him I'm sorry."

"He's not upset with us, Mom. He's upset with the whole darned system. The world has been turned upside down, and it just doesn't make sense anymore."

"I know honey. Believe me I know. Do you want us to wait until you get back before we eat?"

"No, as I said I have no idea how long I'll be. If you're done eating by the time we get back, we will just nibble during Bible study, if that's okay."

"That's just fine, honey. Then we'll see you when you get home. Drive carefully, Anna. I love you sweet girl."

"I love you too, Mom, so much. See you in a bit."

"We've got to get these girls to safety, before those soldiers can free themselves."

"I know, Mom. But, we tied up the two men they left here in camp, so I'm thinking we're safe for a little bit."

Gabby stifled a giggle. "I'm sorry, I shouldn't be laughing, I guess. But, they all looked like piñatas, hanging in the trees like that. I really had to control myself, so I wouldn't burst out laughing in front of them. Two of the girls are having a hard time walking, so they will need help. And, I really think we have to feed all of them before we leave the compound, or they will simply collapse on the way."

"You're right. Let me see what is available in the mess tent. You see about some bandages for the two that are in trouble."

"It's a deal." Grace rounded up some grub for the girls and Gabby located the first aid supplies. Each of them would have to be physical support for one of the two injured captives, but the bandages would help. As soon as the girls wolfed down their food and water, the group was on its way. They had some ground to cover, which would be much harder in the dark. Sounds of the jungle surrounded them, and some of the girls seemed skittish, crying out at every little sound. Gabby and Grace tried to comfort them and simultaneously keep them quiet. Who knew how much time they had before their enemies would overtake them? It would take considerable time before they would be in the nearest clearing large enough for the trucks to get in and pick them up. Time, and quiet, was of the essence.

Dad, Grampa and Uncle Tom had evacuated the extended area. They were heavily armed and on their way to the clearing to provide safe extraction. Everything was going smoothly.

Gabby was especially glad they'd been able to pull this one off without any casualties. She never liked killing anyone; even though rational people would consider these men the bad guys, and she was exceptional at what she did; because, the thought that they would die without knowing Jesus burdened her heart terribly. She didn't want anyone to go to hell, and she knew the only way into heaven is to know Jesus Christ as Lord and Savior. Had these men ever even heard the 'Good News'? She doubted it.

They arrived at the clearing just as gunfire erupted in the jungle behind them. One of the men must have managed to escape his bonds and loosed others for the fight. Bullets sliced through trees around them, and were getting closer by the second. Mike and Uncle Tom proceeded to load the girls onto trucks, while Jason, Grace and Gabby tended to their pursuers.

An interesting fact about doing battle with followers of Allah is that, as a general rule, they do not fear death. Islam guarantees them a place in paradise if they die in holy jihad, which simply means the killing of infidels during a battle. There is no other guarantee of paradise in the Qur'an. So, fighting jihadists can be an especially savage thing. These kidnappers knew the punishment they would face if their superiors discovered the kidnapped girls were missing, so death, and Islam's paradise by its definition, was a much more pleasant thought.

The fight raged on, with more combatants joining the mêlée by the minute. Jason waved the trucks on. They would join the group at a pre arranged site after the conflict. They were very well versed on things that could go wrong on these little jaunts into enemy territory. After all, this wasn't their first, or even their thirtieth rodeo. Prepared with plenty of ammunition and water, should the fight take some time, they used every trick they'd learned in their years of battle training. Angel warriors round about them were engaged in their own conflict with hideous demons from the pits of hell. Grace began to pray out loud for their angelic host, then Jason and Gabby joined in, and as they prayed she could see the tide turning in favor of their soldiers of light.

Gabby decided the best use of her talents might be to

use invisibility to invade their midst and turn these guys against each other. Cloaking herself with heavenly guardians, she moved closer. Breaking off a low hanging branch, she poked one of the soldiers in the back, hard enough to produce a yelp. Startled, he turned suddenly, she ducked and he fired on the man behind him, blowing his head off. Two soldiers, closest to him, confusing his act of surprise as treason, shot him multiple times. Meanwhile, Gabby snuck up on another enemy soldier and whacked him in the back of the head. He turned and sprayed the jungle behind him with bullets, killing several more of his comrads.

Soon there were rival's bodies littering the ground all around. The soldiers of Allah were becoming so confused they began shooting indiscriminately at anything and everything that made the slightest sound. Several took off to save their own hides, evidently not much concerned with getting to paradise today to meet their seventy two virgins. A few clean shots from Jason and Gracie took out those who remained on the attack. Once the shooting stopped, and the jungle quieted, the trio headed off for the pre arranged, final, extraction site. They would get the girls to a safe place, then take off for the airport, and finally, home.

This small band of freedom fighters stayed out of the

country for many months at a time, this time had tallied five and a half, on soul saving missions for the Lord. However, they'd grown very weary, and desperately needed a rest. Agreeing all around it would be good to get back to family; they'd heard recently, from several reliable sources, that things were deteriorating fast back in the states. And, they might very well need to use some of their well honed combat skills to help their loved ones in America.

It was getting more difficult, these days, to travel in and out of the U.S. Much had changed in the land of the free. Passports now included a box that must be checked if you still claimed Christianity as your religion of choice. And, since world governments were pushing hard to ensure growth of the new 'Unified World Church', backed by the U.N.; while squelching the practice of free speech; they would only allow so many 'subversives' through ports of entry each month. Even if those 'subversives' were legal American citizens.

Ironic, how the major win for those in favor of open borders, allowing illegal aliens to flood into the country by the tens of millions, almost a quarter century ago, caused the biggest financial meltdown the world had ever seen. A situation for which those actors, and the entire globe continued to suffer.

They'd imagined, those open borders advocates, that it would amount to more votes for liberals, by herding extra bodies into sanctuary states. But, once political parties were done away with, once and for all, and the 'New Socialist Party' of America took over, only those few deemed most extreme left, anti-Christian and anti-America were allowed to occupy those desirable government seats.

Most of those who'd voted for open borders, thinking it would assure them a coveted place at the table going forward, were now eating from the same communal trough as the rest of the country's nobodies, assuredly regretting their previous sad and unfortunate choices. Surely many were re-thinking their stupidity at giving in so easily to those rampant socialist ideals. After all, and this is widely known, in a socialist government there are very few chairs at the big boy table. This is the only way those at the top can maintain control over the masses from their luxurious mansions in the sky.

And now, those same borders that opened wide for illegal aliens twenty odd years ago, became all but inaccessible to Americans whose religion didn't pass the liberal litmus test. Meaning it could not contain the Name, or person, of Jesus Christ. It was very conceivable that Gabby and her family would have to eliminate their future overseas missions, or risk being shut out of the country all together on one of their return flights home. What a mess.

"Welcome everyone. Anna was called out to run an errand, but she and Luke will be back soon. She made us a lovely meal, for anyone who is hungry," (murmurs of appreciation). "A lovely lasagna; salad of fresh greens; and some delicious, warm, homemade bread. There is plenty for everyone. Brother Dan, would you say the blessing?"

"I'd be happy to, Sister Nancy. Lord...." Just as the blessing was being shared there was a loud boom. Government U.N. soldiers blasted the front and back doors open, at once, and rushed inside. There were dozens of them, heavily armed, in tactical gear, and shouting orders to the members of Nancy's Bible study. The beautiful lasagna was left untouched as every participant was herded off, frightened and protesting, into heavily armored trucks.

Nancy, pushed hard through the back door of the first

truck, landed squarely on her bad hip. In a great deal of pain, she heard others crying out for help, or sobbing loudly, begging to know what was going on. Nancy knew. She'd been warned, but had been unwilling to believe things had progressed this far so quickly. What had her beloved country come to? The doors of the transport trucks were slammed shut and bolted from the outside. Without windows, the inside was pitch black. They were prisoners of the socialist state.

And I said: Hear, you heads of Jacob and rulers of the house of Israel! Is it not for you to know justice?- you who hate the good and love the evil, who tear the skin from off my people and their flesh from off their bones, who eat the flesh of my people, and flay their skin from off them, and break their bones in pieces and chop them up like meat in a pot, like flesh in a cauldron.

Micah 3:1-3

CHAPTER 4

When Anna and Luke arrived home, they saw the front door was quite literally blown off its hinges. The main floor of the house was torn apart, with broken furniture and pictures strewn about as if a tornado had blown through the premises. The food Anna had prepared for the evening's meeting remained untouched. And Nancy was nowhere to be found. Anna was in a panic. She knew the condition of her mother's health, and knew this wasn't a good thing.

It was pretty clear what had happened. She was aware of the cease and desist notices Nancy had received over the past few months, and her mom's attitude toward them. What was it she always said? "As far as I know I still live in the United States of America. And in the United States of America I am free to worship as I choose. They will have to march in here and drag me away, to keep me from sharing my Jesus with anyone who will listen." Well, it appeared that is exactly what they did.

The question was, who had dragged her away, and to where? Well, she was sure it was the new socialists, the ones who'd sent the notices, but who were they exactly? Anna had no real idea. Mom didn't have her high blood pressure medicine with her, and in a stressful situation like this, that could be disastrous. Luke was attempting to talk to Anna, trying to quiet her down. "Sweetheart, we have to stay calm, for your mom's sake. We will figure this out. I promise you. Please don't worry. We will get her back safe and sound."

"How can you be so calm, Luke. You know the state of her health. It looks like the Gestapo marched through here. The whole house is torn apart. How can this even be legal? To blast open someone's door and destroy their home like this. Then to drag them off to who knows where? I wish Dad and Gracie were here. They would know what to do. We have to get her back. How do we even know where they've taken her, or what they're doing to her? Where do we start? Oh, Jesus, help us."

Mike, Uncle Tom, Jason, Gracie and Gabby, were presently in the custody of the airport authorities; with their hands cuffed behind their backs, and left ankles cuffed to the chair where they sat; who were waiting for someone to arrive from immigration and customs. They weren't sure why they would need to be questioned by immigrations and customs; as, per their passports, they were clearly American citizens; but that was their current situation. When the officers arrived, the odd questions began. Why were they out of the country for so long? Who were they working for? Why did they have so many Bibles in their possession? Were they aware of the new rulings concerning religion? And, so on.

At the end of nearly four hours of intense interrogation, by a rather angry duo of, so called, immigration authorities, nothing was resolved. At this point, Mike was getting impatient. "I don't understand what is going on. You can clearly see from our passports that we are American citizens. What is the hold up? We just want to go home."

"Sir, you will achieve nothing by your aggressive and argumentative behavior. If you continue in this hostile manner, we will be forced to restrain you further."

"Restrain me further? I'm not sure how you could restrain me any further than I am. But, aggressive and argumentative? I don't know what you are talking about. I just don't understand what in the world is happening, that American citizens are being held this way. For decades our government has been letting illegal aliens, people who tell us openly that they want to harm this country, into the nation. And you are questioning American citizens? This is unreal." Mike had no idea how much had changed in his beloved country over the past five and a half months.

"That's it. Guards, take this gentleman into custody. We will deal with you later Mr. O'Sullivan. Your outburst will likely cost you dearly."

"Wait a minute. You can't do this! I'm an American citizen. I have rights." As the guards took him by his shackled arms to lead him out, Grace jumped up.

"Dad! No, wait, you can't take him like this. We need a lawyer. He is entitled to a lawyer."

"Ma'am, if you'd like, we can take you into custody as well. Your outburst clearly puts us in danger of violence from you, and we have full authority to take you to detention along with Mr. O'Sullivan."

"Grace, sit down, or they will figure out a way to take you too. Just sit and listen to me for a minute."

"But Jason, we don't even know where they're taking him."

"Mom, dad is right. Let's wait till we are released. We'll have better luck figuring it out from outside the detention center, than from inside it."

"Okay, okay, Gabby, I see your point. But, what the heck is going on here? We've only been gone five and a half months. Can things have changed so much in so short a time? I wish we had called Anna to pick us up, instead of deciding to surprise them. Now, absolutely no one knows we're in here."

"Kakos, Sir, I can't wait to tell you the news."

"Very well, Keres. Spill it. What news have you?"

"Sir, you are going to be so excited when I tell you."

"Okay, Keres, just spit it out."

"Okay, okay, well, the woman's mother and her study group have been taken into custody, by the authorities. And, the girl and her fiancée don't know where she's been taken. But, even better, the travelers have all been detained at the airport; and when the woman's dad got upset, the immigration agents took him into custody, just as they've been ordered to do. Everything is going as planned."

"For once, praise Satan. Things are finally going our way. Thank you for the good news, Keres. Now, I have some great information to take to the boss."

"I will bring you any new news, as soon as I receive it, Sir."

"See that you do." And, just like that, Kakos was back to his old swaggering, sarcastic, arrogant self.

With no windows in the transport truck, Nancy couldn't see where they were being hauled off to. But, wherever it was, it was taking considerable time. She was especially concerned for some of her older Bible study members. Two with diabetes, for example, whose personal belongings were still back at the house. They had all been taken before they could eat the beautiful meal Anna prepared, and without their insulin, they would likely be sick sooner than later. Would their captors care enough to intervene? She doubted that.

Members of the Bible study group had been separated into several different transport trucks, and she couldn't check on those that she was most concerned about, so she prayed for their health and safety. Pain in her hip was almost more than she could bear, but trying to keep her wits about her, she bit her lower lip and prayed to strengthen her resolve. She could feel her heart pounding way too fast and hard in her chest, blood pressure rising through the ceiling. But, her medicine was back at the house, so she wouldn't have access to that. They'd been in the trucks for hours. It was pretty clear they weren't being taken to the local police station, but where?

Nancy noticed the temperature in the truck dropping perceptibly, little by little. Where were they headed? They'd left the sounds of the city behind them long ago, but she didn't know if it was still night time, or had slipped into early morning. Her pervading thought was, "How will Anna know where we are? She's surely home by now and when she finds us all gone, she will be worried." She was right.

Luke found several sheets of plywood in the shed to seal up the hole where the front door had been, and he created a makeshift entry in the back, where the damage was a little less all encompassing. They didn't have a clue where Mom had been taken, but decided to check the local police station first. The officers there didn't know anything about the raid, much less the whereabouts of Anna's mom, or so they said. Anna noticed that U.N. soldiers made up most of the local force now. So, it was more likely that they just had no intention of telling her anything. Anna broke down and cried. "I can't believe this. My mom has always been there for me, and there's nothing I can do to help her. We have to find her, Luke. We just have to."

"I know, Anna. Try to calm down. We won't accomplish anything this way. Someone must know what is going on, and where they've taken her. We'll just keep looking. How far could they have gone?"

It turns out they could go quite a long way in those lengthy nighttime and early morning hours. And, where they ended up was out of the comprehension of most Americans. It seemed the socialists had known all along there would be dissenters in the ranks, when they decided to choose their religion for them, and they'd planned ahead. They'd been building quite a number of detention camps in the mountains, and out in the deserts, for several years. Camps that were only lately being put to use.

Transport trucks arrived at their destination shortly after sunrise, and once the doors were opened, the passengers were unceremoniously yanked out and dumped on the ground. However, they weren't the first to arrive. Even this early in the morning, Nancy could see many others up and about doing chores around the camp. She stood, with great difficulty, and looked around for those members she'd been concerned about for hours. Then she saw them, on two gurneys. The bodies were quickly covered and carried away. With tears trickling down her cheeks, standing in the cold mountain air, she said a prayer for the families she knew they left behind.

They were ordered, by a rather angry looking young man, to line up. He was wearing a uniform she didn't recognize, that she'd later discover represented the U.N. forces, and spoke with an accent she didn't know. What was going on? Where were they? She tried to stand as straight as possible, but was having a hard time. That's when the angry, young man walked up to her and gave her a shove. Falling hard on her hip, again, she stifled a scream. He ordered others to help her up, and then yelled at her to stand straight. She stood straight. Funny how a little painful violence will cause us to do what we thought only moments ago was impossible.

Armed guards were stationed at positions all around the camp; and a twelve foot fence, topped with razor wire, surrounded the entire prison encampment. She thought it ironic; and suddenly had to keep herself from breaking out in laughter; that the government hadn't thought it necessary to give American citizens the wall they wanted over twenty years ago, to keep out terrorists, murderers and rapists. But, now, they found it to be an especially fine idea to use a really nasty looking one to keep their own people caged inside an internment camp.

They were counted, and the number was relayed to another man standing aloofly off to one side. The man walked to a space in front of the group. He began to speak, and Nancy heard the same accent she'd heard from the younger man. "I am your commander. You will follow orders. If you do not follow orders, you will be punished. I do not know you, and I do not want to know you. Nor do I care whether you live or die. So, know only this, that your very lives are in my hands. Each of you has been accused of a crime against the state. I don't care if you proclaim your innocence from the rooftops. No one knows that you are here. As a matter of fact, no one knows that these camps are here. You have been sent to me as an enemy of the socialist state, by proper authorities, for the act of religious treason. And, I will treat you as the enemies you are."

His speech left the new prisoners looking at each other wide eyed and in utter disbelief. If they were looking for answers only moments ago, they need look no further.

Nancy's arms were covered in goose flesh, and it wasn't all due to the cold.

How had their once free country fallen so far? Their family had been warning people for many years about the changes taking place in America, and the creeping rise of socialism in their nation. Many out there thought there was nothing particularly wrong with the idea of socialism, that it might even be a good thing. Others just didn't think it's rise could possibly be accomplished in their lifetime, so they sat back and allowed evil to transpire. Now, here they were, prisoners in their own land, and all for the crime of being Christian. She felt responsible. If she had taken the 'Cease and Desist' orders more seriously, they might not be in this situation. Two of her dear friends were dead. And it was all her fault.

They were led to barracks. Men sent to the buildings across the space, and women on this side. As they walked into their building, they were handed a stack of items, which included: canvas, draw string pants (one size fits all), a canvas, tunic top, and cotton underwear; shoes constructed of rubber soles and canvas tops (again, one size fits all); a towel and face cloth; a bar of soap, a comb and a toothbrush. Ordered to change their clothing, they were then instructed to drop their used clothing into a large rolling bin, which was later pushed into a storage building. Commanded to remove all jewelry, including wedding rings, those were then gathered and added to a collection bucket. Nancy tried to ask how they would get their items back and was struck in the mouth, with the back of a hand, leaving her lip swollen and bleeding. Tears threatened to flood her eyes, but she wouldn't give them the satisfaction of seeing her cry, so she took a deep, shaky breath instead.

Assigned bunks, by a large, very stern looking woman; Nancy was grateful hers was on the bottom, as with her current pain level, she didn't know if she would have been able to climb the rather rickety looking ladder to the top bunk. On each bunk they found a rolled up mattress, a sheet, a pillow and pillow case, along with two rather scratchy woolen blankets. A whistle blew, and they were ordered to make up their beds, being informed that part of their duties, going forward, would involve making their beds each morning, keeping their communal bathroom clean and keeping the building dusted and swept. A door at the end of the building, on the far side, led to the matron's sleeping quarters. So, she would be able to hear everything that went on in her assigned barracks. Another whistle blew, and they were ordered to the mess hall for breakfast.

Nancy was dumbfounded. Women from this side of the compound, and men from the other, walked in orderly lines to the building where they were directed, like angry, confused puppets. They were handed trays and then slid their trays down the serving line, where they received a scoop of soupy oatmeal, a piece of dry toast, and a cup of coffee. Looking around, first at her own table, and then throughout the room at large, she saw faces that seemed as bewildered as she felt. The whole mess was moving rather quickly, and seemed like a terrible, terrible dream.

Mike, who expected to be taken from the airport to the local police precinct, was instead thrown into the back of an armored van. Seeing his likely predicament he fought his captors, but when it looked like he might be victorious, someone hit him, hard, in the back of the head. When he woke, he was still bound with his hands behind his back, and found he was laying flat on the floor of a panel van, hogtied, his feet shackled to his wrist cuffs. With no idea how long he'd been unconscious, he couldn't begin to guess how far they'd gone, or where they were headed. The two men in the front were deep in conversation, and unaware he'd awaken, so he took a moment to look around and assess his situation.

Obviously, these fellows were not from 'Immigration and Customs', or any other normal government department he could think of. The officers back at the airport had seemed all too anxious to accuse him of a crime, any crime. And, the more he thought about it, the more it seemed as though they might be out merely to separate him from his family. He stopped and prayed for Gracie, Jason, Gabby and Tom. Nancy and Anna wouldn't even know they'd arrived back in country, unless the kids could get free somehow. Things looked bleak. And, he had no idea if he would ever see his wife again.

It was his own fault. He'd stayed away so long, too long. Caught up in the desire to 'do' something for God. And then, on top of that, he'd allowed his temper to control him yet again.

He had to admit that the missions he went on with the kids made him feel a little like a super hero. So, it really was all about him after all. And, now his entire family would pay the price for his selfishness.

A slight tinge of pink colored the sky as sunlight began

to register on the back windows of the vehicle. It appeared they'd been driving all night, and the sun was just beginning to climb on the horizon, so, they were currently heading West. Suddenly, the sky was filled to capacity with one of the most beautiful sunrises he'd ever seen; at least what he could see of it from the floor of the van, and he took a deep breath. The officer in the passenger seat turned around and saw that he was awake. "Don't give us any trouble man. We're almost there. You can ask all the questions you want, once we drop you off."

The accent wasn't American, but that was the only thing he knew for sure. These guys must be more of the U.N. troops he'd been hearing about. "Where are you taking me? Can you at least answer that?"

"Hey, man, we were told not to answer any of your questions. Save it for the guards."

Guards? Where were they taking him that was so far away from the city, and where he would need guards? Well, he would have to wait for an answer to his questions, as these guys seemed quite content to ignore him for the rest of the drive.

As the sun rose in the sky, he noticed that they'd been on a constant incline for quite some time. They must be in the mountains. That would also account for the cold. But, why were they in the mountains? Pretty soon they arrived at their destination. Even before the back doors were opened, he could see fences, complete with razor wire and guard towers, through the windows of the van. Once the doors swung open, he was grabbed by his bound hands and feet, and thrown from the vehicle into the dirt. Black boots kicked him in his ribs and back, while a voice yelled at him to get up. He struggled and they laughed. Finally someone removed the shackles attaching his feet to his hands.

He struggled to his feet, without the use of his hands. Someone behind him loosed his bonds, and he began to rub out his wrists and hands and to stomp his feet to get the blood circulating once again. Someone else was yelling at him to line up, so he obliged. He was trying to take in as much of the place as he could, while attempting to get into a straight line with the rest of the guys. Where did all these men come from? They all looked as shocked and confused as he felt, and they looked at one another, as if to say, "We'll talk later, and figure this out".

"I am your commander. And from this point forward, I am your world. You will do as I say, or your punishment will be severe. You have been brought to this internment camp, because you have committed crimes against the socialist state. I don't care to hear your pleas of innocence, and I don't want to be your friend. It will be just as easy for me to kill you, as to look at you, so stay out of my way, and do as you are told. The first shift of prisoners has finished breakfast. You will follow these guards to the mess hall, where you will eat your breakfast. Then you will be assigned to a barracks. Now, march."

Well, at least they would be fed. As a Marine, Mike knew that not all prison camps fed their captives. He still had no earthly idea what laws he'd broken, or what crimes he'd committed, and it didn't look like there were any who wanted to help him clear this whole thing up, so for now he would eat breakfast. His ribs and back were sore from being kicked. But, working out with the kids these last few years, for their frequent foreign missions trips, had left him in better shape than he could ever remember. So, even though he wasn't as young as he used to be, he figured he'd be okay. Scoping out the lay of the land as he walked to breakfast, he was looking for any chink in the armor of this well guarded camp. Aware that no one knew where he'd been taken, he had to figure out a way to escape and get home to Nancy.

A scoop of runny oatmeal, a piece of dry toast, and a cup of coffee later, he was shown to his new accommodations, and handed a stack of supplies. What exactly was going on?

Tears dripping from her eyes, Anna was trying to put the house back into some semblance of order. Luke was doing most of the heavy lifting, while she sorted and swept. They'd made phone calls, the night before, and driven around until there was no gas left in her car, with no answers and no results. Several family members of the Bible study group had contacted them throughout the night, wondering where their loved ones were, and they had no answers to give them either. So, the only thing they knew for sure was that it was likely the whole group had been taken.

They were also aware that the new socialist government had been doing everything within its power to make Christianity a crime punishable by death, as they marched on the route of a one world religion with the U.N. council and the rest of the globe, so it seemed this was just one more step in that direction.

Anna's heart was breaking, thinking about her mother

in a prison cell somewhere, so she didn't even notice the knock on the boards where the front door used to be. She peered through the window to see Jason, Gracie, Tom and Gabby standing on the front steps looking confused. "Oh, I can't believe you're home." She screamed excitedly. "Come around to the back. You can get in that way."

After hugs were exchanged all around, "What's going on, Anna?"

"We aren't absolutely sure, guys. Mom got several warnings from the government, telling her to 'Cease and Desist' from having her Wednesday evening Bible studies. And, you know Mom. She said that nothing would stop her from sharing the Gospel. So, I made a meal, the way I always do. Which, by the way, is still perfectly good, so there's food if you want it. I left to go get Luke, because his car is not working right now, and when we got back, this is what we walked into. Oh, believe me, it was much worse. We've been cleaning up for hours and hours. They blasted the front door open, and kicked in the back, and when we got here, everyone was gone. We called and drove around all night trying to get information about where they might have taken Mom, but no one seems to know, or at least that is what they are telling us. Where is Dad?"

"We don't know, Anna. We flew into the airport, and they wouldn't admit us into the country. I gather that we're labeled as subversives now, because of our Christian faith, so there were men there who questioned us before they would consider allowing us through immigration and customs. You know Dad. He got upset and started questioning them back. They got angry and arrested him. We've checked everywhere, but no one seems to know where he's been taken, or so they tell us. It's as if he's vanished from the face of the earth."

"I'm scared Gracie. Mom's health hasn't been the greatest, and I don't know where she is. What if they hurt her?"

"If they hurt her, they will have to answer to us, I promise you that. We will get this all figured out, Anna. God hasn't left us, or forsaken us. We are still surrounded by angel warriors."

"We should eat, or all that great food I made will be wasted. I'm so glad you are all home. God is good. And, now we can figure out a way to save Mom and Dad."

For behold, the day is coming, burning like an oven, when all the arrogant and all evildoers will be stubble. The day that is coming shall set them ablaze, says the Lord of hosts, so that it will leave them neither root nor branch.

Malachi 4:1

CHAPTER 5

Picking up the tiny rocks and bits of gravel, that littered the internment camp grounds, became a daily ritual for Nancy. She filled her pockets with them. Intending to wrap them in pieces of found fabric, to create weapons of sorts, became her latest goal. Anything to keep her mind off her racing heart and the pain in her hip. She'd been allocated cleanup in the 'Mess Hall', as her duty assignment. So, three times a day, for a couple of hours each, after breakfast, after lunch and after supper, she wiped and swept and mopped and scrubbed. Each of the women had duties to perform, besides keeping their barracks ship shape, so she wasn't the only one. But, she wasn't as spry as she used to be, especially with her hip injury, and the work load was wearing her down.

Cold all the time, these days, and suffering from excruciating headaches due to her high blood pressure, she staggered through her daily duties. But, she wouldn't share that information with anyone. She'd noticed, watching others with health issues, that those in charge of the camp didn't care about any of the inmate's health, as it had become their preferred method of dealing with inconvenience to just let prisoners die when possible. And, she noticed those prisoners who complained of health issues most often were suddenly given work assignments that would guarantee more illness, and an early demise, as a sure way of dispatching those individuals quicker.

After all, only healthy inmates could do the multitude of chores required to keep a camp of this size running. And, if those in charge could manage to assign most of the chores to prisoners, instead of depending on paid civilians as hired help, more of the camp's budget could make its way into the pockets of the commander and his closest aids. It was a perfect, greedy plan, like so much of socialism tends to be. So, Nancy spent a lot of time praying, which helped to ease her pain, and helped her get through her daily work load.

Keeping her little side projects, such as the making and hiding of potential weapons, secret was difficult to say the least. Quarters were inspected daily, with mattress inspection weekly. Her barrack's mates knew about her scheme to make enough weapons to equip each woman, and to develop a plan for escape, so hiding places rotated to provide safety for the whole group. The supply was growing and consisted of sticks, sharpened to a deadly point; pouches filled with gravel; and eating utensils filed to razor sharpness. So far they hadn't hatched a fool proof plan of escape, but when they did, they would have weapons to help execute that plan. Perhaps not sophisticated weapons, but weapons the guards would not be expecting.

Mike was still trying to get someone, anyone, to listen to him. He knew he had committed no crime, and he desperately wanted his due process. Due to his continual complaining, he was being given the dirtiest and most physically taxing jobs in the camp. He didn't mind hard work. It kept him busy. And, it put him in touch with some very interesting items. Items he was sure management of the internment camp would not want him to have, that is, if they had been at all aware of his collection. And, therefore, items he was sure would come in handy at some point. He was building up quite a little arsenal of usable weapons. And, he was determined to use them if he could not get answers to his questions. His desire, no, his need to get home to family was eating at him, as nothing in his life ever had before. Something in his gut told him Nancy, his beloved, was in danger; and that he needed to get to her as quickly as humanly possible.

Snow had begun to fall on the mountain in earnest, and the landscape was sporting a new coating of four to six feet, with more predicted to come. The earth appeared sparkling clean and pristine white, even in the midst of all this evil.

Their previous plans had been to come together as a family for the holidays, but he didn't know how long he would be in this place, and his heart was breaking thinking of how hurt Nancy would be when he didn't show up for their celebrations. He had no way of contacting her to keep her from worrying. And, though she wouldn't be alone, because she'd have the rest of their family there; he hadn't been away from her at Christmas, in all the years he'd known her, except for that very first year when he'd been away at war.

The barracks were cold, but his work outside was much more so, because the coats they were provided were thin and flimsy mere suggestions of outerwear. Coats that were obviously designed for a much warmer climate, perhaps those desert camps he was hearing whispers about, and had probably been sent to this base by an accident of paperwork. It looked to Mike like procuring supplies through military sources hadn't changed much since he served in the Marines all those many years ago. However, when he tried to mention this detail to his guards, they immediately stripped him of the coat he supposedly "Didn't appreciate", and made him work outside all day without it.

That night, he didn't think he would ever get warm again, after being chilled to the bone for so many hours. Next day, he was thoroughly exhausted, reprimanded over and over, and then punished by being sent back to his barracks without supper. He accepted his flimsy coat back with humble gratitude, and decided it didn't pay to be contentious in this place. He knew this was ultimately how the enemy wears you down, so he decided to keep his big yap shut from now on.

"Sir, you will be happy to know that it looks like we are wearing the woman's father down."

"Great news, Keres. What about the woman's mother?"

"The news isn't as good about her, Kakos. Even with her injuries, she remains strong. We've sent instructions down the line to lean on her, so we will see where that goes. But now she has figured out a way to minister, even in the midst of prison."

"Have the woman and her husband figured out yet where her parents have been taken?"

"No Sir, so far they have not. We're keeping tabs on that situation. You know the woman's daughter has more heightened senses, than either of her parents, so we are putting up road blocks everywhere we can."

"Good. Keep me posted."

"Will do, Sir."

Watching through the front window, Gracie could tell the car parked on the curb of their house was there to keep an eye on them. If too many people showed up, such as for a Bible study, they would be raided, and charged with unlawful religious assembly. But, there wasn't much chance of that, because all the Bible study members had been arrested along with her mom. Besides, those neighbors who witnessed the raid taking place a couple of days ago still hadn't come to offer condolences. And not a one had come to help her mother, so they were clearly not interested in doing the right thing. No, they wouldn't have to worry about a sudden influx of concerned citizens flooding their doors, and that was just fine with her.

The whole thing bugged her, if truth be told. Her mom was one of the most loving people in the entire world. She never put herself first. She'd been helping the people in their neighborhood since the economy tanked badly years ago. No one around her ever went hungry, not if she could help it. She was an angel to friend and stranger alike. Yet, when she needed assistance most, where were all those that she'd sacrificed for without once thinking about her own needs?

Well, it was just the way it was, she supposed. She knew that many people are only concerned about themselves. And that most people don't care about anything they see going on, unless it directly affects them. Frankly, this was in large part how their country had gotten into a mess this huge to begin with. They'd been warning people for years, even their Christian friends, about the ripping away of their rights by a rogue government, but very few would listen. Thinking these were matters which didn't relate to them, they looked the other way and allowed the never ending evil to grow. Now they were all paying the price.

With no gasoline credits left on their ration cards, their investigations today would necessarily have to be conducted on foot. Gracie didn't believe for one minute that her mom was being held prisoner locally. She and Jason had been hearing rumors for years about massive building projects going on in the mountains. They'd even taken a drive up there, a year or so ago, when they were home from a mission. But the road was closed and guards sent them back the way they came. They'd wondered then if the new socialist state wannabes were building bases, but had no way to pursue the matter further. So, when their trails led nowhere they concentrated on things they could control, and forgot about those fruitless investigations.

"Are they still out there, Mom?"

"Yep, they sure are, Gabby. And, I'm sure they will be following us everywhere we go. But, we will figure out a way to get the information we need in spite of that."

"Are we going to go out there and try to get Grandma and Grandpa back?"

"You bet we are baby girl. We will not let a few detectives get in our way. God didn't design us to be people who could sit around and do nothing. We're not doing anything illegal, and we will be sure to keep it that way. This way, they won't have a thing on us."

"I love it. Won't they be frustrated? I'm going to enjoy making them suffer in their irritation, when there's nothing they can do to us."

"What do you want me to do, Gracie?"

"Anna, I want you to stay put. I know you want to help, but we need someone to stay at home base, in case there is news of any kind. If somehow Mom shows up, someone would need to be here to fill her in on what's going on. And besides, you and Luke will have your hands full finishing the repairs and clean up of this place." Gracie was afraid that since Anna and Luke had never had any training in the outdoors, or in self defense, they would be clueless in the art of survival. So it was best to keep them somewhere they'd be most safe.

"I suppose you're right. I know I don't have the kind of training the rest of you have, so I wouldn't be much help out there anyway. But, I want to know that I'm contributing somehow. Where are you going to start?"

"Well, we're going to get a real good night's sleep first, Anna. Then we're going to pack up some supplies and head out. I won't tell you where we're headed, because that way if you are questioned, you can honestly say you don't know where we've gone. There won't be a way for us to keep in touch that can't be traced, so you are just going to have to trust us."

"I do, and I will. I just want Mom home, that's all."

That evening Anna made a feast, for the soon to be travelers. From the greenhouse, a variety of vegetables and herbs created a soup, that filled the whole house with sumptuous fragrance, while, two loafs of her finest bread baked in the oven. She also tossed together a rhubarb buckle with some of her remaining flour and sugar, which would bake while they were dining. She had a knack for being able to turn very little into much. Anna and Luke would ultimately be able to eat when everyone around them thought there was nothing of substance available, so Gracie knew she needn't worry about the two of them making do while they were gone.

As she slept that night, Gracie dreamt of days gone by, and people she hadn't thought of for years. In her dream, a little boy ran to her and jumped into her arms, she tried but couldn't see his face. He was bigger than Bobby had been when he died, but she thought the little boy might be her lost brother. She held him as tight as she could, until first morning light caused him to fade away before her still closed eyes. She woke with tears on her cheeks and a wet pillow case. Wondering why she would be dreaming about

her long ago childhood and people who had passed on decades before. She rose, setting off for the kitchen and an
absolutely delicious smelling breakfast, thoughtful about
vanishing dreams.

"Are you okay, Babe?"

"Yes, I guess so. I was just having some odd dreams. I
woke up crying."

"Maybe I should have gotten you up before I came
down, but you looked comfortable, and very much like
you could use the rest."

"That's okay. I just haven't thought much about my
childhood in a long time. It's usually just on the outer
edge of my recollection, and when my brain starts to go
there I shut it down. I suppose bits of it are bound to sneak
through now and then. It was just strange is all."

"I think that is probably all stuff you've never really
dealt with, Mom. That's just your brain's way of making
you look those things right in the face. You know there isn't
any real healing without acknowledgement."

"Thank you Gabby. You are wise beyond your years.
And, perhaps one day I will. For now, I have lots of other
things to keep me occupied. Including this delicious looking breakfast. I don't know how you do so much with so

little, Anna. You are a genius!"

"We all have our strengths, Gracie. But thank you."

"No, thank you for all your hard work."

The table was laid out with their best china, and several serving bowls containing: Oatmeal, with apples sautéed in hand churned butter and vanilla; pancakes, with warm syrup (made by heating sorghum with just a little water); scrambled eggs, speckled throughout with chopped red and green peppers, mushrooms, and scallions from the green house; chicory coffee (since coffee beans were no longer available to them, Anna grew chicory root in her greenhouse, right next to the beets); and a selection of goat cheeses with yogurt with honey. It was a feast fit for kings.

Anna had been up since well before dawn to make dozens and dozens of biscuits, along with all the other sumptuous items displayed before them. Some to enjoy with their meal, along with homemade honey butter and blueberry jam, and more to wrap up and take along for their journey. Those, in addition to portions of hardened goat cheese, sunflower seeds from her eight foot tall specimens in the greenhouse, and the last of her prized apples, would keep them fed, at least for a while. She also wrapped up some ground chicory root for coffee, and some dried crushed dandelion leaves for tea. The travelers ate, laughed and acted as though they weren't at all about to leave on a very dangerous trip. They didn't want to worry Anna with talk of the mission, so they would go over details after they left. Clearly she was already tearing up, off and on, while trying so hard to keep it together and be brave.

After their delicious meal, the travelers checked their gear. Backpacks loaded with filtering water bottles, first aid supplies, hunting and fishing equipment, solar blankets and bedrolls, plus the food Anna had wrapped up for them. Tom's pack was equipped to carry the ax and shovel, while Jason's held the tent. The women carried firearms. While it was true that the new socialist government had confiscated all registered guns (another reason why it had been relatively easy to take control of the teaming masses), these were rifles bought before registering was mandatory, and they had been hidden in the basement against prying eyes.

Thankfully, they had also purchased plenty of ammunition, before it became unavailable to civilians. They wouldn't use these munitions unless it became necessary to do so, as the attention they would draw would likely give them away. So, they also carried knives; and miniature, but very powerful, crossbows, which had been custom made for them before one of their overseas missions. These crossbows would allow them to remain quiet, but provided the deadly force they would likely need to exert on this perilous journey. Of course their angel guards would travel with them, and that would be their best protection of all.

After their meal, the entire family stopped to pray together. Jason began, "Lord God, thank you for providing your protecting angels to see us safely on our way. We ask you to watch over Mom and Dad as we try to discover where they are and how to recover them. Also please watch over Anna and Luke, as they guard home base and await our return. And, Lord, give us the strength we will need for this trial and the wisdom to await your word on any decision we need to make along the journey. In Jesus' holy Name we pray. Amen" Hugs were exchanged, along with promises to be careful.

They couldn't simply walk out the front door with their loaded backpacks, or they would risk being stopped and searched. So, they went out the back, through the yard, into the greenhouse, and under the vent flap clear in the rear of the unit. From there, they made a B-line for the trees, in the same forest where Satan had once held Anna captive so many years before. Gabby's heavenly warriors stood between her group and any possible prying eyes as they entered the trees, to shield them from view. If they got enough of a head start, the officers in front would never be able to track them down.

"Kakos, Sir, there has been a new development. And, I'm afraid you aren't going to like it."

"What is it this time, Keres? Why is it that every single time I think we are getting ahead, you come to me with bad news?"

"I'm sorry, Sir. I just thought you would want to know."

"Tell me, Keres. Get it over with!"

"Sir, the woman and her husband and daughter have decided to go out and find her mother and father. We will do all we can to keep them in check, but you know I can't promise anything."

"I told you before not to tell me what I know. I can't tell you how angry this makes me. You continue to disappoint me, Keres. And, now I have to relay this news to Satan. What do you think his reaction will be to this news? The same reaction I am having. I can't believe this. Can't you do anything right you stupid wench?"

"I'm sorry, Sir. We will try to put up roadblocks, and trip them up if we can. If they didn't have that blasted group of winged warriors with them, our job would be much easier."

"I don't want excuses, Keres. And nobody ever promised you 'easy'. I want results. Do you hear me?"

"Yes Sir. I will do my best Sir."

Come now, you rich, weep and howl for the miseries that are coming upon you. Your riches have rotted and your garments are moth eaten. Your gold and silver have corroded, and their corrosion will be evidence against you and will eat your flesh like fire." You have laid up treasure in the last days.

James 5:1-3

CHAPTER 6

Nancy was holding her own. Publically, she was obeying all the rules, and doing more than her share of the workload. She took care of several ladies who couldn't quite manage on their own, and the guards had no reason at all to suspect her of anything. Privately, she was doing the very thing that had gotten her locked up in the first place. After the barrack's matron was off to sleep each night, she was conducting a 'lights off' Bible study. Now, since no Bibles were allowed in camp, all scripture was quoted from memory. And, she was grateful to have had the opportunity to memorize so many great verses over the years. As a group, they praised God quietly, but the ladies also came up with some excellent questions.

"Nancy, if God loves us so much, why would He let these monsters lock us up for merely worshipping Him?"

"Gwen, I don't have all the answers. But, we do know that not everyone follows the Lord. In 1st John 3:10, John says, "By this it is evident who are the children of God, and who are the children of the devil: whoever does not practice righteousness is not of God, nor is the one who does not love his brother." Timothy has a number of scriptures that are helpful in seeing this as well. We know from reading scripture that some will leave the faith, 1st Timothy 4:1-2 says, "Now the Spirit expressly says that in later times some will depart from the faith by devoting themselves to deceitful spirits and teachings of demons, through the insincerity of liars whose consciences are seared." And others were either never followers to begin with, or had never really fully committed their hearts to the Lord, so they were easily led astray. 2nd Timothy 3:1-4 tells us, "But understand this, that in the last days there will come times of difficulty, for people will be lovers of self, lovers of money, proud, arrogant, abusive, disobedient to their parents, ungrateful, unholy, heartless unappeasable, slanderous, without self control, brutal, not loving good, treacherous, reckless, swollen with conceit, lovers of pleasure rather than lovers of God."

"I just don't get it, Nancy. Wouldn't you think everyone would want to know Jesus? I mean, don't we all just really want to know the truth?"

"Actually, Lois, the answer to that would be a resounding no. Listen to what we're told in 2nd Timothy 4:3-4, "For the time is coming when people will not endure sound teaching, but having itching ears they will accumulate for themselves teachers to suit their own passions, and will turn away from listening to the truth and wander off into myths."

"I know I sound bitter when I say this, Nancy, but how can these people continue to get away with this? Why does God let this go on? I just get tired of doing the right thing, while they get away with murder."

"It isn't as simple as that, Maryann. These people are sealing their own fate. Galatians 6:7-10 tells us, "Do not be deceived: God is not mocked, for whatever one sows, that will he also reap. For the one who sows to his own flesh will from the flesh reap corruption, but the one who sows to the Spirit will from the Spirit reap eternal life. And let us not grow weary of doing good, for in due season we will reap, if we do not give up. So then, as we have opportunity, let us do good to everyone, and especially to those who are of the household of faith."

"So, I'm supposed to do good to my brothers and sisters in Christ, I get that, but you're not suggesting that I should do good to these horrible people who are holding us prisoner and keeping us from our families also, are you?"

"Yes I am, Betty. Who knows why these men and women are here to guard us? Many of them have accents, haven't you noticed? What if they were pressed into service by the U.N. council? They may not want to be here anymore than we do. I am suggesting that if we are kind to them, we may make a friend or two. And, that could come in handy down the line."

"I think I'm just getting tired of being treated badly, just for being a Christian."

"I think the Christians in the first century; the ones who were thrown to the lions to be ripped to shreds, or crucified, for their beliefs would most likely agree with you. Wouldn't you think? But, we serve a God who will see all things made right. Remember what Romans 8:28 says, "And we know that for those who love God all things work together for good, for those who are called according to His purpose." Our God doesn't leave us to suffer in vain. If we can persuade even one to follow Jesus, in the midst of this chaos, what a victory that would be. And for those who refuse to ever listen to the truth? Isaiah sums it up in the 20th verse of the 5th chapter, "Woe to those who call evil good and good evil, who put darkness for light and light for darkness, who put bitter for sweet and sweet for bitter." You don't have to worry about whether or not things will all work out in the end, ladies. God is good, and He will have His way, regardless of the intentions of man."

On the other hand, Mike just continued to get into mischief. The guards considered him to be a trouble maker, but that was fine with him. The slop jobs they gave him to do continued to put him in touch with tools, materials, and other items that he wouldn't necessarily be in contact with under ordinary circumstances. He'd managed to squirrel away a number of useful items, and the numbers grew every day.

Of course the jobs he had to do for that advantage were horrendous, but he would deal with all of that in order to make a way of escape. His schedule was a little different than the other fellows in his barracks, due to some of those chores. For instance, digging out the out houses was easier to do at night, when people weren't using them.

He'd grown accustomed to the cold, for better or worse, and his thin coat wasn't an issue anymore. As a matter of fact, he'd lost some weight since being brought into camp, and the looseness of the jacket made it easier to smuggle items to his secret hiding spot, behind the mess hall, buried beneath the refuse cans. On a particularly cold morning, after he'd successfully hidden his latest acquisitions, he was coming around from the back of the building just in time to see the work crew leaving the mess after breakfast clean up. His heart almost stopped in his chest. For there in front of him was Nancy. He was sure it was her, even though she looked thinner and very tired. She was walking with a pronounced limp as well, in case he needed any further verification. But, she was every bit as beautiful as the day he'd married her. She hadn't seen him yet, and that was probably best, as her reaction might just give them away. He decided quickly that he didn't want the guards to know they were married, because it might cause them to be harsher on her than before, just for her association with him.

She was smiling. That great smile she had. The one that went clear up to her eyes and made them twinkle with joy. That was Nancy. She always could make the best of any situation. Even in this freezing cold and in these wretched circumstances she simply shone with the love of Christ. She was his sunshine, his meaning and the love of his life. Had been since the first day he met her. He hated that she was in this terrible place, but happy to have seen her. Then he wondered if Anna and Luke were here as well. He'd have to keep his eyes open.

He watched while she entered her barracks. And now that he knew where she slept, he would figure out a way to contact her. Mike smiled, which was especially strange considering he walked back to his barracks covered with human excrement, in the freezing cold.

Gracie, and the travelers got as far away from the house as the short winter's day would allow, before they sought out a place to hole up for the night and grab a bite to eat. They'd covered over thirty five miles in those hours of daylight, Attempting to stay out of sight first, in the forest, and then in the miles of turkey foot grass laid out before the base of the mountain. Even with almost constantly falling snow, they'd held their own, so this had been a very productive day. Filling their water bottles in a nearby, icy stream; they searched for cover in the lowlands that stretched out before the mountain. Once they reached the behemoth they would have plenty of cover to choose from, but that might take another day or so. The mountain, with its many plateaus, was riddled with small caves and convenient cubby holes throughout its height and breadth. Their biggest concern, once they arrived there, would be to make sure they weren't disturbing any hibernators in their search for a place to take refuge.

For now though, any shelter would do. Tom spotted an abandoned farmstead not too far a hike in the distance. The house was gone, burned to the ground from the looks of it; and the barn looked downright dangerous, with its roof falling down in several places; but there was a silo on one side of the yard that might make a good place to rest.

It was fully dark by the time they reached their destination, so they crept inside the silo and used their flashlights to look around. Other than disintegrating, windblown leaves' drifted to the far side of the structure, they appeared to be alone. The door scraped a bit on the concrete, but the place seemed dry. The first order of business would be to bring in old wood, dry enough to burn cleanly. Too smoky a fire would be an invitation to unwelcome visitors. Luckily, there was half a cord of wood stacked on the side of the dilapidated barn, seasoned for decades. So, brushing it off to keep moisture to a minimum, Tom built a small fire on the cracked concrete floor of the hidey hole they'd chosen for the night.

Jason got busy laying out bedrolls and blankets, since this would likely be an early evening for all of them. They would need their strength again for the walk tomorrow. Who knew exactly how far up in the mountain the hostages were being held?

Gracie and Gabby began unwrapping the rations they would eat for supper that night. "I have to say, this looks delicious, and I'm starved. Skipping lunch saved us time, but I feel like my stomach is ingesting itself."

"Me too, Mom. And, these biscuits don't look a bit like the rations we've been known to eat on our missions rescues. Anna surely is a treasure."

"I agree with everything you just said, ladies. Should we eat? I'm as hungry as a bear. You just about done, Jason?"

"I'll be there in a minute, Tom. I just want to get some branches in front of this opening, where the door doesn't shut tight, to dissuade any night prowlers. Go ahead and start without me."

"That's okay. It won't hurt any of us to wait a couple of minutes, Honey. I'd like it if we prayed together before we eat."

"Okay, Gracie. I'm coming."

Jason quickly finished up what he was doing and joined the group for the blessing. Gracie began, "Lord, thank you for the success of today's journey, and thank you for your favor. Bless this food to our bodies, which we gladly dedicate to Your service. And, Lord, keep all of our loved ones safe, wherever they might be. In Jesus' precious Name. Amen."

"Do you think it's much further?"

"I don't really know, Gabby. When your dad and I went out for a drive a couple of years back, we tracked for several hours before we were stopped by those guards we told you about. We'd heard talk about some major building going on in the mountains, while we were all off on missions trips, and we wanted to take a look for ourselves. Who knows how much further the actual buildings were, from the place where we were stopped. They didn't let us get past their check point.

"We'd wondered if the self proclaimed 'New Socialist party', that was trying so hard to take over the country at that time, was preparing for future plans. Was it a series of training centers, bases, or something else? Now, it appears they were building prisons, or internment camps, for those of us who don't agree with their ideology and communist propaganda. They were so secretive in those days.

"They don't seem to be as reluctant to show the world the rest of their evil agenda now, right out there where it's as plain as the nose on your face, now that they have U.N.

troops to back up their big talk. I guess It's just the arresting of Christians they are interested in hiding, at least for the time being.

"I'm so angry that they took your Grandma, Gabby. We don't bow down to their godless philosophy, so I guess we don't fit in snugly with their 'One World Religion', and that's just fine with me. It appears that since we weren't converting at a rate fast enough for them, they are going to try and ram their agenda down our throats. Well, I've got news for them. They will have to kill me, because I will not renounce my Lord Jesus. I'm sorry, I'm ranting."

"That's okay, Mom. I don't mind your ranting. You're angry about the same things I'm angry about. But, you still didn't tell me if you think it will be much farther."

"Sorry baby girl. Well, at thirty five miles a day, if we can continue this pace, two hours of driving time would equate to around four days, more or less, plus any additional time it might take to get up to the prison encampments. That's just a rough estimate, but it should be close."

"Okay, then we will have to be on the lookout for game. Our supplies won't last long enough, unless we supplement with hunting along the way. Especially after we find Grampa and Gramma. I'm just saying."

"You're right, Gabby. I will put you in charge of that. You're an excellent shot. But, use your crossbow, for now, and not your gun. We don't want to attract any unwelcomed attention."

"Sure thing, Mom. I'll just keep my eyes open as we hike. Roasted rabbit sounds great. Especially in a world that limits ration stamps for meat. Whose idea was that anyway."

"I'm not sure. I think it was that last 'green' bill they passed in the Senate. I've heard that some of the folks, in the socialist congress, are vegan or vegetarian or something, so they don't think any of us should be eating meat."

"I heard a joke a while back. What's the difference between a liberal and a conservative?"

"I don't know. What's the difference between a liberal and a conservative, Jason?"

"If a conservative doesn't like something, they stop doing it. If a liberal doesn't like something, they pass a law that stops everyone from doing it."

"That would be funny, Jason, if it weren't so true. What a world we live in, huh?"

"Well, I still live in a world that has rabbits, plenty of rabbits, so let's have roast rabbit for supper as soon as possible!"

"I'll second that, Gabby! Roasted rabbit sounds terrific. And, your mom makes a great roast rabbit."

"I'm sure she does, Dad. Though, I don't remember ever tasting that growing up."

"Just trust me, it's the best you will ever eat."

"Good to know, Dad. Good to know. Now, I just need to find a couple of the critters."

"Quietly ladies. I thought I heard some scratching noises earlier. I want us to be ready to jump into our bunks if someone surprises us. Why don't we all pull the blankets down on our beds? Then we will have faster access, should that occur."

"Good idea, Nancy. Can I ask you a question?

"Sure, Lois. What's your question?"

"You were talking before about being nice to the very people who stole us away from our families. The same monsters who treat us so badly every single day. You said that we might make friends with someone who could turn out to be an ally down the road, and perhaps we could lead them to the Lord? Well, I might be the worst human being in the world for feeling this way, but I don't want to make friends with these people. I don't care if they come to know the Lord. They can all go to hell for all I care. That's what they deserve, isn't it?"

"Lois, I understand your feelings. But, we aren't supposed to live by our feelings, remember? Romans 3:10-12 tells us, "As it is written: 'No one is righteous, no not one; no one understands; no one seeks for God. All have turned aside; together they have become worthless; no one does good, not even one." So, you see, we are all guilty. We all deserve hell. None of us is righteous on our own. We all need Jesus, and the free gift of His sacrifice, to make us whole and give us eternal life. And remember, we were each where these people are at one time in our lives, before we came to know the Savior. I don't want anyone to be lost, not if I can help it anyway. God feels the same way, I promise. Listen to 2nd Peter 3:9 as we remember, "The Lord is not slow to fulfill His promise, as some count slowness, but is patient toward you, not wishing that any should perish, but that all should reach repentance." So, you see, it is our job to share Christ with everyone, whether we think they deserve forgiveness, or not. We are not to think of ourselves as better than others. God loves them too, just as He loves us, and has made provision through us to lead them into the saving Grace of the Gospel message. We are admonished to be kind, no matter how we feel. In Romans 12:20-21 we can clearly read, "To the contrary, if your enemy is hungry, feed him; if he is thirsty, give him something to drink; for by so doing you will heap burning coals on his head. Do not be overcome by evil, but overcome evil with good." This is a spiritual battle that we find ourselves in, ladies. And it will be won by doing the will of the Father, not by depending on our own human devices. So, let us be the ones God uses to bring someone home to Him."

"Wow, I see what you mean. Now I really feel like a jerk."

"Now, stop that. Lois, I really wish you would quit relying on your feelings so much. None of us is perfect. And, we can't depend on ourselves for salvation and peace. We are, all of us, just human. But, we can be instruments of His love, and we can have the peace that only comes through Him. When we truly know Him, that peace is with us, no matter the circumstances."

"Is that why you are always smiling, Nancy?"

"I guess it is, Doris. No matter what is going on in my life, I have Jesus, and He has me. No one can take that from me. And, at the end of it all, He will still be my Lord.

So, if I already have everything in the universe that matters, then it really doesn't matter what is going on around me, does it?"

"No, I guess it doesn't, I suppose. But I sure wish I could see my kids again."

"Now, I didn't say that there are not people I miss, or situations that I would rather be in than this one. But, if I were to die today, I will eventually see all those people that I love, because they all know Jesus. He has been so good to our family, and they have all opened their hearts to Him."

At precisely that second; two floorboards nearest the wall, and closest to the bunk where the women were congregated for their meeting; lifted. "Shhhh, ladies, please don't give me away. I mean you no harm. I'm here to see my wife, Nancy."

"Mike? How on earth."

He left the boards up, for easy access, and came to her with his arms open wide. He lifted her off her feet and they hugged and kissed, with the soft sounds of, "awww", surrounding them. "How is this possible? The last I knew you were still out of the country on a mission. How did you know where to find me?"

"That's the strange thing, Nance. We came home early,

because we were going to surprise you. With the holidays getting closer, and the airports getting tighter about allowing Christians access to ports of entry, we thought it would be a good idea to make our way home. Airport security called the folks from 'Immigration and Customs', or at least that's who they told us they were, and they were questioning our right to be here, our loyalty to the country, and making some other pretty ridiculous insinuations."

"Let me guess, Mike," Nancy said with a chuckle, "You got insulted and let your temper get away from you again. Oh Mike."

"Well, Babe, you do know me better than anyone on this earth. Anyway, they got upset with me, after I got upset, and I was arrested. They threw me into the back of a van, and the next thing I knew we were driving all the way up here. How did they get you? I can't imagine you were doing anything too threatening."

"I was simply having my usual Wednesday night supper and Bible study. Now, it's true that I had received several 'cease and desist' notices from the state, telling me to stop conducting illegal religious meetings. But, I just didn't believe things had gotten that far out of control, or that we suddenly live in a country where I can't share Jesus? I couldn't fathom that. So, Anna made us a lovely lasagna and some homemade bread, and she left to get Luke. All of my regulars arrived, plus a couple of new guests, and we were just about to sit down to supper, when the doors blew in.

"We were rounded up like cattle and thrown into transport trucks. My two ladies with diabetes, Barb and Chris, passed away in the trucks on the way up here, and I don't have a way to tell their families, but no one seems to care. I'm very sad about that. I felt the most angry about not being able to let Anna and Luke know what was going on. I can't imagine how worried she is. I learned very quickly, from watching others, not to rock the boat. We've been hiding away things to use as weapons, so we can use them when we finally get an escape plan put together."

"Well, I'm one of the people who leads by example, Babe. I've intentionally gotten on the bad side of most of the guards. This way they have me doing all the crap jobs that no one else wants to do. I'm on a different schedule than the rest of the camp, and I have access to tools and things that I will be able to use when we do get an escape plan put together. I have to say that most of the time I don't smell very good, but that aside, I'll be prepared when the time comes."

"So, where are Jason, Gracie, Gabby and Tom?? Do they know where you are?"

"They were still in the airport interrogation room the last time I saw them, so I don't know about now. I have no idea if they were arrested, or set free, but I haven't seen them here since I arrived. I know there are other detention centers around the country, or so I gather from listening to the guards, but it wouldn't make sense to send them to a different district. So, I would say they are probably still free. None of them have my temper, so they wouldn't have gotten into a mess the way I did. Or, at least that would be my guess. Only, now that I know you are here, I think me being brought to this camp was a God thing. He wanted me to be close to you, so I could protect you."

"You should go, Mike. The ladies and I are usually done with our Bible study by now. There is too much risk of being caught, and with all the chores they have us doing first thing in the mornings, we need our rest. Go down the hole, and I'll secure the boards after you. And, from now on, until we get a plan put together, we will figure out a different way to communicate. I don't want you to get caught."

"I'll tell you what. Just leave me a note in the back of

the mess, where the garbage cans are located, I'll find it. Then I'll get a response to you as quick as I can."

"Okay, that will work. I can be sure I'm the one to take out the trash every day, so it won't seem strange when I head out there. I love you, Mike. God is good, and I'm grateful to see that you're okay my love."

"I love you too, Nance. I was feeling pretty dead up until I saw you again; thinking you would be heartbroken when I didn't make it home for the holidays and you didn't know why; and now I know I have my heart and my purpose back. Don't worry, I'll be in touch." With a long hug, and a drawn out kiss, he was back down the hole and gone. The ladies helped Nancy close up the floorboards after him, and then they all made their way to their beds. Most of them smiling because of the loving scene they'd just witnessed. This must be proof that God was still working on their behalf.

You are the Lord, You alone. You have made heaven, the heaven of the heavens, with all their host, the earth and all that is on it, the seas and all that is in them; and You preserve all of them; and the host of heaven worships You.

Nehemiah 9:6

CHAPTER 7

"I'm sorry, I don't know what you're talking about."

"Listen Miss, we didn't bring you in here today to play games."

"Just exactly where is it that you have brought me today? This isn't the local police station, so obviously you are not police officers. I don't understand what right you think you have to bring me in for questioning?"

"We are with the U.N. global socialist initiative. And we do have the right to question you. We work for the New Socialist Party, which is now the governing body in the area. So, unless you want to be arrested and imprisoned, you will answer our questions. Where have they gone?"

"Excuse me? Where have who gone?"

"Again, we are not here to play games. Your sister, your brother in law, your niece and your friend. Where have they gone?"

"Oh, now I see who you're looking for. I assure you that I don't know where they've gone. I suppose they are out on another humanitarian mission. That is what they do after all."

"Again, where have they gone. And when did they leave."

"And, again I assure you, I don't know. They merely come home to re-supply. They don't fill me in on their itinerary, because there would be no way for me to contact them, even in the case of an emergency. And, now that you have taken my mother, to God knows where, I would have no need to contact them at any rate. Where was it again that you have taken my mom? You still haven't given me that information."

"You will not ask the questions. We ask the questions."

"Oh, I see how this works. Well, I have no information for you. You have come to the wrong place."

"How could you not know when they left? Did they not even say goodbye? Did they simply slink off into the shadows? I don't believe you. We know for sure that they were there at your house."

Anna shook her head and smiled. At that point the officer slapped her so hard, her head snapped sharply right. Seeing stars, Anna gasped and tried to raise her hands to her face, only to be reminded that her hands were tightly cuffed to the table.

"You can't do that. I'm an American citizen. I have rights, and we have something called due process in this country. How dare you hit me." He hit her again, but this time harder. She tasted blood, lots of it, and spit a mouthful on the floor beside her chair.

Where mere moments ago she was only a bit frightened by the whole ordeal, now she was terrified to her core. Then, as quick as the fear had come, it was suddenly replaced by righteous indignation. Her jaw stiffened, and her eyes glared daggers, as she slowly turned her head to look at her attacker. Things going through her head, violent things, about the way she would take care of this later, became downright dangerous to even think.

These men clearly did not know who they were dealing with. She'd been through much worse than this in her life, and their actions only proved to make her stronger in her resolve not to help them in any way. She wasn't going to take this, and wasn't going to let her loved ones endure this either.

"I want answers lady. And if you do not give them to me, I will......"

"You will what? I already told you. We said our goodbyes over a meal. They come and go as they please. We are all grownups here, so I don't keep tabs on any of them. Now, if you will kindly release me, I'm sure my fiancée is worried sick by now and has probably already begun making phone calls and searching for me." Somehow, that last statement said without a hint of fear in her voice, and perhaps more than a suggestion of threat, caused them to release her on her own recognizance.

"We will be watching you. Don't believe for one moment that there is anything you can do that won't be tracked."

"Enjoy yourselves. I'm glad you have so much time on your hands."

Anna made her way home. Of course the U.N. officers who'd knocked on her door, and snatched her as soon as she opened it, didn't offer her a way back. And, cowards that they were, they'd waited until Luke was away from the house before kidnapping her, so he didn't know where she was. She was right though. He was frantic by the time she returned.

"Oh Anna, I've been worried sick. Where have you been? What happened to you? You're bleeding."

"I've been cooling my heels at the local U.N. facilities. Did you know we had local U.N. facilities? Nope, neither did I. As soon as you left they knocked at the door and the second I opened it they put cuffs on me and dragged me to their headquarters. They were looking for Gracie and the gang, and they wouldn't believe I didn't know where they'd gone. They got a little physical, that's all. So, Grace was right. It was a good thing I didn't have any information. Not that I would have ever given it to them, but if I'd known anything they might have been able to read it in my face. We need to figure out what we're going to do next. It could be dangerous to continue staying here."

"I get what you're saying, honey, but where would we go? How would your family know where to find us when they get back? And remember, we don't know where they are either, so if we leave and they come back, we may never be able to find them again. No, I think we ought to stay right here. Even though you've had to close the restaurants, we still have the goats, the chickens and the greenhouse, so at least we won't starve. If things get worse, we can always change our plans later."

"Okay, you're right, I guess. These guys just really made me mad. I kind of lost my head for a minute. So, what are we going to do?"

"I'll tell you what I'd like to do. I'd like to go down there and give them a little of what they clearly gave you. How can any of that be okay? It can't be legal, that's for sure."

"Well, you know you can't go down there. They would

just arrest you, and then where would we be? And, I don't know if what they do is legal. As the socialist party has taken over the country they've changed laws to benefit their agenda. We are no longer living in a free America, Luke, and it gets scarier and scarier by the minute."

"I do know one thing. From now on, if either of us has an errand to run, or any place to go, we go together. Agreed?"

"Agreed. I love you Luke."

"I love you more, Anna, and I don't ever want anything to happen to you again. Now, come here and let me put something on your lip and your eye. I can't believe they did this to you. What a bunch of cowards. Notice that they didn't come for you until they saw that I was gone. Nothing but a bunch of worthless bullies and cowards. The next time I go to my meeting, I'd like you to come. I want you to meet the guys I've been talking to. They have some pretty interesting ideas about a few things."

"Sure, I'd like that."

Mike couldn't believe his luck. He'd found a back way, under the floor, into the armory, and he was positive those in charge would never even know he'd been there. Sure that the guards must keep some kind of inventory, or at least he sure would if the building was his responsibility, he'd be careful to begin removing things slowly, just a little at a time. Only to see if they noticed, at first. Finally, real weapons to back up his home made ones. They would never know what hit them.

The amount of ammunition available in the store room was mind boggling, so he checked and matched carefully, and then tried very hard not to break out in girlish giggles for the excitement it caused him. His hiding place behind the mess would have to be upgraded with more plastic, or perhaps even changed altogether, that was an absolute necessity. These rifles would have to be kept dry at all costs, or they wouldn't be any more effective than a rudimentary club. He couldn't wait to tell Nancy. She would be so excited about his find. Now they needed to start working on a plan. He couldn't help but wonder how Tom and the kids were doing.

Their fire had gone out in the middle of the night, and they woke to a cold silo. Jason started a small fire, so they could make some dandelion tea to drink with biscuits, and the space warmed up quickly. Gracie came up behind him and wrapped her arms around his neck. He turned and gave her a long kiss. "Good morning gorgeous."

"Good morning yourself. Have you looked outside?"

"No, I was going to get the tea started. Are you worried?"

"I just wondered if we got more snow. It was getting deep out there when we stopped for the night, and if it gets much deeper the going will get awfully rough."

"I'll go check."

"No, I can check. You just finish up with the tea. I'm going to fill a pan with snow, so I can melt it and wash up a bit."

When she looked outside, Grace gasped and smiled. Sunrise was breathtaking. In the hue of first morning light the fresh ice and snow sparkled like drifting pink piles of diamonds and rubies. It appeared they'd gotten at least several more inches throughout the nighttime, so all their tell tale footprints were covered nicely. But, the additional snow would make their travel today more difficult. Well, at least they'd packed all the right cold weather gear, so they were completely prepared for whatever nature threw at them.

She couldn't help thinking though; standing with her arms crossed, in the cold morning air, her breath escaping in small puffs of white vapor; that God was good. So good. Strange, that even in the most dire of circumstances, she could know without a doubt that He was with them, and would never leave them or forsake them. She looked to her side and saw that even her heavenly guards were gazing up at the beautiful sunrise. Yes, absolutely, God is very good indeed.

Luke and Anna woke to a commotion in the back yard. When they opened the back door to check, they were confronted with an odd sight. A young boy, of about seven or eight years, with a chicken under each arm. He was struggling to keep the girls in check, but still managed a bold and defiant look when his eyes met theirs. "Well, hello there." Anna chirped as she tried, without much success, to hold back a smile.

"Hello." The boy shot back in his gruffest tone. He was wearing tattered clothes and sneakers wrapped in knotted, plastic bread bags. An old towel wrapped around his head was meant to keep his neck and ears warm, and a holy, stained blanket over his shoulders kept some of the snow off.

"May I ask what you are doing young man?"

"I ain't doing nothing."

"Well, it appears you are holding two of my chickens. May I ask where you were thinking of taking them?"

"I'll give 'em a good home. I promise. Looks like you got more than enough to share."

"You are correct in the fact that we have enough to share. And we do share all the time. However, what you are doing is called stealing. There is a big difference. Do your mom and dad know where you are?"

"They got shot by the police a while back. I'm on my own now."

"We're very sorry to hear that. But, I don't know what you were thinking you might do with those two chickens. Do you know how they work?"

"Yeah, 'course I do. You just squeeze 'em and eggs come out, right?"

"Actually, no, that's not exactly how that goes. And unless you have food for them and a place for them to do their job, they won't make eggs at all. Why don't you put the chickens down and come inside. We were just going to make some breakfast. You're welcome to join us."

"How do I know you ain't going to call the U.N. police when I get in there?"

"You don't have to worry about that. Some of our friends, and even my mom, were arrested by the U.N. police. So, we are not big fans of those guys. Just come in and get warm for awhile. You can have a nice breakfast, and then we'll decide what comes next, okay?"

"Sure, but if I see any cops, you best be out of my way. You understand me?"

"Agreed. No police, I promise. Can I ask your name?"

"Sure, I guess so. I'm Daniel, but you can call me Dan."

"Hi, Dan. We are Luke and Anna, and we're pleased to meet you."

Anna prepared scrambled eggs and French toast, with thick slices of homemade bread, lots of hand churned butter and warm syrup. Big glasses of cold goat's milk accompanied their meal. And warm tea with honey; to top it off; left them all sitting back in their chairs. Dan, who was obviously half starved, had eaten them both under the table. And, now that his tummy was full for the first time, in who knows how long, his eyes looked heavy with fatigue.

"Do you have a place to stay, Dan?"

"I got places."

"Are they safe places, son?"

"They're safe enough."

"We won't press you any more, Dan. But, this is a big house, and we have plenty of room. It's gotten pretty cold outside lately, and we wouldn't want you to freeze. So, if you ever need a place to stay, you are welcome here. No police, no strings attached."

"Okay. I'll think about it. Thanks for breakfast."

"It was nice to meet you, Dan."

"You're really going to let me leave? No police?"

"Hey, we promised, didn't we? No police, and we won't stand in your way. But the offer still stands if you ever need a place."

"Thanks. You got any kids?"

"No we don't, Dan. We aren't even married yet. We hope to be married soon, and have lots of children later, if that is what God has planned for us."

"You're kinda old to start having kids, aren't you? I mean, especially now with the world the way it is. It'd be kinda dangerous, wouldn't it?"

"You do have a point. And, yes, I guess when I was younger I thought I would have kids by now. But that just wasn't God's plan for me at the time, so here we are."

"Yeah, I'm just saying. You know, maybe you ought to think about getting a kid that's already around. You know, since there's plenty of 'em that don't have a place to stay. Besides, kids that have already been around for awhile have some experience, if you know what I mean. Like chores and stuff."

"Would you consider staying here with us, Dan? I mean, we could really use the help, couldn't we Luke?"

"Yeah, we sure could. It'd be great to have an extra pair of experienced hands around here. The police did a lot of damage when they blew our doors in and trashed the place. You could help me fix things up, and I could teach you how to take care of the goats and chickens. What do you say?"

"Yeah, okay, I could maybe do that. But, I want you to know it's nothing permanent. If a better deal comes along, I'll be gone."

"Oh, we understand. And, we certainly wouldn't ever want to stand in your way if something better comes along. So it's a deal?"

"Sure, it's a deal."

"Good. I'll show you where you can sleep. I might even have some things that would fit you. All the stuff I brought home when we had to close the soup kitchen, after our do-nations stopped, are upstairs in boxes. You can get cleaned up and I'll see what I've got."

After a bath Dan dressed in the clothes Anna found in the attic. They were a tad big, but nothing that one good growth spurt wouldn't fix. The shoes were new too, and very, very comfortable. He couldn't remember the last time he'd had shoes that he didn't have to cover with bread bags. Anna showed him to his room, and his eyes practically exploded out of his head. "In here? This is my room?"

"Yes, if that's okay."

"I just ain't ever seen a room this big before. Even when I was at home with my folks, I slept on the couch. It folded out to a bed, you know?."

"Why don't you get settled in? Lunch will be at noon, in case you want to rest for awhile. We're glad you decided to stay, Dan."

"Yeah, thanks for asking me. Remember though, this ain't nothing permanent."

"Yep, we remember. Nothing permanent."

When Luke and Anna peeked through the door fifteen minutes later, he was sound asleep, his face bathed in a peace that caused him to look every bit the sweet, innocent little boy he was. A look they were sure he'd hate with every single ounce of his 'big boy' bravado. They turned to one another and smiled.

Finally, be strong in the Lord and in the strength of His might. Put on the whole armor of God, that you may be able to stand against the schemes of the devil.

Ephesians 6:10-11

CHAPTER 8

"Keres, come here, NOW!"

"Yes Sir, what can I do for you?"

"What is this that I'm hearing about the woman and her team heading up to the mountain? And, why, may I ask, am I not hearing this from you?"

"Sir, I just got confirmation myself. I don't know who told you, but they could only have known for mere moments." Keres knew there were others gunning for her job, and as far as she was concerned, they could have it. They'd regret it soon enough. However, this meant someone was out to get her in more trouble than she usually already was, and that made her angry.

"It doesn't matter how long they knew it. They were quicker to get me the information than you were. Should I give this demon in question your position?"

"Sir, if that is what you deem fit, then that is your prerogative."

"No, you sound much too eager to pass your responsibilities along to someone else. I believe I will keep you right where you are."

"Whatever you say, Boss. Is there anything else?"

"Of course there is. Why do you think I called you in here?"

"To tell me you already had the information I was about to bring you?"

"Watch your mouth, wench. You will speak to me with respect. Do you understand me?"

"Yes Sir. Respect Sir. Well, I have no more information for you at this time. I will keep you updated on any new developments."

"See that you do."

Their exodus from the silo into the Plaines area, covered with the remains of summer's turkey foot grass, was relatively uneventful. They'd prepared for the day and left their shelter very early in the morning. With winter upon them, the grasses were dormant, and colored a peaceful sort of maroon-tan hue. However, the plant's meek appearance belied its true aggressive nature. And by the end of the first day there were not enough angry adjectives in their vocabularies to describe the terrible, abusive weed.

With miles of frozen ground to cover, and millions of

three pronged barbs whipping up to dig into any and all exposed flesh as they made their way through the infernal foliage, they were at wits end by the finish of that first painful day. Thankfully they would only have to endure a couple of days of the dreadful plants before gaining the less offensive vegetation directly at the base of the mountain.

Already exhausted, clearing out an area big enough for all four bedrolls was grueling. The nature of the evil plant was to send shoots and runners out in every direction in order to start new growth. So the thick, twisting root structure was mostly buried just beneath the surface, and proved to be a total disaster to sever, even with the sharpest of knives. The two men took turns sawing with their knives, and finally turned to the ax, until they were just too tired to continue. Then the ladies tried their luck. After a combined effort of a couple of hours of chopping, they'd cleared an area that might barely accommodate the four bedrolls. There wouldn't be a fire tonight. Not out in the open. It was too risky. So, later in the night they would be very grateful for the close proximity of their fellow travelers, as the temperatures dipped into the teens.

Supper was more of Anna's wonderful biscuits, cheese and fresh apples with plenty of water. Later, as Grace laid beside her husband until his breathing became deep and even, she stared at the sky and marveled at the stars. Wondering how the universe could look so normal, when their country was in such turmoil, she shook her head and went to the Lord in prayer. She didn't know how long she'd spoken with the Lord this time, but the stars had moved significantly in the sky by the time she was finished. She looked around, and acknowledged her band of winged warriors, before she quietly commented. "Thank you Lord for always sending angels to watch over us as we sleep."

One weapon and one box of ammunition at a time, over the past several days, had proved too build Mike's arsenal more than he could have dreamed. He'd moved the rifles and ammo to a hollowed out tree in the woods; behind the camp; when the pile became large enough to distort the flat landscape behind the mess hall. He'd dug a hole under the twelve foot fence out back and filled it in with loose dirt. That way, when he went in and out, the hole would fill quickly. Since there were fewer guards at night, and he was just one worker going about his business, he didn't draw much attention. He lined the hollow tree with plastic he pilfered from the camp kitchen. Now, he took trips out to his hiding spot every night with his new acquisitions. So far, no one was the wiser. Obviously people weren't doing their jobs correctly in the armory, but that was to his advantage, so he certainly wouldn't complain. Someone should have caught the discrepancies by now if they were doing any kind of inventory, and so far no one had raised an alarm, so all appeared to be well.

Perhaps, Mike reasoned, the individual in charge of the armory was even so confident his supplies were safe, that he didn't feel the need to spend time endlessly checking inventory. And, if that was the case, then that was just fine with Mike. This revelation caused him to be even more bold, taking more than one piece of equipment at a time. What Mike didn't know, was that the base commander knew exactly what was going on. He'd known since the first item was stolen from his supplies. And, soldiers had been quietly watching Mike, from a safe, discrete distance right from the beginning.

Nancy was tired. With her blood pressure wrecking havoc on her body, and the ever growing pain in her damaged hip, it was almost impossible for her to get any significant sleep on the hard bunk she was assigned. But, just as she always had, she would push on. Now that she knew Mike was accumulating an arsenal of weapons, and that they would be devising an escape plan soon, she had more hope than at any time since her capture. Still conducting Bible studies, and still answering difficult questions for confused and angry women, she felt her usefulness was not at an end. But, the sheer effort of rising each day, to go about the chores she was assigned, was becoming more difficult.

Ever the encourager, she could do with a little encouraging herself these days. Oh, she knew God loved her, that wasn't the issue. It was just different here. And though she got an occasional brief visit with Mike, she really would have loved to fall asleep in his arms. She missed the kids, especially Anna who had become her invaluable friend and helper, and wondered often how she and Luke were getting along. She was sure the girl was more than concerned and she wished there was a way to get word to her. As she bowed her head to pray, before she began her day, she saw a sudden flash of a vision. It was a young boy. He was carrying chickens; one under each arm; in her back yard, and wearing a big smile. She shook her head and wondered where in the heck that odd vision came from.

Finally out of the infernal turkey foot grass, they would camp for the night; before undertaking those last miles to the base of the mountain, and ultimately, the long climb upward. Of course it would have been easier to take the public road leading into the mount, but that road was manned by well armed guards, probably supplied by the U.N. forces. No, this would be the only way of reaching the camp without being detected. For this last night on the plains they would place their bedrolls in the lower vegetation between the turkey foot grass and the plethora of boulders and scrub brush on the long expanse at the base of the mountain, thus maintaining at least a little cover from prying eyes.

Supper consisted of some of the last of their biscuits, sunflower seeds and water. It would be nice to be on the mountain, where they could light a small fire, roast fresh game and fish, and make some hot coffee or tea. For now this would have to do.

Even with good sleeping bags, and severe winter garb, it was downright cold out in the open. Jason, ever the strong one; and always willing to sacrifice himself for her; took the outside position and formed himself to her back to provide a little body heat for shared warmth. However, even with that, and though she would never tell him for fear of hurting his feelings, Grace felt as though she would never be warm again. In her very brief moments of sporadic sleep she dreamt of hot baths and fire places. Directly on her other side, Gabby was tucked in as close as possible, and Uncle Tom was close to her back. She knew everyone was at least as cold as she was, so she didn't complain, but the night couldn't end quickly enough for her. During the few moments of her only real rest all night long, she had the strangest dream. She dreamed of a young boy in their back yard back home. The oddest part of the dream was that he held one of their chickens under each arm as he walked to the greenhouse with a huge smile on his face. Once she was awake the vision nudged her memory. Was it possible that this child was the same one she'd mistaken for her brother in a dream not so long ago? She wondered.

Out of the kitchen window. "Hey, Dan."

"Yep. I'm here Anna."

"Oh." Chuckling. "Are you with the chickens again?"

"Yep. I think they like me. They don't fight me when I carry them now."

"Well, that's good. But, you have to give them enough time on their nests, or they won't lay eggs. We won't have anything for breakfast."

"Oh, I collected the eggs first. The basket is on the table on the side porch. And I'd like mine scrambled please."

"Well, thank you for getting on that first thing this morning. And those scrambled eggs are coming right up."

"The little guy seems to be fitting right in, don't you think?"

"Oh my, you frightened me. I didn't know you were up yet. Yes, he seems to have made himself right at home. Did you sleep well?"

"I'll sleep much better after we're married. The beds here are so big. I think I'd be much warmer if I had you to snuggle up with. Doesn't that sound nice?"

"Yes it does. But, it would be really sad for me to marry without my mom here. And, I'm not even sure where Pastor Roy is these days, since the government closed the church up, so there's that."

"I know, I know. And I will wait. You are absolutely

worth waiting for. But, know this, you are not going to get rid of me so easy."

"That is the last thing I could ever want is to get rid of you. I plan to spend the rest of my life with you, remember? Besides, I've always planned on wearing my mom's wedding dress when I marry, and who else would have me in that old thing?"

"Don't talk like that. Any man would be happy to have you. I'm just the most blessed man in the world, because you have agreed to marry me. I don't want you to worry. We are going to find your mom soon, and when we do, we will have the nice wedding you always dreamed of."

"Thank you, Luke. How did I ever end up with such a wonderful man?"

"I don't know, just lucky I guess. I am meeting with my friends tonight. I'd like you to come with me if that's okay. I want you to meet them, but I also don't want you to be at the house alone."

"Okay, I know we talked about that, but what are we going to do with Dan?"

"We'll just bring him along. Most of the guys are married and many have kids. He'll fit right in. I think you're really going to like these people."

"I'm sure I will. I can't help but like them if you do."

Gabby was ready to go before dawn, her teeth chattering so severely she was sure she'd break an incisor if she didn't get her blood stirring as soon as possible. Oh what she wouldn't give for a hot cup of coffee or tea right about now; and a hot shower. A hot shower would be great. Maybe by tonight they would be in a cave on the mountain. Then they would at least be able to start a fire. That would be terrific. She wasn't a wimp by any means. She'd been going on missions trips to dangerous parts of the world since she was a teen. But, cold was cold, and she had little tolerance for any of it.

As the rest of the group crawled out of their sleeping bags, and rolled up their beds for transport, Gabby pulled out some of the last of their biscuits and cheese. All the food they had left in the bag was a few of those biscuits and a little cheese, some sunflower seeds and a few packaged MREs, left over from their last mission trip. She'd necessarily have to start doing some hunting, as soon as they got up on the mountain, or they'd all be hungry soon.

Grace came up behind her daughter and hugged her

tight, hoping to warm them both up a little. Then, Dad grabbed them both and squeezed tight. "Can I get in on some of that, or would it be weird?"

"Get on in here, Tom. There's a tiny bit of room right here." They all huddled close for a bit, and then started laughing, until their blood was pumping hard. They would eat on the go. Knowing they would be finished long before they achieved the base of the mount.

"Kakos, I have news."

"What news have you, Keres."

"There is a new entity involved."

"What entity is that, Keres?"

"It is unclear, Sir. Perhaps I shouldn't have even come to you yet, but I didn't want you to get the news from some-one else first. This one might be more dangerous than the woman, her husband and their daughter."

"This makes me very uneasy."

"Yes Sir, I knew it would. But, I figured it was better to know, than to be surprised later."

"Yes, you're right, Keres. We will have to keep our eyes open on this one, and watch out for this new entity. Thank you for your focus."

"Certainly Sir. I'll let you know if I hear of anything that might be helpful. Meanwhile, the woman and her husband, their daughter and friend, have achieved the mountain. Should I warn those who are waiting at the camp?"

"No, wait on that a bit. Let the woman's father think he is safe, in his deception, for just a while longer. The result will be even more enjoyable to see, if we wait till he thinks he's home free, don't you think?"

"Yes Sir. I'll keep you posted."

"Good. I may even let you come with me to watch this time. We will need plenty of troops on the ground when we step in to squash them all."

"Thank you Sir. I would be grateful for that. I seldom get to see final results."

"Hey, Jim, I want you to meet my fiancée. Anna, this is Jim. He's kinda in charge of the group."

"Don't let him fool you, Anna. Nobody's in charge around here. That's why we're such a mess."

"Well, I'm pleased to meet you, Jim, whether you're in charge or not."

"Who's the little guy?"

"This is Dan, he's seven."

"It's nice to meet you, Dan. My kids are over by the big game table, if you feel like joining in?"

"I don't know. I ain't going to do any baby stuff, but I'll check it out."

"Good. You can play whatever you'd like. And, there's all kinds of big kid stuff over there too, so feel free to look it over."

"You going anywhere, Anna?"

"Nope, Dan. Luke and I will be right here when you get done. We're just going to talk to some people. We'll let you know when we're finished, okay?"

"Okay." Dan walked away reluctantly, but with his best 'self confident' swagger, to stand by some others in the 'kids' section.

"I brought a snack for everyone, Jim. I hope that was okay. Just some biscuits and vegetables, but there should be enough for all."

"That was very kind, Anna. I'm sure everyone will appreciate that."

"So, you never said you had kids, Luke."

"This, my friend, was a very recent acquisition. We found

him in our backyard a few days ago. He was hungry and trying to walk off with a couple of chickens almost bigger than he is. Quite comical really. He's a good kid, and a hard worker. It's actually been a blessing to have him around."

"If you say so. Now would not be the time I would be taking on extra children. I have enough to worry about with my three."

"Well, we don't have three others, and he really has been no trouble at all."

"So, is your wife here, Jim?"

"No, Anna. She stayed home with the little one tonight. When he gets tired he's a handful. I can handle the two older ones, since they mostly play anyway, but I am woefully underprepared when it comes to the baby."

"We all have our strengths, Jim, as I was reminded recently. And, we all have a purpose to fulfill."

"Just a minute, Anna. I'm going to get everyone together. Hey folks, I think that's everyone who was coming tonight. Shall we gather around?"

"Where do you want us, Jim?"

"Let's just sit right over here, Carl. That way we can keep an eye on the kids, but still be out of earshot. What do you think people?"

"Yep, this is good, Jim. So, what have you heard?"

"I've been hearing quite a bit through the grapevine and I think you are all going to be excited. There are more and more small groups and even few larger chapters springing up around the country. Who would have thought there'd be that many munitions left out there after the government grab programs that have gone on in the past couple of decades? But I guess there are literally tens of millions of arms, bought before mandatory registration, that are still in the hands of solid patriots.

"When gun laws began to change, I guess we weren't the only ones who knew the socialists were up to something. Many of us hid our weapons and ammo away, instead of turning them over to the bad guys. I mean, I knew we would need these someday, didn't you?" Agreement all around. "I'm hearing more and more that Americans everywhere are ready to take our country back. People are sick and tired of the mess this country has become in the hands of these liberal, socialist enemies, and they are organizing. I'll be hearing more soon, so we should meet again on Monday. Is that good for everyone?"

"Sure, I think we can all make that work."

"Well then, get something to eat. Thank Anna for

bringing the biscuits and veggies, and visit for a while. But, when you leave be careful out there, we might be watched, and we'll see you on Monday."

"It was nice to meet you, Jim. I hope I'll get to meet your wife next week."

"I hope so. We'll have to see how the little one is doing. And, it was good to meet you too, Anna. You've got a good man there. Be safe and we'll see you next week."

"Thank you, I know, he's the best. See you Monday. Dan, we're going now. Come along buddy."

Back at home, Dan took a bath and got ready for bed. "Anna? Would you read me a story?"

"Sure buddy. I'd be happy to. I'd like to read you a story from the Bible. Would you like that?"

"Yeah, that would be great. My mom used to read to me out of the Bible. Jesus is my all time favorite. He lives in my heart you know."

"No, I didn't know that, Dan. I was just about to ask you if you knew Jesus. And, I'm very glad that you do."

"Yeah, I asked Him to come into my heart when I was almost three, but I think He's always been my friend. That's why I can see stuff. You know, like at the meeting."

"What do you mean, "Like at the meeting", did you see

something at the meeting?

"Yeah, everybody there had angels, except that one guy. He was Mindy's dad. And, I think he was mad. I kinda felt like he was anyway. It made me want to stay far away from him."

"So, you can see angels, Dan?"

"Yeah, since I was a baby I guess. That's why I knew you and Luke were good. Because you both have angels. My mom always told me not to say anything about it to folks, because they might think I was crazy. But I see the bad ones too. You know, the demons. And, I usually know when the bad ones are going to do something to hurt somebody. That was the way I felt at the meeting. Mindy's dad was planning to do something bad to all the people there."

"Dan, do you mind if I read to you later? I need to talk to Luke about something very important. I promise I'll be back, okay?"

"Yeah, are you going to tell him about Mindy's dad?"

"Yes, Dan, I'm going to tell him. I hope you don't mind. He will know your secret now too. But, I promise he won't think you're crazy, and he won't make fun of you. Is that okay?"

"Yeah, but don't forget my story, okay? You promised."

But you, Oh Lord, are a shield about me, my glory, and the lifter of my head.

Psalm 3:3

CHAPTER 9

"Nancy, we're almost ready. I'm getting excited. We've got quite an arsenal out there in the woods. We're going to get out of here yet, and those socialist jerks are going to get what's coming to them."

"Are you sure no one knows, Mike? I don't understand how you can take that many weapons without anyone being the wiser."

"Well, all I can say is that someone isn't doing their job right. But that is going to come back to bite them in the butt, not me. We need to call a meeting with the ladies, so we can plan some strategy. I will have to talk to the men by myself. As long as we can get everyone on the same page, I don't see any reason why we couldn't be out of here by the end of next week."

"I can't wait to get home. I've been so concerned about Anna. I know she's been worried sick about me since I was taken. And, my oh my, Just to sleep in my own bed again."

"Nancy, Babe, I'm sorry, but we can't go home. We will never be able to go home again, not unless someone unseats this current government. The minute we leave this place, we will be wanted fugitives."

"Oh Mike, I hadn't even thought of that. You mean we will never see our kids, or our granddaughter again? I don't know if I can stand the thought of that. Maybe I shouldn't go. Maybe I should just stay here and tough it out."

"Nancy, it is only a matter of time before this government decides they have no earthly use for us anymore. Just like the Jews in the Nazi concentration camps. Why do you think they built these detention centers so far away from prying eyes? You know, "out of sight, out of mind". For anyone out there who might have cared two cents worth about what the government was doing with all the Christians and the political dissidents, all they had to do is keep us locked away until no one is asking about us anymore. Then, no one will raise a stink when we disappear for good."

"Do you really think it is that dire, Mike? Do you think they plan to kill us?"

"What do you think, Nancy? Have you seen them raise a finger to help anyone who is sick, or in trouble? Or, do those people usually just die? Of course they plan to kill us. After all the genocide we've seen in foreign countries that have fallen into socialism, or communism, there is no other conclusion I can come up with. Besides, my love. Even if all we ever had again was each other, would that be so bad? We've raised some strong kids, who have amazing talents and abilities. They will be able to take care of themselves. And, if all goes as planned, perhaps we will even be able to take back our country. Then we can search out our kids and be together again."

"I didn't mean to imply that you wouldn't be enough for me, Mike. You are the love of my life. And if I don't see my kids again, before I see them in glory, then I know I'll see them there. Just tell me when we need to meet with the ladies, and I'll see that everyone is ready."

"So he sees angels, like your sister and your niece do?"

"Well, and Jason too."

"Yeah, yeah, I forgot. Does he see the demons too?"

"Yes, that's how he knows Mindy's dad is a bad man. I promise you that this guy is not part of the same movement you guys are part of. If he's there, and he's covered with demons, then he's either a spy for the socialist party, a maniac who intends to do us all harm, or both."

"What do you think we should do?"

"Well, I think we have to talk to Jim. And it would be

best if we did it when Mindy's dad isn't around. I don't know how to get a hold of him if it's not at a meeting, do you?"

"No, he used to work at the foundry, but it closed down. No one could get materials anymore. I think most people are having an impossible time finding employment, now that most of the businesses in the area have failed. That's part of what has all these men, here and around the country, upset enough to start meeting and organizing.

"Not everyone wants to sit around doing nothing and have the government telling them what to do. Especially after said government runs out of money. People are getting tired of being hungry and seeing their kids go without. I'd sure like to get the names and numbers of all those ignorant people who voted for the Democratic Socialist Party, and ask them how that's working out for them now. I'll bet they wouldn't have so many takers for their stinking socialist agenda now, huh?

"You know, even if I had a cell that worked anymore, and Jim's number for that matter, it wouldn't be something I'd do over the phone, knowing everything is likely being tapped by the feds."

"Yeah, I agree. Well, then we'll have to wait till Monday's meeting. I hope Mindy's dad doesn't decide to do anything before we meet again."

"If he's a plant by the socialists, he won't do anything. Jim didn't give out enough information at the last meeting for him to take back to his handlers. He'll want more details than what he has to pass along to his superiors. However, if he's just a guy who wants to blow some stuff up, we could be walking in to a trap on Monday. Maybe I'll have you and Dan stay home, and I'll go try to explain to Jim what's going on."

"Okay, so how are you going to tell him we got the information?"

"I don't think he'll be as freaked out as you might think. He's a Christian, so he's probably heard of your sister and her husband."

"Jason, even if he's heard of Gracie, that still doesn't explain anything in a way that regular people would understand. It has never been advertised that my family sees into the spiritual realm. I don't know. I don't want him to think you're just some nut case. I think it would be better if we all went, so we can explain these special abilities a bit better."

"Okay, I just wanted to keep you safe, that's all."

"I know. I love you for that. You are now, and always

will be my hero. But you can't be the only one sticking your neck out. We all have a stake in this."

"Okay, Monday then. We should go and ask Dan if he's okay with that."

"You're right. I owe him a bed time story anyway."

It wouldn't be an easy climb, but they had experienced worse. At least if wasn't a sheer drop like Mount Thor on Baffin island in Canada. That climb had been nearly impossible to navigate. This mountain was much different. It consisted of vertical climbs, level ridges and plateaus. It was on the level ridges that they would find small caves, holes and crannies in which to hide. There they would be able to build small fires for cooking and warmth.

They were hoping to find the detention camp, where Mom and Dad were likely being held, within the next few days. So a quick, but safe, climb was absolutely necessary. In the cold the assent was taking much longer than anticipated and they'd had more than a couple of close calls. But, some of those close calls had to do with the evil interference from demonic forces.

Satan had obviously called for reinforcements to conduct attacks on the travelers, and they were running into obstacles of all kinds along the way. A loose boulder here, sliding shale there, a root that looked like a sturdy hand hold suddenly pulling loose. But, the travelers had two advantages. And no amount of evil intention could take them away.

First, they could see the demons who were perpetrating the assaults. So, they were better prepared to resist. Second, they had angels surrounding them on every side, angels who would even keep them aloft if that's what it took. After all, in these times and circumstances, the message of the Gospel was in serious danger. The devils didn't have a chance, not with the forces of the Lord to contend with. All their evil interference did was confirm to the travelers that they were on the right track. So, their resolve was merely strengthened.

Just as the sun was beginning its winter descent in the Western sky, they climbed over a jutting, rock ledge that put them directly on a ridge peppered with possible places to set up camp. In no time at all they had ferreted out a cave big enough for all four bedrolls and a modest fire. They were ecstatic, and went about setting up to cook supper. Tom filled the water bottles from a nearby icy stream, and Jason got a cozy blaze started. Grace sharpened a couple of sticks with which to skewer rabbits for roasting, and built 'Y' structures in the fire pit on which to hang them, ever the eternal optimist.

Gabby headed out with her weapon, just as the sun was beginning to set, and happened upon some unsuspecting prey within yards of their cave. Her shots were quick and her aim true, and in no time at all she'd bagged, skinned and cleaned their meal, throwing the furs and innards over the cliff's edge, so as not to attract any carnivorous, night-time visitors.

As they all sat facing the fire, salivating over the wonderful aromas filling the cave, Jason prayed. "Lord, we are thankful and grateful for your abundant love and favor today. Thank you for your angels that surround us. Thank you for the wonderful meal you've set before us. Thank you that we are one day closer to finding Mom and Dad. Thank you for keeping us healthy and safe. And thank you for keeping those that we love healthy and safe as well. Lord, we give you all the praise and all the glory for all these things and more. For only you are worthy. In Jesus' wonderful Name we pray. Amen."

"I hope they're okay. Mom and Dad I mean. With

Mom's health being the way it is, I worry about her. And, if Dad is being held anywhere near her, and he sees someone treating her with anything but total respect, I'd be willing to bet he'd get himself in more than a little trouble trying to protect her."

"I agree that your dad would do anything he could to protect your mom. There's is a special love bond between those two. However, I don't think you give your mom enough credit. I think she is a lot stronger than you know. And, as far as your dad goes. We might think he's a bit of a hot head."

"Hey, I didn't say that. I just meant he tends to find causes in which he can use his justifiable anger in a positive way."

"Okay, I agree that he's a good guy to have around in a fight with the enemy. But, I think he can lay low too. You know, choose his battles wisely. I don't think he would risk both of their safety and freedom doing anything stupid. Don't worry. We will find them, and soon we will all be together and safe."

"Kakos, Sir, I have news."

"Good news I hope."

"No Sir. I'm afraid not."

"Why, why is it you are always bringing me bad news?"

"Well, Sir, it has to do with the people we are up against. We simply don't have the power to overcome the guardians who surround them. I've told you that over and over." She didn't see the blow coming until it was too late. When she hit the far wall, with a loud thud, the sound resonated throughout the halls of hell.

"You don't get to speak to me in that manner, and with that familiar attitude, wench. And, how dare you try to 're-mind' me what you've said before. As if you are intending to make me look stupid, or small. You do not command me. Do you hear? Now, get up and get something figured out. Send more troops, if that's what it takes. I do not want them to reach the woman's mother and father."

Keres rose slowly, wishing with everything inside her that she had the power to take him down. For millennia she'd had to endure his abuse. And, to think, there was even a time when she felt a little sorry for him. No, he deserved to be here more than anyone, and she was tired of dealing with him. The end of all things could not come quickly enough for her. No matter how much pain and suffering it caused her, it couldn't possibly be as bad as what she put up with from this maniac every single day. Why had she ever followed him as he followed Satan? These were decisions for which she would pay for all of eternity.

"Dan? Hey, Dan, are you up yet?"

"Yes ma'am. I've already been outside. The eggs are in the basket in the kitchen."

"My, aren't you the industrious one? What are you doing upstairs again?

"Anna, who used to live in this room before me?"

"I'm pretty sure that was David's room."

"Who is David?" As he walked down the stairs with a small box in his hands.

"David is my older brother, but he died before I ever got a chance to meet him. What have you got there?"

"After I collected the eggs, I went back upstairs to dress and I stepped on a floorboard that squeaked. It's the same one that always squeaks whenever I step on it. So, I figured I'd better find out what the deal was. It lifted up pretty easy. This box was in the hole. It must be his treasures, don't you think?"

"I don't know, Dan. Maybe it is."

"Do you think we should look?"

"Somehow, I don't think he'd mind. Go ahead and open it up buddy."

"Hello ladies. I've already talked to the men on the other side of the camp, so I will mostly be filling you in on what we've decided. I'm hoping you will all want to be a part of this. We plan to fight our way out of this prison camp at the end of the week. Come in close. I don't want to be overheard, and I don't want to take a long time in explanations. It wouldn't do anyone any good if I'm caught in here.

"Yes Sir. I've been following him. He had a meeting with the men last night and he's in with the women right now. He thinks he's pretty slick."

"Did you check his weapons stash?"

"Yes Sir. I've been emptying them out as he brings them in. I put sticks in the bottom of the pile, so there are only two real rifles in the whole stash, and those are on top. He wouldn't ever know unless he lifts the plastic, and he's usually in a rush to drop off the munitions and get back to camp before someone notices he's gone."

"So, you've left him with two functioning rifles?"

"No Sir. I removed the firing pins in the two weapons that are left in the hollow tree. I've also been removing ammunition, and filling the shell boxes with gravel, in case he picks one up to move it. He's going to have quite a surprise in store when he attempts to arm his insurgents. I will almost feel sorry for him, when he has to look them all in the eyes to tell them he's been duped, and he's gotten them all killed."

"Good job, soldier. Keep tracking him. I want to know everywhere he goes, even before he knows he's going there. You got that? We will stay on this until they make their move, then we will bury them all."

"Yes Sir. On it Sir."

Waking in a warm cave was a blessing. Gracie rolled over and watched her husband's chest rise and fall in rhythm to her own breathing. From the beginning he'd been there for her, protected her and adored her. They truly were kindred spirits. And, not just in the fact that they both had the gift of spiritual sight, but in the way they thought and believed. She ached with love for him. And then when she looked at her daughter, tears sprang to her eyes. She was almost perfect. God's instrument on earth, and a product of their undying love. What a true miracle she was. Grace knew she was blessed among women, and owed every single bit of it to her Lord. Oh, how often she just stopped and thought, these days, "God is good".

Jason opened his eyes. "So, how long have you been laying there staring at me?"

"Not long enough. You are very cute when you sleep."

"What about when I'm awake?"

"You are also cute when you are awake."

"Come here you." Jason grabbed her and pulled her close. Wrapping his arms around her tiny frame, he kissed her long and hard."

"Mom, Dad, hey, you are not alone, you know. I would say "get a room", but that is kind of out of the realm of possibility, so please stop before you make your daughter ill."

"You hush now, baby girl."

"Okay everyone. I won't ask what's going on, but please remember there are others in the cave." Laughing, Tom rose and tossed more sticks on the fire. "Anyone for coffee or tea?"

"That sounds great. We only have a few biscuits and a little cheese left. But we do have some sunflower seeds left in the bag."

"Sounds good to me. We should save the MREs for later. How much longer do you think, before we reach the detention camp?"

"Gabby, I already told you we've never been there. I'm not sure about the distance. But I do know you're starting to make me remember the little girl who used to ask, "Are we there yet?" from the back seat of the car, within five minutes of leaving the house. And I will remind you of what I told you then."

"I know, Mom, I know. We'll get there when we get there. I'll have to come up with more wild game for supper, so if anyone sees a likely target, let me know."

"Sure thing baby girl."

Consider how many are my foes, and with what violent hatred they hate me. Oh, guard my soul, and deliver me! Let me not be put to shame, for I take refuge in you. May integrity and uprightness preserve me, for I wait for you.

Psalm 25:19-21

CHAPTER 10

"Anna, this is really weird."

"What is it buddy?"

"There's only two things in the box."

"That's not so weird, Dan. What are the two things?"

"Well, one of them is a dead butterfly. It's a really pretty one, but it's dead, and kind of crunchy."

"Of course it's dead, silly. I think it would be much weirder if it was alive inside that box. What is the second thing?"

"It's a letter."

"A letter? Does it say who the letter is for?"

"Yeah, that's the really weird part. It's for you, Anna. I thought you said he died before you ever met him?"

"He did. Hand it here, Dan, please. Oh, you're right, this is highly weird. Where is Luke? I need him to see this."

"Kakos, Sir, you are going to want to hear this."

"More bad news I take it?"

"Yes Sir, really bad news."

"Well, spill it wench."

"Sir, they've found the letter."

"I thought we decided that letter was lost. Didn't we have Anna looking for that thing when she was in our control all those years ago?"

"Yes, Sir. At our direction she looked all through the house and couldn't find a thing. But, now she is grown and the little boy she and her fiancée have taken in has discovered the letter in a box under a floorboard. What can we do?"

"I wish there was something we could do, but I don't have any answers. Now I'll be forced to tell the boss. He is going to be singularly displeased about this. Everything is disintegrating around us."

"Do you have any orders for the troops, Sir?"

"Yes, tell them to stay on the travelers. We must keep them from reaching the woman's parents. This plan is getting away from us, and we can't allow that. Tell them they have my orders to throw everything we have at their targets."

"Yes Sir. Right away Sir."

"Nancy, are you alright?"

"Yes, Doris. I was just thinking about my kids and doing some praying."

"Do you really think we're going to get out of here?"

"I believe that whatever God has planned for us will happen. I'm hoping that his plans for me are to see my kids again, but if that doesn't happen then I will see them again in glory."

"I'm kind of scared. I mean about the fighting. I'm not really afraid of dying, I guess. I know I'll be with the Lord when I die. But I'm afraid of letting people down. Mike is expecting us all to fight, and I don't think I'm very good at that. Do you think you can fight right along with the men?"

"I'm going to try. I've never really been in a physical fight before, so we'll see. And, I think you might surprise yourself. When you are backed up against a wall, another part of you will emerge. A part you never knew existed. You know, like when a car rolls onto a child. That child's mother is suddenly filled with superhuman strength and is able to lift the car and save her child."

"Well, we'll hope so anyway. I will pray too. I'm going to pray for God to give each of us superhuman strength to lift ourselves out of this prison."

"That's good, Doris. He is the only one who can do

that. Just like Pastor Roy always says, we must never, ever, ever, ever stop praying."

Their morning was filled with more climbing, and more walking. They stopped for a tasty lunch of MREs, and Gabby bagged, and cleaned three squirrels. Along with the four handfuls of frozen, dried berries she'd found along the way, and the few remaining sunflower seeds, they would make a tasty supper.

As they progressed into the afternoon, strange things began to take place. First, a boulder seemingly 'slipped' from a ledge above, and tumbled toward them. They barely escaped, and that, only with the help of their heavenly soldiers. Next, the ground gave way, to create a hole beneath their feet, almost swallowing Gabby alive. Again, if it had not been for their winged warrior guard, they would surely have fallen to their deaths. And then, a giant tree suddenly cracked and fell, almost crushing the group beneath its enormous branches. Quick action by their angel guardians thwarted another disaster. It was abundantly clear that these 'accidents' were contrived by demons, some seen and many hidden. In other words, the travelers must be getting closer to their destination, and Satan has given the order to pull out all stops.

Completely exhausted, by the time they reached shelter for the evening, they found a sizeable cavern in which to camp for the night. Jason gathered wood, enough to last through till morning, and some pine branches with which to secure the cave opening. Tom filled water bottles and pots, while Grace started a nice blaze. Air temperatures had fallen as the group rose higher on the mountain, so a good fire would be much appreciated.

Gabby skewered two of the squirrels to roast on the fire, and cut the third up for the largest pot of water; breaking up the bones to add their flavorful marrow. A nice soup, filled with tender chunks of meat, would provide a great protein boost in the morning. Perhaps not a conventional breakfast, but tasty nevertheless. She added the berries to a little water and mashed them before warming them over the flames, adding the seeds at the last moment.

With bedrolls laid out, and the front door protected, the travelers stretched out to await their supper and plan strategy. But first, they would pray. Tom began. "Lord God, we want to thank You for our safety today. We know we wouldn't be here without Your divine intervention, and that of Your angels. We are eternally grateful. Thank you for the delicious meal we are about to eat. We ask you to bless it to our bodies, to make us strong, and to help us in the work You have given us to do. We pray, Lord, for safety on our trip, and success in our mission. In Jesus' Name. Amen."

None of the four had ever eaten squirrel before, but they all agreed it was delicious. They cleaned up and settled in for the night. But, Satan's minions had one more surprise for the group that night. The biggest wolf any of them had ever seen, or even imagined, like something out of a science fiction novel. It scratched and pawed, growling ferociously, at the pine boughs in the cave entrance, all night long. Probably only deterred by the blaze inside. They agreed that they would take turns on watch throughout the night, keeping the fire burning. But, with all the scary noise, none of them rested well.

In the morning, the wolf was gone like smoke in the wind, but even with breakfast in their systems exhaustion, and frustration, seemed to be their constant companion all morning.

"That is the strangest thing I've ever heard. So, he was

dead before the family adopted you?"

"Yes, that's what I'm saying. He died years before I came along. He and my sister Bella both died long before I was on the scene. Don't you think it's odd that he would write a letter addressed to me?"

"I absolutely agree. However, all we know so far is that the envelope is addressed to 'Anna'. Is it possible that there was another Anna? You are not the only person with that name, you know."

"You're right. I guess I jumped to conclusions. I'm seeing coincidences where there are probably none to be found."

"Now, having said that. You haven't even opened the envelope yet. We aren't ever going to know what's in the letter unless you read it, don't you think?"

"Yes, of course. I'm a little afraid, if truth be told."

"Do you want me to read it?"

"No. I should read it, I guess. He is my brother after all. Okay, here it goes." Anna ripped off the end of the long envelope, blew in the end, and retrieved the two pages tucked inside. The message was hand written, in almost impossibly, neat, cursive script.

"Dear Anna,

"I'm sure this letter will seem strange to you. After all, to receive a communication from someone you've never met is unusual. But I have been instructed by the Lord, yes the Lord, to deliver a message to you, little sister. What an odd statement, huh? I thought so too, so I guess I should explain a little.

"I've always been a bit of an outsider. That is, until Mike and Nancy took me in, along with our sisters Grace, Lilly and Bella. I've never felt so loved, as I do in this family. And I will be eternally grateful for their compassion and kindness. I want you to know that even though the people who will kill me, try to make it look like I died by my own hand, I didn't. Bella introduced me to Jesus, who I asked to be my Savior and Lord, and I would never so disrespect Him.

"Anyway, on with the story. I went to bed one night, and in my dreams I met with Jesus, who told me of some future events I needed to share. First He told me that when I woke I would think the entire encounter was only a dream, but not to believe that lie.

"He told me about my death, Bella's death, and Grace's abilities. He told me about Jason, and Tom, and Grace's marriage to Jason. He even told me that Grace would have a daughter, named Gabriel, whose powers of sight would far surpass those of her parents. He told me about you and Luke, and the little boy, Daniel, who you will eventually adopt. I know that Daniel has the gift of spiritual sight, just as Grace, Jason, and Gabriel have.

"The Lord also told me about what would happen in our country and in the world, during your lifetime, Anna. And, He wanted me to tell you that, though it may seem like the end of the world, the time is not quite right. Not yet. This time will, instead, be a test of the nation. A nation founded on the Word of God, but overtaken by those who oppose Christ. Our country has gone through many tests, but this one will bring the faithful together as no other has. Not in the history of our great nation.

"The country has been cruelly tricked into the deadly vacuum that is socialism, and is dying a slow and painful death. But, it can still be revitalized. This is a time of great revival little sister.

"The new socialist government has built prison camps in the mountains, and they will be out to imprison all Christians. Using lies and deception to do so. Yes, Satan has been up to his old tricks again. Mike and Nancy will be taken, and you will be their only hope of escape.

"I've been asked to give you this message. "Tell Jim, at your next meeting, that he is to take a group to the mountain, to free the prisoners there. Tell him that God will see him through. And that he should know Mindy's dad is a spy."

"A new grassroots movement will spring up around the country. You and Luke will become involved, and you will do things you've never dreamed you were capable of. Don't be afraid to take Daniel with you. He has spiritual sight, and will be of great help to you.

"I know how crazy this all must sound. Even as I write this letter, it sounds insane to me. But, I believe the Lord has actually spoken to me and given me this message to pass along to you, little sister.

"I wish we could have met in life. But, I know we shall meet in glory. Peace and Grace in Jesus.

David"

"Wow, Anna. That is some seriously weird stuff."

"But, it has to be true, doesn't it?"

"I don't know. How could he know any of that, all those years ago?"

"That's why it has to be true, Luke. There is no possible way he could have known all those details, unless he was getting them from someone who knows everything. Don't you see?"

"Yeah, I guess you're right. Holy cow, Anna."

"I'll tell you what I found strange. He said I would be Mom and Dad's only hope. How can that be? Grace, Jason, Gabby and Tom went after Mom and Dad. Surely they will find them and bring them home, won't they? I don't understand."

"I don't know if we're supposed to understand, Anna. I think we're just supposed to obey, don't you?"

"Hey, you guys. Remember the letter talked about me too. I'm coming, and we're going to save everyone."

"No, Dan, I don't think it's safe for you."

"No, Anna, I agree with Dan. His sight will be invaluable. We will be meeting with Jim and the rest of the guys in a couple of days. We need to start getting our ducks in a row, so we will be ready to go when the time is right. I am greatly encouraged. It sounds like God is as sick of socialism as we are. And, it also seems as though He has a plan to get us out of the middle of this mess we've gotten ourselves into. We need to get out the weapons your dad hid away, and begin getting things ready."

"Oh, Dad didn't have any weapons hidden away. He

turned them all in when the government held the manda-tory gun collections few years ago."

"Actually, Anna, your Dad saved back quite a few of his favorites, and plenty of ammunition too. Where do you think Jason and Grace got those rifles they took with them? I believe he knew a time like this would be coming. He used to tell me that, "The right of the people to keep and bear arms shall not be infringed. A well regulated militia, composed of the body of the people, trained to arms, is the best and most natural defense of a free country." That is a quote from James Madison, so I know he believed in the old adage about prying his weapons out of his cold dead hands."

"I don't believe this. He told you, but he didn't tell me? Why would he do that?"

"Babe, it's not like you've ever shown any interest in weapons, or war, is it? He just wanted you to be protected."

"Who else knew?"

"Well, Grace and Jason, and Gabby, and Tom, and probably Lilly."

"So, I'm the only one who didn't know? I find that highly insulting."

"Don't be angry, honey. You never showed an interest in

learning to shoot, did you?"

"And you did?"

"Well, yes."

"I didn't even know you knew how to shoot. Am I living in the twilight zone?"

"I'm sorry, Anna. No one was trying to leave you out. You just always seemed much more interested in running the restaurants, than training for war. We should go downstairs and take inventory, so we know how much fire power we have before the meeting on Monday."

"Okay, it just might take a minute or two for me to get over the shock of all this. Lead away, since you seem to know where this arsenal of weaponry is."

Down in the basement, way in the farthest back, behind a false wall, was Mike's collection of firearms. Shotguns and rifles galore, along with hand guns. Anna wondered how he'd managed to hold onto the pistols since, before confiscation, registration for handguns had always been so much more stringent than it was for rifles and shotguns. Boxes and boxes of ammunition, a few compact bows with a plethora of arrows, and a vast assortment of other camping and survival gear filled the space. Anna's mouth dropped open. How could she have never known about all this?

Gather up your bundle from the ground, O you who dwell under siege! For thus says the Lord: Behold, I am slinging out the inhabitants of the land at this time, and I will bring distress on them, that they may feel it.

Jeremiah 10:17-18

CHAPTER 11

Mike was readying the men for their coming insurgency, while Nancy was working to calm the women. It wasn't that they didn't want to participate. It was only that they were frightened. Most of them had never been in combat of any kind. The closest they'd been to war, was raising teenagers. And, as scary as that might be, it usually didn't involve bullets. Everything was set for tomorrow night, and nerves were frayed all around.

What none of the revolutionaries knew, was that security on base was all set and ready for them. They would be shut down before their rebellion began. The base commander had plans for them. And, there would likely be injured among them for their trouble.

Mike made one more trip under the floorboards of Nancy's barracks that night, just to confirm that they were all on the same page. He was being watched. As he came up from the floor, his wife approached. "Is everything okay?"

"I'm just checking to be sure everyone is ready for tomorrow."

"We are, Mike. We're just waiting for your word."

"We're all set as well. Are you okay? You look skeptical."

"I am, Mike, and I'm frightened. You know I've been uneasy about this from the start. I don't want anyone to get hurt. But, I also don't want to spend the rest of my life in here, or to die by the hand of the government, because I am no longer convenient for them."

"Then it's all set. As we're coming back to the barracks from supper, when everyone is in the yard, I will have rifles hidden around the compound in designated spots. I'm going to go out with a couple of the guys, after lights out tonight, to bring the rifles and ammunition back in. Be sure your ladies know when to duck for cover, and be sure they have their weapons at the ready, for when we start clearing the guards out of the way."

"Mike. I know you're trying to do what's best for everyone. No matter how this turns out, I love you."

"I love you too, Nance. And, it's all going to turn out fine. Don't worry. If I don't see you before, I'll see you tomorrow night."

Their whole day had been filled with one disaster after another. Some of the mishaps were caused by demons stalking them and stirring up trouble. But, others originated from decisions made through pure exhaustion. They were getting closer by the minute. Grace could feel it. But, it was clear there were forces who did not want her parents rescued. She was more determined than ever now to see this through.

As dusk set in, an accident caused by a misstep almost took Gabby from them. Whether it was through the work of demons, or just being plain old tired; ground shifted and her feet slipped from the ledge. She hung by one hand from roots jutting out of the side of the cliff. With her shoulder wrenched out of socket, the pain was so excruciating it took her breath away, and it took the last of her strength to hang on as she awaited rescue. Quickly the other three travelers used ingenuity and speed to devise a plan that would save her from certain death.

Rope was fashioned into a harness. One end of the rope was draped around a boulder, and then wrapped around the trunk of a nearby, dead tree. The two men held on with their whole strength. Grace put her legs through the holes designed for that purpose, took a firm hold of the remaining rope; looping the slack through her fist; and lowered herself gingerly down the cliff face. When she got to Gabby, who, in spite of help from her angel guards, was barely holding on any longer, she put her daughter on her lap and tied her in. From there it was mostly up to the men. She tugged the rope and they began to pull with all their might, until they could see evidence of the girls at the edge of the jagged ledge. They tied the rope off and ran to grab the girl's hands to help them over the tangle of rock and roots, on to the ledge.

Once they were safely topside, the women stood hugging and shaking uncontrollably. Their group decided that was enough excitement for one day. And, since they still had MREs in Gabby's pack, there would be no hunting tonight. They found a nearby cave and set up for the night. Gabby thought that this was probably the closest she'd ever come to death, even considering their foreign missions trips, and came to the realization that she'd probably considered herself more indestructible than she actually was, all things considered. She'd just naturally assumed that her guardian angels would always be able to save her, no matter the circumstances. She would never make that assumption again.

That night her mother prayed. "Heavenly Father, we

thank You for Your favor and help in the time of trouble. We praise You for Your rescue of Gabby today. We know that You love her Lord, and that You alone are good. Father, keep us safe as we get closer to the camp where Mom and Dad are being held, and help us Lord to overcome our enemies. We do pray Father, that Your will be done in all things. Thank you Lord. In Jesus' Name. Amen."

Jason collected enough wood to see them through the night, and once again placed pine boughs, in the cave opening, but, as on previous nights, nocturnal visitors made such a ruckus that none of them slept well. Again, they would rise in the morning, even more exhausted than they'd felt going to bed the night before.

Mike waited until the entire camp was sound asleep, or so he thought. With three volunteers, he snuck out of the camp by way of his usual route, and made his way to the hollowed out tree where his weapons cache was located. When he unveiled the stash, the men gasped. So many weapons. This was going to make their justified uprising much easier. They were all excited, until Mike lifted the two rifles from the top of the stack. Beneath the two rifles on top was plastic, and under the plastic was only piles of sticks. Mike's mind whirled in disbelief. "How can this be? I put them all right here. Where could they have gone?" At that moment he knew. Nancy had been right all along. It had been much too easy to walk off with the camp's armory. He knew now that he'd been followed, was probably being followed right now. He'd not only put himself in danger, but those men who volunteered to follow him out here. So many were counting on him, and he'd let them all down. He grabbed the two, and only, rifles and handed one off to the nearest man. "We've got to get out of here. They know."

As they turned to run, lights flooded the area. They couldn't see into the lights, but Mike had no doubt the base commander was at the end of the glare. "You may as well put the weapons down, Mr. O'Sullivan. The firing pins have been removed for your safety. Now, turn around, so the officers can cuff you. If you cooperate, it will go much easier on all of you. And yes, we know all about your plans. We have been following you from the beginning. I guess you aren't quite as smart as you thought, huh?"

In the morning the ladies walked to the mess hall for breakfast, completely unaware of the previous night's goings on. When they walked through the door, they stopped dead in their tracks. Nancy, and the wives of Mike's three volunteers, gasped. Nancy wanted to run to Mike, but he stopped her with a look. He still thought the base commander didn't know she was his wife. He was wrong about that too.

The four men were displayed at the front of the building like bloody hunting trophies. Beaten so badly, they were barely recognizable. Chains held their hands, attached to rings in the wall, high above their heads. The floor beneath them was covered in blood and small bits of flesh from the flailing they had undergone, for hours and hours, throughout the night.

One of the men was missing an eye from the beating. All were missing teeth. And, none of them would have been able to stand on his own, if those chains were not holding them up. So, their shoulders and wrists were supporting their entire body weight, making it difficult to breathe and causing excruciating pain. They were, every one of them, in unimaginable agony.

They hung that way, helpless, as the ladies walked through the food line to get their scoop of oatmeal, piece of dry toast, and cup of chicory coffee. Nancy couldn't imagine eating. Her stomach was rebelling enough just to see her husband, bloody and bruised, hanging like so much butchered meat in front of the whole room. And, she knew her husband well enough to know, he was much more upset about being tricked, than he was about the beating. He would feel that he failed, that he'd let everyone down, and that everyone blamed him for whatever came next.

Her heart broke for him, as well as for the other men and their wives who also endured so much suffering. She didn't want to leave him there, but then, what could she possibly do? She couldn't wait to get out of the building, to go somewhere, anywhere that she could cry. It was impossible for her to watch him in so much pain and shame, knowing she couldn't do a thing to help him. And, just the effort of not letting the tears behind her eyes fall was giving her the most painful migraine she'd ever endured.

Neither Nancy, or Mike, would ever know what had gone wrong with their well laid plans. They didn't have spiritual sight like their daughter, so they couldn't have seen the red eyes and the demons with long talons guarding those traitors who walked in their midst. One turncoat in the men's barracks and one in the women's barracks. Mike simply never had a chance.

Anna and Luke were relieved to see Monday roll around. After supper they made their way to the local meeting. The first thing they did was take Jim aside and try to explain spiritual sight to him. It was clear that Mindy's dad was trying to get close enough to hear their conversation, but they kept their distance, their voices low and their information as simple as possible. When they were done Jim approached Mindy's dad. Voices started out mostly controlled, but quickly picked up pitch and volume, and ended with yelling. Mindy and her dad were escorted out of the meeting. But, now it was imperative that the group make some quick decisions, before the spy had a chance to make a citizen's complaint to authorities, about the purpose of their meetings.

If authorities got wind of Christians holding meetings in town, they would all be quickly arrested. And, if it got out that the purpose of their group was to plan a nation-

wide civil war, to take their country back from the socialists, well, let's just say that wouldn't play very well with the
powers that be.

Though the spy didn't know the details of their plans,
he did know the group's members were in possession of
'unlawful' weapons and ammunition, so they were sure a
visit from officials would be coming in pretty short order,
if they didn't take quick action.

Jim stood in front of the large group, Luke, Anna and
little Dan by his side, and explained to the members what
had just happened. Instead of jumping to the conclusion
that young Daniel was a freak, they chose to be grateful his gift had saved them from a terrible fate. Together
they quickly arranged for another, more secluded, meeting place, and set out for their individual homes to collect whatever weapons and meager supplies they might be
able to put together to take with them on a mission of
this magnitude. Thankfully, Jim had been in resent contact with other groups around the country, through what
many would consider 'old fashioned' means, and found
there were hundreds of thousands of homegrown militia
ready to do whatever they needed, to take back their beloved country, in the Name of the Lord Jesus. The revolu-

tion was growing rapidly.

"Kakos, Sir, I have some excellent news, Sir."

"At last! Tell me, Keres. What good news have you?"

"Sir, the escape plan devised by the woman's parents has been discovered and thwarted. Her father has been severely disciplined, along with his accomplices, and he is currently on display in their mess hall, for all to see."

"Hoorah! Finally, some news I can take to the boss. This isn't just good news, this is great news. Keep me posted on every detail."

"Yes Sir, absolutely!"

Throughout that day, and into the evening, the travelers made slow progress. Gabby's shoulder was badly injured, and she and Grace were both still shaken from the previous evenings near fatal mishap. Jason and Tom were keeping close tabs on the girls, as they'd both noticed a lack of critical attention from the ladies through the day's journey.

It would serve no purpose to show up at the camp and be unable to fight. They agreed this evening would be for rest and recuperation. The urgency of their mission had not lessened, but their fitness to do the job certainly had. A night's rest would be the best cure.

They found a cozy cave, and set up camp. Jason hunted while the women rested and Tom built a fire. He came back with two rabbits, and they all ate their fill before turning in. If night prowlers made noise that evening, it wasn't detected by the group. They were much too exhausted to notice the racket.

"Are we going camping, Anna?"

"Yes, Daniel. We are going to meet with our group, but then we are going to save our family."

"You mean like David said in the letter?"

"What?"

"He said you were their only hope. I think we should save them, and then save the country!"

"That sounds like a good plan to me."

"I agree, Jason. That does sound like a good plan, Dan. We are glad to have you on our side young man."

"I'm glad to have you on my side too."

Nancy's entire day had been an emotional roller coaster ride to hell and back. The four injured men were left hanging in the mess hall until after supper. A whole day. Nancy tried to claim sickness, to get out of her mandatory chores, hoping to avoid the horror of seeing her husband hanging, and bleeding, from that wall. But, her matron wouldn't give her leniency. She was probably following orders in that regard. They must know, she concluded. They have to know I'm Mike's wife, and aren't going to let me escape the punishment of being his coconspirator. She wasn't afraid. And, she wouldn't have minded the punishment. It would be better than standing back and watching him suffer.

After supper she watched through the window as the four men were dragged back to their barracks. They weren't transported to medical. So, she could only assume that meant they would receive no treatment. After all, the commander certainly wouldn't be anxious to see any of them recover. That would only make his job easier.

Mike's injuries were painful, considering the beating

he'd taken, but couldn't compare with the guilt he felt at leading his three friends into that trap. True they had volunteered, but only on the assurance from him that all was well. Les and Bill were as bad off as he was, but Pete. Pete's right eye was gone, and he seemed to be in much worse shape overall than the rest of them.

Actually, It was hard for him to believe they'd been spared death, and he wasn't altogether convinced that wouldn't still be an option, from some of the comments he'd heard from the guards who dragged them back to their barracks. It seemed there might be an inquiry into other conspirators, leading to an ultimate hanging, of any found guilty of treason, by the board.

Mike knew he couldn't let that happen. He also knew the rest of the guys felt the same way. They would never let their wives be implicated. So, they would assume all the blame, no matter the torture or threats of death.

For these things I weep; my eyes flow with tears; for a comforter is far from me, one to revive my spirit; my children are desolate, for the enemy has prevailed.

Lamentations 1:16

CHAPTER 12

By midday the travelers had gone nearly fifteen miles, a much better show of effort than the previous day. Gabby's shoulder was still aching from her accident. But, after Mom and Dad managed to get it seated back in socket properly, the pain had subsided significantly. Breakfast was sparse that morning, dandelion tea and a few seeds, and it would appear lunch was heading in the same lackluster direction. They did still have four MREs left in her backpack, which was now being carried by her dad to save the strain on Gabby's shoulder, but they'd decided as a group to save those emergency rations in case of a real emergency.

Grace spotted a couple of rabbits and slowly pulled out her crossbow. With speed and precision supper was secured, so at least they wouldn't starve tonight.

Off in the distance they saw a column of smoke rising into the cold winter air, and knew instinctively that it must be coming from the prison for which they had been searching. They would set up camp early, eat and get some rest, then scout the area in question during the dark of night.

Once they could get an idea of what they were up against, they'd have a better idea how to proceed with this life saving mission.

Gabby was fine with the short day, and looking forward to getting in out of the cold to rest her aching shoulder. Grace was behaving like the proverbial mother hen, hovering over her daughter to make sure she was doing okay. And Dad was shaking his head and chuckling.

The smell of roasting rabbit, filling their small cave, was heavenly. They were all starved half to death by the time the meat was cooked. A half a rabbit each was just the right amount of succulent, greasy, moist perfection to fill each of them up nicely. And once they were done eating, and licking their fingers clean, they sat back to plan that night's surveillance expedition, before settling down for a nap.

Anna was amazed at how much equipment her dad had packed away in his secret stash. They loaded up all the supplies they would need for themselves, and then they grabbed as much extra as they could fit in the wagons to help other families who might not have enough. Luke, pulling a vegetable cart to and fro, took several trips to the agreed upon meeting site for that night. Taking a huge risk, he had to be careful not to be followed. He hauled load after load of weapons, ammunition, bullet proof vests, cartons of MREs, water purification equipment, blankets, tents and every manner of camping gear and survival paraphernalia one could imagine.

Mike had obviously been collecting for years. Aware of the direction their government was headed, for quite some time. A Marine, Mike was, and always had been a patriot, and a man who wanted to keep his family safe. He'd bought and squirreled away anything that looked like it might be useful someday, planning for just such an event. That's what a Marine did.

Once the wagons of equipment and supplies were off loaded at the meeting site, Luke came back for Anna, Lilly and the boy. They loaded the last of their supplies, then took time to have a last meal in the home they loved, knowing they would most likely never see the place again. It was a simple meal of vegetable omelets, yogurt, and biscuits, but it was delicious. Anna washed up, and put everything away lovingly, and neatly. That was just who she was. She wouldn't have dreamed of leaving a messy kitchen for anything in the world. Not if she could help it. Even though she would likely not be the one coming back to use it again.

Luke watched her with tears stinging his eyes. He knew how much it was hurting her to leave the only place she'd ever really thought of as 'home'. Anna didn't know when she might have another kitchen to cook in, but she would always remember that this one was where her mom and dad taught her just about everything she knew concerning the culinary arts.

They would bring the two goats and all the chickens along, plus as many of the fresh fruits and vegetables as they could load into the back of the wagon. Daniel would ride in with the animals, to keep them calm, and Luke would pull the wagon, with Anna and Lilly walking beside him. There would be children in the group who needed milk, and the eggs and fresh produce would always come in handy.

They'd contacted Lilly before they decided to leave with their new friends. Poor Lilly hadn't wanted to trouble them with her problems; and they'd not been aware that she was one of those whose clinic had recently been closed by the government. Yes, closed down for good, for the terrible sin of treating people that they had not authorized her to treat. She'd argued that she was not billing the government for the treatments she provided, and had assumed all costs herself, but evidently that wasn't enough to satisfy them. Socialists want to be in complete control, so anyone moving outside their purview, is instantly shut down.

Lilly had come to realize that even if what she was doing as a doctor was purely for humanitarian reasons, and not for personal profit, she would eventually be arrested. As long as her actions didn't align with their socialist agenda, she would be halted immediately, and made to pay the consequences.

As fed up, with this farce of a government, as the rest of the nation, Lilly had decided enough was enough.

She was angry that so many ill informed young people had voted to put this governing body in power, with its unsustainable policies and programs. And knew that over the past few years they had slowly, but surely, seen the folly of their decisions, and the error of their ways. Those misguided people were discovering what others had known for centuries. Socialism doesn't work. It makes those powerful individuals at the top, more powerful, and richer, each and every day; while the common man starves to death in the streets. If only they had listened before it was too late.

For those many reasons, Lilly would be coming with

them. It would be good to have an experienced doctor on board. When she arrived for supper, she came with several bags of medical supplies from her closed clinic. The guards who'd come in to shut her place down several days before, had been instructed to seize all of her supplies and equipment. And they did. Well, most of them anyway. She thought it was terrible that they could just march in and take things that she had worked and paid for, out of her own pocket, over these past many years. So, knowing ahead of time what they would do, she'd hidden as many items, as she could ferret away, to take with her. Especially important were the lifesaving medicines that could work miracles for those afflicted on their journey.

Once they arrived, for the final unloading, at the meeting site, Jim greeted them warmly. He'd never met Lilly before, and instantly wanted to introduce her to his brother, Max. Anna smiled. "Hmmm," She thought, "This just might prove to be a match made in heaven, for the sister who thought she'd never marry." At least judging by the shy smile blooming on her lovely face.

Instantly the work began. Making sure that any adult or older teen, who was even mildly proficient with firearms, had a weapon and ammunition, was their first effort. They divided supplies and equipment among families, for the purpose of carrying it to the next station. With no gas rations; now that Christians had been cut off from what remained of the nation's existing supplies; this journey would be on foot and with wagons pulled by strong men. It would be absolutely necessary to hide weapons beneath various household items, as the wagons were likely to be searched at every junction from here to there.

Jim, and the group, agreed they would travel to the base of the mountain; since they were as interested in finding the detention center as Luke and Anna were. There they would set up camp and get the women, the elderly and the children settled. Then, a large group of armed men would make their way into the mount to the hidden prison camp. Many of the group had family members who'd also gone missing, and they were sure those loved ones were being held at that same facility.

As a united force they would raid the base, cutting off communications to the outside world to protect their actions, restraining the guards or killing them if absolutely necessary, and they would free all their family members. Once that was done, they would rejoin those in the lower base camp, and go on to meet up with other rebel groups who were set to free other prison camps and join the revolution. They were bound and determined that they would take their country back, one detention center, and one city at a time. And, if they had anything at all to say about it, America would once again be a nation under God, "Of the people and for the people".

Nancy hadn't seen Mike all day, and was worried about what might have become of him after he was taken off display. Then, at supper, the four in chains were paraded, like ragged, bloody puppets, before the women in the mess hall who were attempting to eat their meal. The men were a pitiful sight, bruised and battered in their dried blood encrusted clothing, as they came shuffling in. Handcuffs on their wrists and shackles on their ankles.

Commander Ford delivered an impassioned speech about loyalty to the socialist state, and what would happen if anyone ever tried to escape again. Then he stepped up behind Pete, grabbed him by the hair, pulled his head back, and slit his throat so deep he nearly severed his head from his body.

As he released Pete's hair, and the injured man dropped

to the floor; vainly groping at his fatal wound, blood pouring from his neck to pool on the concrete floor; the commander smiled. Women screamed, several vomited, and many backed up as blood flowed closer to their slippered feet. Pete's wife fainted, hitting her head on a nearby table as she went down. And, as Nancy's eyes met his, the commander's smile turned into the most vile grin Nancy had ever seen on a human being in her life. But, then, perhaps he wasn't human after all. She and her family had certainly encountered enough demons in their years of ministry. After all, how could any human garner so much joy from the suffering of others?

The four men were still chained together, so, as Pete's body convulsed in death their legs were yanked from under them to tumble to the blood soaked floor. The commander put one foot on the back of the dying man; who was gurgling through rivers of blood as he tried, and failed, to breathe; and pushed down hard. Pete soon gave up the struggle and succumbed to a hideous death, as women in the crowd wailed and cried and tried to revive his wife.

"Let this be a warning to all of you. This man, with his damaged sight, would've been of little use to me going forward. It was easy for me to kill him. I have told you all before that I do not care about any of you, and if you are not be able to pull your weight in this camp, you will be of no use to me either. At that point you may as well be dead, and I will see to it that you quickly are.

"I assure you, that if you attempt escape, you will be caught. And, if you are caught, your last moments on this earth will not be pleasant. There is no one out there in the 'real world' who cares about you anymore. There is no one searching for you, to set you free. You will be here until you die, one way or another. There is no hope of freedom. And, I promise you, every one of you. You do not want me as your enemy. As I said before, I will never care about you, but if you are useful to me you may live. However, if you cannot work you are my enemy, and I will make you wish you were dead."

At the very same time Pete's throat was being slit in the internment camp just North of their location, the travelers were settling down for a most needed nap. They would grab a few hours sleep, and then do some necessary reconnaissance, in the wooded area that surrounded the prison, in the blackness of night.

"Anna, are we almost there?"

"Daniel, it's going to take us a few days; with this many people to move; to make it all the way to the base of the mountain. You'll be able to tell when we're there, because there will be a big mountain in front of the wagons, and we won't be able to travel any further. Try to be patient, okay?"

"Thanks a lot. I was just wondering 'cause I'm hungry."

"I made that big bag of biscuits, Dan. Just nibble on one of those for now. I'm going to guess that everyone is hungry, and we all must wait till we set up camp for the night to do anything about it."

"Okay, I'll eat a biscuit."

"Well don't make it sound like eating one of my biscuits is some kind of a punishment."

"Hey, hey, hey, you two. It's getting late and we're all tired. It sounds like some of us are getting a little cranky too. I'll ask Jim when he's planning to stop for the night. Do you think you two can be nice?"

"Yes Luke, we can be nice. Can't we, Anna?"

"Sure we can, but tell him I hope it will be soon. I'm sorry, Dan. I shouldn't have snapped at you."

"I'm sorry too, Anna."

Setting up camp that night was easy. Out in the open this way, the group didn't want to attract undue attention, so supper would be MREs and plenty of water. It was cold, with a couple inches of fresh snow on the ground, so hopefully, waterproof tarps would act as insulators between the snow and the collapsible tents; and would create an additional layer of warmth before bedrolls and sleeping bags were laid down. Thankfully, between supplies other families brought, and all the extras Luke and Anna donated for the journey, every family had a tent. It would be imperative at night that they cuddle close, to share body heat, with nighttime lows currently in the single digits.

Luke and Anna slept with Dan between them; and, though he was a 'big boy' now, he didn't argue about the sleeping arrangements one single bit; because, for added warmth, they magnanimously allowed the goats and chickens to bunk in with them too.

Back in his barracks Mike was frozen to the core. Not from the cold, but from guilt and shock. His breath was coming in chest convulsing, heaving, gulps. He knew Pete would still be alive, if he hadn't hatched that whole stupid escape plan, and put all of their lives at risk. It should have been him. He'd said as much to the commander. Telling him that the plan was his alone, that he'd talked the other guys into helping. And, that if anyone was to blame, or to be punished, it should be him. That was why the commander chose Pete. He could tell that this one vicious, impactful act would make more of an impression on Mike than all the beatings in the world. This might be the one act that could squelch his 'hero' instincts for good. Knowing that his actions would have this much impact on those he cared about, would certainly make him stop and think before doing anything so foolish again.

This was the biggest reason Commander Ford had been chosen to warden the mountain encampment. His ruthlessness was well known among the U.N.s military elite. They'd simply chosen someone who could work with Christian prisoners, without getting taken in by their 'goody two shoes, Jesus wants us to love the world' temperament. Let's face it. It is darned hard to incarcerate and police people who haven't really done anything wrong; and only want to help everyone they meet; without getting inadvertently sucked into their strangely peaceful world.

This challenge was met in part by employing U.N. troops from non-Christian countries. Putting non-American, sometimes even anti-American, atheist personnel in charge of the Christian prisoners in camps around the country. The command believed they didn't have to worry about the possibility of bonds forming between the incarcerated and the U.N. workers in these cases.

However, command wasn't accounting for the power of the Gospel message, or the influence of the Holy Spirit.

On this pitch black, moonless night, with snow lightly falling, the travelers packed only their most essential gear and readied for their reconnaissance mission. Leaving most of their equipment in the cave, to keep their load as light as possible, would be vital while scouting the area. They'd be coming back this way later, to bed down for the remainder of the night and to ready themselves for the rescue mission tomorrow night.

For now, they needed only light weapons and water, and the warm boots and clothing they currently wore. Snow and clouds would cover their movements this night, and their tracks back to the cave upon completion of their mission, but made it more difficult to navigate the mountain in the dark. The weather could be a blessing in disguise, it would likely keep the guards inside tonight, which might give them time to look around unhindered, and then give them a chance to get back to home base where they would plan their attack.

Nancy woke with an uneasy feeling. She hoped that didn't mean Mike was in trouble again, and worrying brought on another high blood pressure headache. A pretty nasty one. Ashamed any time she worried, because Christians weren't supposed to worry, she reached out to the Lord, praying. "Lord, I know You love me. I know You love Mike too. Please forgive me for moments of doubt. I know that we can count on You to see all things to an outcome, which will be best for us, and will give You all the glory You deserve, Father. Remind me daily that You are still in control. That You are still on the throne. And, that Your will shall be done on earth as it is in heaven. Thank You for caring enough to listen. In Jesus' Name I pray. Amen." And then she mentally reached out to her husband. Hoping they might connect in some way. "Mike, feel the nudging from

Donna M. Young

the Lord. Please don't do anything else that will put you in harm's way. I need you to come out of this with me. I can't imagine my life without you. Please remember that God is good, and that He loves you, my wonderful husband."

At that moment, Mike did feel a nudging in his spirit. One that he knew was from the Lord, and his breathing calmed. He and Nancy would get out of this together. He could hear Nancy saying, "God is good." And, he countered. "All the time, Babe, all the time."

Proclaim this among the nations; Consecrate for war; stir up the mighty men. Let all the men of war draw near; let them come up. Beat your plowshares into swords, and your pruning hooks into spears; let the weak say, "I am a warrior."

Joel 3:9-10

CHAPTER 13

The mountain loomed before them. Those who would be on the team going to free the prisoners would ascend tomorrow at first light. Luke was already filling his backpack in anticipation of the mission. "Is that going to be enough for all three of us?"

"What do you mean, all three of us?"

"Daniel and I are going with you."

"No you are absolutely not going with me."

"Luke, there is no way I'm letting you leave me behind while you go off and rescue my family. And, without Daniel's sight, how will you know who are the bad guys? No, we are going with you. And, if you persist in arguing about it, we will just wait for you to leave and follow right behind you, so you don't really have a choice."

"You really are impossible, Anna."

"Oh, I know. You aren't the first person to tell me that. But, isn't it better for you to find that out now, instead of after we get married?"

"Okay, just pack a bag so you two will be ready to go first thing in the morning. I hope we don't all end up regretting this. You know we're most likely just going to be following right on the heels of Jason and Gracie anyway. We'll probably arrive just in time to clean up the mess they make capturing the base."

"I don't know, Luke. I've been getting a very uneasy feeling the last couple of days. Like maybe they are in trouble too. We might be rescuing more than just Mom and Dad. We will have to play it by ear, but we could be the only rescue coming for the whole lot of them."

"I think you're being paranoid, but let's be prepared for anything. Make sure you have a firearm too. And handle it first, so you'll know it's one you can make use of."

"Yes, Sir. Right away, Sir."

"Very funny, Anna. Very, very funny."

"I have another very serious question, Luke."

"What's that, Anna?"

"Will you marry me, and make me the happiest woman alive?"

"You know I will, Anna. What a goofy question. I already asked you, remember?"

"No, I mean tonight. I want to get married tonight, Luke. I don't know how this whole rescue mission is going to go, and if anything were to happen to either one of us, I want everyone to know that I am your wife. What do you think?"

"I think we should find Pastor Roy."

In the freezing cold, On the windswept plains of the mountain's base, Pastor Roy spoke anointed words of hope to the new couple, and they were joined in holy matrimony. It wasn't the wedding either of them had dreamed about, but it was one they would certainly never forget. That night Daniel slept in Lilly's tent with his animal menagerie.

Tens of thousands of groups, just like this one, some with hundreds of members and some even with thousands, were gathering all over the country, to raid, occupy and destroy socialist run detention camps filled with family and friends. Americans were finally, after all the pain and suffering they'd endured, finished with the socialist dictatorship that was keeping them starved, fearful, and beaten down. They would no longer be prisoners in their own country. These Americans knew their nation had only ever been the home of the free, because of the brave. And they finally decided to step up to the plate and be those brave who would fight to the death to make her free again.

Most of these patriots had not been foolish enough to turn over all their weapons to the rogue government now ruling their lives, no matter what those in power supposed. The rebellion had begun, and there would be no going back, not ever again.

These God fearing, America loving patriots, couldn't possibly know how many had answered the call for freedom from tyranny. For all they knew, there were only a few bands here and there, who were ready to take up the gauntlet and battle with them.

This lack of information truly made their sacrifice all the more heroic, because they supposed themselves a minority, and yet marched on, in spite of their supposed, underwhelming numbers. In truth, however, their members numbered in the hundreds of thousands. And, though they didn't have the communications, and tech to back them up the way their U.N. foes did, their hearts were filled with the strength that comes from knowing you are on the side of truth.

As the travelers, scouting the woods behind the prison camp, drew near enough to see guards in the tower, they heard a sudden noise behind them. As they began to turn, floodlights clicked on and they were instantly blinded. They had no way of knowing, that on a recent cold night, when they could see a large column of smoke rising from the prison miles away, the guards there also saw a smaller column of smoke rising from their own cave. Commander Ford had been waiting patiently for these visitors to finally show their faces since that night.

With nowhere to run, and hands bound behind their backs, the travelers were marched off to the nearby camp. Once there, the barracks were roused and all the prisoners called to the courtyard, to witness the welcoming in of new prisoners. Thankfully, this wasn't a nightly annoyance, due to their remote location. But, it happened often enough for them to know Commander Ford was simply showing off his hunting prowess to intimidate the inmates.

Nancy limped her way to her regular, assigned position, and Mike hobbled to his. When guards marched the new prisoners into the empty square, Nancy almost cried out. Mike averted his gaze, hoping he hadn't given anything away with his eyes. What was going on?

From the way the new prisoners were dressed for the weather, Nancy could tell they'd come out to the mountain willingly. Not the same way she and Mike had gotten there. And, the way Gracie was grinding her jaw, in that particular way she had, Mike could tell she was frustrated. Gabby, on the other hand, stood defiantly beside her parents and Tom had that, 'you're not going to lock me up again', look on his face.

When Gracie finally locked eyes with her dad, she gasped. He looked terrible, beaten bloody and bruised. But, she knew it was imperative that she keep her cool, and not allow her desire to destroy whoever had so badly beaten him to show through, so she took a deep, regulating breath and controlled her anger. She couldn't let this commander know she was related to any of the prisoners, or it might cause things to go even worse for them. Then she saw her mother, and knew, by her eyes and complexion, that this place was literally killing her. She had to figure out a way to get them both out of here. And, that might be difficult considering her own current situation.

Gabby saw her grandparents and her heart broke for them, but then she gazed around the compound and saw the same thing that was evident to her parents. It was clearly the age old adage of the fox guarding the hen house. Angels surrounded those innocent Christian captives, being held prisoner by evil forces; while demons, with yellowing talons firmly attached to their U.N. hosts, hissed and spit as they all marched past. The commander in charge, was accompanied by one of the largest and most hideous devils she'd ever seen in all her years of traveling for missions. Meanwhile, this demon seemed truly uncomfortable at the sight of the new prisoners, as well he should, and that made Gabby smile. Her spontaneous smile causing a flurry of grey leathery wings throughout the camp.

The commander spoke, "As a warning to all of you. And as a further hindrance to those who would attempt acts of sedition, in the future, I have a special treat. In two nights we will be executing these four who have dared to invade our camp. I would proceed with the execution tomorrow, but I'm waiting for a special implement I ordered a while ago. A guillotine. I was actually wondering who I would sacrifice to demonstrate my new toy. So, thank you, to the newcomers who have so graciously provided appropriate guinea pigs for my pleasure. I'm especially excited about this new implement, I expect it will supply a great many thrills for many of us who have become bored with your country, and I think it will be great fun for all. Until then, these four will be on display for you to see in the mess hall."

"Kakos, Kakos, I have some truly amazing news!"

"Well, out with it, Keres."

"Sir, the woman and her husband, their daughter and their friend, have been captured. They are in the hands of the guards, in the same prison that holds her mother and father. Sir, we've done it."

"Amazing! This is great news. Now I can finally go to Satan and tell him what a wonderful job I've done. I'm sure he will want to reward me for this. Marvelous news! Do you have any other word?"

"No Sir. Just that. We will keep you apprised of any new developments."

"See that you do. Now go about your business."

"Yes Sir." Keres was forever amazed at how quickly Kakos took credit for any accomplishments achieved by her team, and how hastily he passed off any blame for failures. Oh well, really, what was she expecting from one of Satan's regional Lieutenants? This was hell after all.

Having finally achieved the mountain heights, Jim and

his group looked for a place to hole up until they could decide on their next step. They'd brought plenty of weapons, and ammunition, but without knowing the layout of the prison, they had no real plan.

Marching as far as they dared before sundown, and the sure arrival of sub zero temperatures, they found a couple of caves large enough to house their substantial group (almost thirty individuals) out of the cold. Jim had decided they would forgo campfires, knowing that in the cold, the heat distortion of a fire would give evidence of their location. So, they ate MREs and bedded down together in close proximity for warmth.

Luke and Anna laid down with Dan between them, to keep him warm. Then they told him stories of their childhoods; stories of the times before madness turned the world upside down; until he fell fast asleep. "Those were simpler times, weren't they?"

"Yes, they were, Anna. You know, sometimes I forget how recent those times actually were. The world has become much more dangerous, way more quickly than I'd ever imagined it could. I'm sure many people feel that way. Even including all those very folks who voted for socialism, while we warned them of the destruction it would bring.

Now that we're married, I dream of being able to give you a wonderful life. The life you deserve, and I wonder if that will ever be possible."

"I know what you mean. And, I always dreamed of my life being a certain way once I got married. You know, children and all. But, if all we ever had, from this point forward, was each other, that would be enough for me. I love you Luke."

"I love you too, Anna. And I feel as though little Dan here has become part of us too. Don't you?"

"Yes, I do. But I do hope to give him a little brother or sister some day."

"My sentiments exactly."

Scouting teams went out very early the next morning and came back by the following sunrise to report. "Yeah Jim, the camp is pretty heavily guarded during the day, but sentries are cut back by half after sundown and the place gets pretty sleepy. One side of the prison sits near a cliff edge, so access from that direction would be practically impossible. Two sides are pretty wide open. Approaching from there would be suicide as well. The fourth side is semi protected by woods. Those woods could be an advantage to us, as long as we advance quietly enough. They could provide some pretty good cover. The guards are all heavily armed, but if we surprise them, that might not matter as much. Looks like they've all gotten pretty used to being out here away from the action. I didn't see a single rifle poised, or a finger anywhere near a trigger. I think they've all gotten pretty lazy, if you ask me. We know where the U.N. soldiers sleep, and where the commander's quarters are located. If we wake the captives, we will add to our ranks, and we can arm them with weapons we remove from the enemy troops."

"That sounds like a plan to me. Good work, men."

A meeting took place, with all those who would be involved in the raid, and Jim spoke. "Men, and, of course, Anna, our scouts returned early this morning with what I consider some pretty good news. I think we have the ability, and all the right circumstances present, to surprise our enemies. We are going to have to be very careful, but I don't think they have any inkling at all that we are on our way. "Now, I won't sugarcoat anything. This is going to be a fight, a big one. These people aren't going to go silently, I can promise you that. But, they are only U.N. soldiers. The truth is, they don't have any skin in the game. This isn't their country. We, on the other hand, are Jesus loving, American patriots who happen to love those people they have foolishly locked away in their prison camp. We also love this great land, and we want to restore her to her former glory. Isn't that right?" Agreement abounded from everyone present.

"Okay, folks. We're going to leave the bulk of our supplies right here and travel light. Take water bottles, protein bars, and every bit of your ammunition. When we go in, we're going in hot."

Without any incidents, such as those that had plagued Gracie and the travelers on their journey through the mountain, this trip went much more quickly. And before any of the men realized, it was dark and they were hunkered down in the woods outside the prison camp awaiting instructions from Jim.

The camp guard was already diminished by half for the night, and the prison population appeared to be headed toward sleep. Dan was with the men, and filling them in on what he'd seen along the way. Anna, sitting beside him, could see the seriousness in his eyes, and reached over to take his hand. He began, "When we were walking through the mountain I looked up and saw a cloud over the camp. It was dark, and I thought it was pretty funny that it looked that way. Then when we got closer I could see it wasn't regular old clouds. It was demons. The sky is thick with 'em, all around the camp. And they are there, even in the dark.

"The guards in the towers have demons too, I can see them because of their red eyes. Ugly ones with long fingernails dug deep into the guard's backs and shoulders. But, I'll bet the prisoners have angels too. At least the ones who know Jesus. I can't see them right now, 'cause none of those people are outside, but they're there. We can fight the battle with the guards. Guns will work in that one. But this battle isn't just with people."

"What do you mean, Dan? I don't understand."

"Maybe I can elaborate."

"Sure, Anna, jump in here anytime you think it would be helpful."

"I believe what Dan means is that even though there is a physical fight to be won, there is also a spiritual battle taking place. And, not just here, but in our country. Grace used to tell me that the only way to win a spiritual battle, is to pray. As we pray, God will send angels to our aid. Satan has already delivered his troops. Now we need to ask God for deliverance from our enemies. He will never leave us, or forsake us, but we have to ask, believing. Would you like me to pray?"

"Yes, please."

"Guys, please bow your heads and pray along with me. Lord, we come to You as a needy people. Here we sit outside this camp, where our loved ones are being held prisoner. Lord, our country is desperate for You. We are desperate for You. We need Your help, Lord. First to liberate this camp, and then to liberate our country. Father, send us aid. Send us legions of angels to assist us in this task. We know that nothing is possible without You, and that all things are possible through Christ, Jesus, who strengthens us. Give us this battle, Lord. And we will give You all the glory. For only You deserve the glory, the praise and the honor. In Jesus' Name we pray. Amen." Through the trees and from all around came whispered prayer, followed by a resounding amen.

"Anna, it worked. I see angels. Thousands and thousands of them. They are lined up all around the circles of demons, and they are covered in light. I think they are ready to fight." Anna nodded to Jim and Luke, and they smiled.

"Are we ready guys? For God, for our families, and for America!"

Two men quietly shimmied up the back of the towers.

They surprised the guards; knocking them unconscious, binding their hands and feet, and gagging them, before they could get off a shot. Then they climbed down the towers into the encampment. Once there, they opened the gates for the raiders. The men came from the woods like a silent rushing wave.

Several men made their way to the barracks where prisoners were kept, and entered quietly. They tied and gagged the guards and matrons in each barrack and woke the captives. Once awakened, the men and women awaited further instructions.

Luke and Anna were shocked to see Gracie, Jason, Gabby and Tom when they looked into the darkened mess hall. They were all four beaten within a half inch of their lives and bloody, tied and hanging from the same rings as the four men before them had been. Their angels stood silently by.

"Anna?"

"Yes, Gracie, it's me."

"What are you doing here?"

"We came to free Mom and Dad, but it looks like we're going to be saving you too."

"I would scold you, but I'm so happy to see you, I

think I'll let it go this time. Who knew you had this much chutzpa?"

"Well, not me, that's for sure. You know Luke, my husband, right?"

"Yes, what? Your husband?"

"Conversation for later, big sister. We have a camp to liberate. The guys have weapons for you outside."

Mike joined Luke and the rest of the men, even in his injured state, ready for battle. Nancy sought out Gracie and Gabby, Jason and Tom, and in the process found Anna and Daniel too, recognizing him as the boy from her vision.

What followed could only be accredited as a miracle of God. Due to the complete surprise of their attack, the raiders were able to subdue all the camp's guards with no fatalities, and very few injuries. Commander Ford, refusing to go down without a fight, was another story. He was alerted to the raid when he heard people congregating, though quietly, outside the mess hall. Looking out his bedroom window, he deduced very quickly the situation he was in, and grabbed a loaded gun. Ready to take out as many foe as he was able, he ran to the back door of his cabin. Forgetting the wire laundry line, his aide had hung there, he rushed out the door. The result just so happened to resemble the effects of the guillotine fun he'd spoken of, but probably hadn't meant quite so literally. He would be a problem no longer.

Heavenly host, fortified by the multiplying prayers of the people, defeated their demonic enemies with little difficulty. Kakos could be heard wailing throughout the halls of hell.

No one managed to get off a distress call to U.N. headquarters, so the freed prisoners and their liberators had some time to organize what would be a huge undertaking to get this many people off the mountain. First they would share a meal, from the base mess. Funny, but there seemed to be many more supplies than they'd ever been led to believe. Obviously food meant for Ford and the guards, but not for those lowly prisoners. They put together a huge celebratory meal, and packed supplies for their trip. But, there would also be a little time to share. "So, married, huh?"

"Yep, you know we always wanted to get married, Grace. Luke just wanted to be able to give me a certain kind of life. That's the only reason we waited."

"So, what changed your mind, Luke?"

"Situations changed, so plans had to change too."

"So, I didn't get to see my baby girl get married?"

"I knew you'd be upset, Mom. We can have another celebration later."

"I know this young man."

"But, I don't get it, Mom. How do you know Daniel?"

"I had a dream, and he was in it."

"I had one of those too!" Gracie exclaimed.

"Well, Luke and I have decided to give him a permanent home, that is, if he'll have us."

"Heck yeah! Of course I'll have you. Can I call you Mom and Dad?"

"We would be very pleased if you would call us Mom and Dad. And, Grace, Daniel has been a great help to us through all of this. He is also blessed with spiritual sight, just like the three of you."

"Imagine that. Well, Dan, I hope I can be a wonderful aunt to you. I've never had a nephew. I'm sure we can learn a lot from each other."

"I'll bet, Auntie Grace. That makes you my cousin, right Gabby?"

"Yes it does. Welcome to the family, Dan."

"I don't know if you've ever had a grandma to spoil you